HEXED

D0320083

HEXED

JULIA TUFFS

Orion

ORION CHILDREN'S BOOKS

First published in Great Britain in 2021
by Hodder and Stoughton

1 3 5 7 9 10 8 6 4 2

Text copyright © Julia Tuffs, 2021

The moral rights of the author have been asserted.

All characters and events in this publication, other than those clearly
in the public domain, are fictitious and any resemblance to
real persons, living or dead, is purely coincidental.

In order to create a sense of setting, some names of real places have been
included in the book. However, the events depicted in this book are
imaginary and the real places used fictitiously.

All rights reserved.
No part of this publication may be reproduced, stored in
a retrieval system, or transmitted, in any form or by any means, without
the prior permission in writing of the publisher, nor be otherwise circulated
in any form of binding or cover other than that in which it is published
and without a similar condition including this condition being
imposed on the subsequent purchaser.

A CIP catalogue record for this book
is available from the British Library.

ISBN 978 1 51010 932 2

Typeset in Adobe Caslon Pro by Jouve (UK), Milton Keynes
Printed and bound in Great Britain by Clays Ltd, Elcograf S.p.A.

The paper and board used in this book are made
from wood from responsible sources.

MIX
Paper from
responsible sources
FSC® C104740

Orion Children's Books
An imprint of
Hachette Children's Group
Part of Hodder and Stoughton
Carmelite House
50 Victoria Embankment
London EC4Y 0DZ

An Hachette UK Company

www.hachette.co.uk
www.hachettechildrens.co.uk

To Teenage Me – who would lose it at
seeing her name on a book

And to teenage girls everywhere – hold tight,
it gets better

CHAPTER ONE

The first time came out of nowhere. Like, totally left field, Meghan-and-Prince-Harry-hooking-up type out of nowhere.

It was a Wednesday morning, two weeks after we'd moved down here. I was sitting in double Maths – I know, double Maths first thing – harsh. My choice of seating, if I'd been given one, would have been towards the back of a classroom, around the middle. Not the very back, as that's prime mess-around real estate and not anywhere in the front half, as that risks teacher eye contact. The key is to exist with minimal, but not total, invisibility – a lesson Mum had instilled in me.

I hadn't got off to the best start with the 'new girl with blogger sister and weird family who've bought the haunted house on the Island' whispers doing the rounds, but I was doing a good job of keeping my head down and averaging it out. Middling. It's all about the middle. That's me: Jessie Jones – perfectly comfortable middle-of-the-class, middle-of-the-road, middle-of-everything girl.

But latecomers can't be choosers so this Maths I'd ended up in the second row – a situation made worse by the fact I had to look at the overly gelled back of Callum Henderson's head. (Callum had been moved to the front the week before for flicking ink on the back of Mr Anstead's shirt, a move that seemed to have upped his legend status amongst the boys. I mean, seriously, are we six?) I didn't know the names of many people at school, but Callum's was one you couldn't avoid. Callum, the star of the football team, Callum, whose dad is the MP for the Island, Callum, who struts through the canteen like he owns the place, Callum, who gets told off at least five times in every lesson but never ends up being adequately punished, Callum, who seems to have different rules to everyone else. Callum, the king of Queen Victoria Academy.

So there I was, in Maths, minding my own equations business, trying to look just the right amount of confused at the numbers and letters as they were scribbled on the whiteboard, concentrating on Mr Anstead's monotonous drone, when there was a knock at the door and a girl walked in. She mumbled an apology for being late, blushed furiously and practically ran to her seat, which was somewhere behind me.

It's never nice walking into a classroom and having thirty pairs of eyes staring at you, so I tried to catch her eye to shoot her a smile of solidarity. She was determinedly focused on the floor. After a confused moment, Mr Anstead launched back into variables and exponents and normality resumed. I was getting back into my faux confusion when I noticed Callum passing a note to Freddie on the desk next to him.

I didn't mean to look at it, really. I was just drawn to it, my eyes rebelling against my head-down protocol. Callum had drawn a picture of a stick figure with a pepperoni pizza for a face. Underneath was written, *'Down to a 3? Bet you still would!'* Freddie gave a half-hearted chuckle and passed it back.

It took me a second to get it. It was a drawing of the girl who had just come in. The exaggerated pepperoni pieces represented her fresh bloom of bad acne. I didn't understand the lowered number *exactly*, but I could hazard a guess – some sort of score they were keeping had gone down because she had more spots than usual?

What total morons.

I must have let out a groan, because Callum turned round and caught my eye. Taken by surprise, I gave him an accidental death stare – obviously a not very effective one, as he smirked in response. Ugh, if only he had any idea what it was like – to have bad skin, or a not-perfect face, or any kind of flaw. Idiot.

What happened next happened in a flash, but also, weirdly, felt like a long, protracted, slo-mo section of a movie. I got a sudden wave of really intense, shooting cramps – period pains – that made me double over, clutching my abdomen. Next thing I knew, there was a roar of horror from the table in front of me and Callum was standing up.

The cramps subsided and I looked up. There was commotion all around, a mixture of shrieking and gasping and laughing, chairs scraping back. A wave of excitement. Callum had his hands up to his face but, through his fingers, I could see fear and confusion in his eyes. Muffled moans were coming from behind his hands, which were grabbing at his face – his fingertips running over his cheeks, brow, chin and neck and pulling back in disgust. He whipped his phone out and looked at himself, gave one long scream and then ran out of the classroom.

Him and his bright red, angry, acne-covered face.

So yeah, that was the first time.

CHAPTER TWO

Five Things About Me:

1. As I said, I'm a middle-of-the-road kind of girl. I learned a while ago it's better to keep your head down and coast.

2. I moved down to the Isle of Wight from Manchester – or rather, I was moved down by my mother – all of a sudden, halfway through Year Ten, with just two weeks warning. (I was used to it, sudden moves was Mum's thing.)

3. I'm very good at Maths. I mean, freakily good. I don't know why, I just get it. I love numbers, they make sense. But I hide this. I've learned my lesson (see Point 1).

4. I have a super annoying older sister called Bella, who is an uber-popular Instagram make-up influencer and thinks that makes her better than anyone else. Guess that's more an interesting thing about her than me . . .

5. There is nothing else to know about me – no hobbies, no passions, no loves, no secrets (see Point 1). I hate black pepper and parsley. See? Even that's boring.

Back in Maths, the classroom was buzzing. And I felt weird. The adrenaline had faded and in its place I felt a wave of utter exhaustion, like I could have lain on the floor in front of everyone and fallen asleep. I knew I needed to get out of there, ASAP. Amid the chaos, I managed to mumble something about going to the bathroom to Mr Anstead, who was shouting 'Silence!' on repeat with about as much success as someone collecting sand in a sieve. I legged it to the toilets – which were empty, thank God – locked myself in the furthest cubicle and pulled down my tights and pants to inspect the damage.

I knew I'd leaked – you just do, don't you? Fabulous. I was five days early and had no tampons with me. I was never early! I was on-the-dot, set-your-clock-by-it regular. Luckily, it hadn't gone through my tights or skirt so I didn't have to do any kind of hideous period walk of shame through the halls. A normal person would have just asked a friend for a tampon. But me? Old Billy No Mates newbie loner over here? No friends, no such luck. So instead I did what every self-respecting female in this situation is forced to do: I shoved a massive ball of tissue in my knickers.

Just as I was finishing up, I heard someone run into the bathroom. A moment later the door in the cubicle next to me banged, and there was an outburst of snotty tears. A proper cry, one that had obviously been held in for a while and was now being let loose in all its heartfelt glory in the knowledge that no one was around to hear.

Except, I was.

I felt bad. I silently brought my feet up to the toilet seat, not wanting the crier to know anyone was there. I should have left, but if I had, she'd know someone had heard her crying. I considered asking her if she was OK and came up with a strong no. I was not the person for that particular job at that moment in time.

I just had to sit-squat and wait it out, hoping that she had friends who could help her. I focused on breathing as silently as possible. Some movement in the corner of the cubicle caught my eye; a fly was trapped in a spider's web, furiously kicking and struggling for its life. I felt for it. I was that fly, that fly was me – one and the same. Except my fight was against human interaction, not quite escaping from the literal jaws of death. I gently, silently, picked off the web around the fly, trying not to do it any more damage. It spun around a bit on its back, and I managed to flick it the right way up with the edge of my fingernail. It paused, confused, then gave me what I'm sure was a little *thank you* look, before flying away.

So there I was, with limited options once again. Story of my life. Either stay and be as silent as possible until she cried herself out and left, or sneak out super quietly, tip-toe stealth style so she'd never know I'd been there. I decided on the latter, but as I was silently lowering my legs down, the bell went and within thirty seconds the toilet was flooded with the standard break time stampede of girls. Perfect – now I could just walk out like a normal person.

'Oh my God! Libby, have you seen Callum?' a high-pitched voice shrieked among the throng of doors opening and closing, taps running and general bathroom noises.

My ears pricked up and I decided it wouldn't hurt to stay a minute.

'Not yet, why?' Libby replied.

There were excited sniggers and an explosion of voices talking over each other.

'Have you not heard?'

'Clearly not, Sadie. Just get on with it and tell me.'

'OK, so, in Maths, he just—'

'He broke out in some kind of acne rash,' another voice pitched in.

'You mean, like some kind of allergic reaction?' asked Libby.

'No. Literally, like, acne *all* over his face, suddenly.'

'It was so weird.'

'It was just after Tabitha came in – do you think that face rash of hers is contagious? She should be put in quarantine.'

I heard a tiny intake of breath from the cubicle next to me.

Ah. Hello, Tabitha.

'I have no idea what you're on about,' Libby said, sounding annoyed. 'I'll go and find him.'

I willed them to leave so me and my now aching legs could escape the confines of the cubicle. But then the toilet door opened again, and brought with it a whole new drama.

'Tabs! You in here?' I heard a different voice ask, accompanied by loud bangs on all the cubicle doors, including mine. I flinched. 'Tabs! I know you're in here.'

The girls at the sinks sniggered.

'What are you gawping at?' the voice said. 'This doesn't concern you, get on with attempting to fix your fake faces.'

Wow. This girl was badass.

'You'd know all about being fake,' sneered Libby. 'C'mon girls, it's gotten *way* too crowded in here.' I heard a rush of movement and then the door shut again.

So now it was me, Badass, and Tabitha in the toilets and I was still squatting on the seat like a total lemon. I didn't see a way out other than officially moving in and making the cubicle my new home. I'd learn to love it, probably more than my real home.

'Tabs, seriously, come out,' Badass said, her voice softer. 'He's a prick, they're all pricks. Everyone except them knows they're pricks. Don't let them get to you.'

There was a sniff and a creak as the cubicle door next to me opened.

'I'm OK,' Tabitha said. 'Honestly.'

'You don't look it. Come on, let's sort you out.'

I heard taps running and tissue being taken from the toilet next door.

'Rumour is you put some kind of a curse on him and made him break out in acne,' Badass said, laughing. 'That's pretty hardcore. Can I give you a list of some other hex-worthy aresholes?'

'I wish. I honestly don't know what happened,' Tabitha said, her voice sounding paper thin. 'One minute I was walking to my seat, hearing him snigger as I passed, the next minute everyone was going crazy and he was running out. Apparently he's saying I've done it to him.'

'Maybe it was his conscience, finally manifesting itself through the medium of a skin condition.'

'Whatever it was, he deserved it.' Tabitha sniffed. 'There was a note. A picture of me with a pizza for a face and . . .' Her voice wobbled. 'A score.'

'They're not still on that, are they? They're idiots. Come on, hold your head high, ignore. Don't let the bastards get you down and all that.'

Her voice was getting farther away as she headed towards the door. My heart thumped at the thought of finally being able to leave the cubicle. But, as I was silently stretching my legs, trying to get the feeling back in them, preparing to flee before anything else could happen, there came a parting line from Badass.

'And to whoever's been in here listening the whole time, hope you enjoyed the show. Next time I'll charge.'

CHAPTER THREE

By the time I made it home after school, I had never felt more relieved to see our manky, flaky front door. It was the first time I'd ever felt anything other than hatred at the sight. The house, big and old and crumbling, was about as far as you could get from the sleek, minimalist chic that had been our normal. We'd been here two weeks and it still felt unfamiliar and other. Like we were on a shit holiday, the travel company had gone bust and we were trapped. Except this was home now, according to Mum. I still had high hopes we'd put our time in here, as we did everywhere, and then move on – maybe even back to Manchester – but the fact that this was the first place Mum had actually bought, rather than rented, didn't bode well for that theory.

Five Things About Mum:
1. She grew up on the Isle of Wight.
2. She was, until a few months ago, a high-powered media lawyer who could win the ass off basically any case.
3. She's recently taken to wearing kaftans;
4. And trying to cook.
5. She's totally having a mid-life crisis.

She'd had a health scare. A minor, turned-out-to-be-nothing health scare that had apparently led to some kind of epiphany that she needed to return to her childhood roots. Practically overnight she had gone from designer handbags to wholesome tote bags, from ready meals to nutritious home cooking and from sitting stooped over her computer to demanding we all partake in 'quality family time'.

She was clearly losing her mind.

I'd petitioned to move to Dubai to live with my dad in his brand-new swanky apartment with pool and his brand-new shiny family, but Mum wasn't having any of it. She said we needed to stick together, the three of us.

Past the front door, I waded my way through the usual dozens of freebie packages for Bella and ran upstairs before anyone could catch me for any kind of interaction. I spent the rest of the afternoon in my bedroom, claiming homework, but essentially hiding out, cuddling our massive, ancient, black rescue cat, Dave (female – the name had stuck by the time we realised), and feeling sorry for myself. I think she knew. She always seemed to know when I was upset, and would give me extra cuddles. She even licked away my tears once . . . though I *had* just been eating chicken.

I had a lukewarm, shallow bath (knackered old water system – and don't even get me started on the shower, it's like standing under a peeing ant) in the avocado-suited glory of the first-floor bathroom. Then I sat shivering under my duvet in my attic bedroom while the seagulls squawked incessantly at me through the window.

What a day. That 'incident' in Maths had been so . . . strange. No one had seen Callum for the rest of the day, but man, did people talk about it. In fact, it was *all* people were talking about. In addition to the rumour that Tabitha had infected, or hexed him, other theories doing the rounds were:

1. It was leprosy.
2. Callum was Patient Zero of a Black Death resurgence
3. He had felt-tipped the spots on to bunk off.
4. It was some kind of new wave, Super STD (this was my personal favourite – though not Libby's).

I felt sorry for Tabitha. She was getting a lot of whispering and unwanted attention solely, it seemed, for the crime of having walked into her lesson a bit late. Marcus (Brainless Henchman No 1) was spreading it about that Freddie (Brainless Henchman No 2) said that Tabitha had seen their note and taken her revenge. I had seen her at one point in the canteen looking thoroughly miserable. Part of me had wanted to go and say something to her, but the other bigger and more sensible part of me told me she was best avoided. So I did what I do best – kept my head down, moved on, faded into the background, became invisible – until it was home time.

I tried to block out the seagull soundtrack and forget about the day when I was hit by a surge of period pains – bad ones, though nowhere near as freakishly bad as earlier. I pulled my knees into my chest, and breathed through the pain.

Dave jumped off the bed with a yowl. Oh, how I hated this stupid, big, old, cold, probably haunted house on this stupid, small, old, in-the-middle-of-nowhere island. I thought back to a month ago, to Manchester, where I really felt like we'd finally found our place. To our gorgeous flat on the fifth floor of a warehouse conversion looking out over the city centre, to my pristine, fully-functioning en suite bathroom, to heating that actually heated, to seagull-free mornings and to my friends. Hmmm, friends. Maybe not *friends* exactly; one of the 'perks' of moving schools every few years (thanks, Mum) was that close friends were hard to come by. We'd done north (Lake District and Manchester), east (Suffolk), west (Cardiff) and now south, never staying in a place for more than four years, which was roughly the point at which I started to feel like I was making friends. So yeah, friends weren't really my strong suit. But at least at Ashvale no one had threatened me through a cubicle door.

Mum called up the stairs, summoning me to dinner. I reluctantly emerged from my duvet cocoon and plodded my way down the stairs. I'd seriously considered missing it, but my stomach was making all kinds of mad 'feed me' noises. Bella's door was ajar as I walked past and I caught a glimpse of her sat at her mirror, doing her make-up wizardry. My sister, aka 'HellaBella' the beauty Instagrammer, aka the perfect student/daughter/granddaughter, aka self-appointed mature adult. Every time I see her now my stomach does a little angry churn – anger with a side order of longing. For the old Bella.

We used to have so much fun together. Wherever we were, Mum always worked long hours so it was pretty much just us two together, always. We'd dress up in Mum's posh dresses, raid the freezer and make ourselves a 'banquet' (which mainly consisted of out-of-date vol-au-vent cases filled with icing sugar and too-posh crisps). In Manchester, we'd go to the corner shop and spend all our money on sweets and junk food and feast on it in the bath, fully clothed. We'd come up with dance routines and shows and play music so loud our grouchy downstairs neighbour would bang on the ceiling. They were happy times, when we felt like a team. We had a secret code – be ourselves at home and blend in at school. Before Bella broke it by starting that stupid make-up channel and drawing attention to us. And before she crossed over to the Dark Side and decided to ally herself with Mum. It used to be us against the world and now it had shifted, seismically, to Mum and Bella against me.

I knew Bella was making a video because she was using her cheesy, high-pitched Instagram voice.

'Bellaaaaa! Dinner!' I shouted, from right outside her room, before running swiftly down the next flight of stairs.

'Daaaarling!' Nonna said as I walked in to the faded un-glamour of the dining room. Dave wound herself around my feet, nearly tripping me up. Mum was bent over the stove, furiously stirring something and looking worriedly at it. Nonna waddled over to me, clasped my face in her hands and closed her eyes, frowning and shaking her head. I stood still; I knew the score.

'Oh dear, oh dear, oh dear. This is bad. You are blocked. Your aura is sad.'

Five Things About Nonna:
1. She's a 'healer'. Crystals, auras, chakras, everything along those lines. I don't really get it, but she does good business so she must be doing something right.

2. She met Gramps when they were five. They lived opposite each other, got together when they were fifteen, got married when they were eighteen and they were *the* most in love couple I've ever seen.

3. She had my mum when she was seventeen (yep, *before* they were married) – didn't even know she was pregnant, went to the bathroom thinking she was going for a really big poo and out came Mum. Great Grandad was mean and scary and basically locked Nonna and my mum in her bedroom for a month until Gramps came to rescue them. It was, like, the Island's biggest scandal.

4. She wears so many bangles that if you were to line them up they would probably go all the way around the Island.

5. She has uncontrollable grey frizzy hair and a mole on her face that she's named Oscar that I used to be really frightened of.

I resisted the urge to say, *of course my bloody aura is sad, anyone who has been dragged away from their life to the arse-end of nowhere would have a Christmas-turkey-sad aura.* She released my face and started flapping her arms around me, her collection of bangles clanging round my ears. She wafted the air away from me, as if it were a particularly potent fart. Finally, taking a deep breath, she smiled. 'That's better. You can sit down.'

'Thanks, Jessie, really helpful,' Bella said, storming in.

'What? I was just calling you for dinner, which actually *is* helpful.'

She glared at me, a glare that then turned into a weird pitying, patronising look, like I wasn't even good enough for a glare.

'Do you want me to lay the table, Mum?' Bella asked, in that relentlessly perfect-daughter way of hers.

'If you could grab the plates, that would be lovely, thank you.' Mum plonked a big bowl of something semi-food-like on the table. 'How were your days, girls?' It was still weird to see Mum in a paint-spattered kaftan – her new uniform – rather than her tailored power suit of old.

I grunted and mumbled, my standard response when I really didn't want to talk about anything. Nonna caught my eye, staring at me inquisitively, clearly trying to access my soul again.

'My day was fine,' Bella answered, tucking into what I think was meant to be dahl, flinching slightly. Whatever it was, it was burnt. 'Hey, what happened with that boy in your year today, Jessie?'

I looked at her perfectly made-up face, trying to work out if she was deliberately trying to cause me grief. It's a well-known fact I have an almost physical aversion to discussing school in any kind of family setting. She looked genuinely interested, which, in some ways, was *more* annoying, another reminder that she'd totally joined the grown-up team now. I shot her a 'don't go there' glare, but she was oblivious. Or choosing to be.

'Dunno.' I shrugged, serving myself the smallest amount of dahl possible, which I fully intended to just push around my plate (I'd eaten Mum's home-cooked creations before).

'Yeah, you know, Callum I think his name is? The really full-of-himself one.'

'Ooh, is that our not-so-fine-and-upstanding MP Bob Henderson's son?' Nonna asked, frowning. 'Awful man.'

'Yeah, I think so,' I mumbled. *Like father like son.*

'Apparently he broke out in some crazy rash in the middle of a lesson or something.' Bella continued, still looking at me for a response. I sensed Nonna and Mum sneaking a quick look at each other.

'It was nothing,' I said firmly. 'He just . . . had some kind of reaction to something and had to go home. Not the drama everyone is making it out to be. How's the house stuff going, Mum?'

I had no actual interest in hearing how the never-ending house renovations were going, but I knew it was the best topic for a subject-change and I really could not be bothered to even think about Callum Henderson, or anyone at that school, any more today.

'Did the rash come out of nowhere?' Mum asked, refusing to be derailed.

'I guess, I don't know, can't say I was watching him every second.'

'So you were near him?' Nonna asked.

'What's with the interrogation? Yes, I was sat behind him, yes it was sudden. I don't know anything other than that so can we leave it please.' There was a silence, another look between Nonna and Mum, and some awkward clunking of cutlery.

'Well, I've found some builders to meet who are available,' Mum said, eventually. 'And I've been getting creative again, reading through some home décor magazines, ooh – and as I was going through a box of old stuff from Manchester, I found some clothes I made for you girls when you were little and do you know, it made me think I quite fancy getting back into . . . something like that. I used to enjoy it.' She looked wistfully into the middle distance, like she was fantasising about clothes patterns.

'And she stripped the wallpaper in the back room,' Nonna added, attempting to smooth down her errant hair that was frizzing enthusiastically over her face. 'Gone is the textured diarrhoea shade of old.' She put a forkful of dahl in her mouth, trying not to grimace.

'How is it?' Mum asked, eagerly.

'Mmmm,' Nonna said, nodding.

'Oh good! I got a bit sidetracked, I was worried it hadn't turned out right. I'm enjoying this cooking thing. So much better than ready meals and takeaways every night, isn't it girls?'

Mum was really trying to embrace this stay-at-home Earth Mother role, but from what I'd seen so far, it was so not her style. The house was always a tip, piles of unwashed dishes were standard and the cooking was ... something else entirely. I looked down at the unidentifiable mass on my plate. My mouth watered at the thought of a Ruma Lebanese, or a Papa J's pizza, or a Prem Indian, or any of our old favourites that Bella and I used to eat in front of the TV while Mum sat at the table, consumed by work. I flicked a tiny bit of dahl down to Dave, who sniffed it and scurried away. Not promising. Mum launched enthusiastically into hers. A big forkful, two chews and what looked like an excruciating swallow later, she reached for her glass of water and downed it.

'That is utterly disgusting. I'm so sorry,' she said, looking crestfallen.

Nonna and Bella muttered some non-committal words of encouragement, obviously not wanting to be too supportive in case they then had to eat more. I sat there, trying to push thoughts of pizza away.

'It's fine, perfectly salvageable,' Nonna said, standing up and scraping everyone's dahl back into the serving platter in the middle of the table. 'I can sort this out, no problem.' She grabbed the mountain-high pile of dahl and headed to the kitchen.

'You *really* don't need to do that,' Mum said, a warning tone in her voice.

'All fine!' Nonna shouted through.

'Mum! Don't . . .' She sighed. 'I really am sorry,' she said. 'I followed the recipe . . .'

'It was a good first try,' Bella said. 'And it can only get better.'

There she went, sucking up like a max-strength Henry Hoover. Ugh.

'Why don't we order takeaway?' I suggested, more bluntly than I'd intended.

Mum sighed again. The soundtrack to our new life – sighs and seagulls.

'Jessie, we've been through this. We're not doing that any more. No more takeaways and ready meals every night. Quality food, quality family time, quality—'

'Connection,' I finished. 'Yeah, I know. I'd just like to eat something edible.'

'Here we are then,' Nonna said, coming back in with a bowl of steaming hot, delicious-smelling food. Same bowl, definitely different food.

'*Mum!*' Mum said, practically glaring at Nonna, which seemed a bit rude seeing as she'd totally just saved the day.

We tucked in. It was gorgeous. Dahl and then some. Super

dahl, bearing no resemblance to the weapon of mass destruction that had been on the table ten minutes ago.

'This is delicious! How did you make a whole new one in that time?' Bella asked.

'I didn't,' Nonna said, avoiding Mum's eye. 'I worked with what your mother had done and . . . zhuzhed it up a bit. A few spices, bit of extra stock, that kind of thing. She'd made a great base.'

I looked between the food on my plate and Nonna and Mum. This food had no black burnt bits. It was almost an entirely different colour. It tasted like food. It was way more than zhuzhed.

'Anyway, isn't it lovely to be eating together?' Nonna added quickly.

I was too busy eating to respond.

***

Finally, enforced family dinner came to an end and I was allowed, after clearing up, to escape back to my attic icebox.

'Oh, meant to say, we need some more tampons, Mum,' I said as I was halfway out the dining room door.

'I got some the other day,' she said. 'In the cupboard under the bathroom sink.'

'I looked, there are only a couple.'

'I've used some,' Bella said. 'I'm on too.'

Mum and Nonna shot yet another look at each other. This time it was totally obvious.

'You're both on?' Mum said.

'I guess so,' I said. 'No need for the dramatic looks though, it's a period, not Chernobyl. We just need some more tampons.'

Mum stood there with her mouth slightly open. Then she blinked and shut it.

'Yes, of course. I'll get some in the morning.'

'Thanks,' I said, running up the stairs, trying not to break my neck on the loose flaps of stained deep green carpet.

CHAPTER FOUR

My Thursday went like this:

Registration – in which a random stupid boy did a random stupid thing (not unusual). This time, loudly reciting a poem that rhymed 'toosh' with 'bush' and 'Ruby' with 'do me' to a girl named (no surprises here) Ruby. Practically Oscar Wilde levels of wit.

Maths – where Callum was back, clear-faced and, as was his way, revelling in his fame. The Incident appeared to have done nothing other than grow his already substantial ego even more. It's a superpower that boys have, managing to turn any event in their favour. I could feel sniggers and whispers aimed at Tabitha, who was the first in and the last out. I guess she didn't want a repeat of walking in late. I kept my head down, as per, and continued to pretend to not know all the answers immediately.

English – which involved boys being silly, including speculating on the possible size of Jane Eyre's boobs.

Break – when I walked slowly between my locker and the toilet and back again so I didn't have to sit obviously in the corner like a loner.

Double Science – where I got mansplained chemical reactions by my lab partner (who had most of it wrong).

Lunch.

Lunch is where things got interesting.

The problem with lunchtime is that there is no avoiding it. Unless you lock yourself in the toilet cubicle for the whole hour (which, trust me, I have considered). Walking through a high school canteen carrying your tray of beige, stodgy food, searching for a 'safe' spot to sit, is about as desperate and nerve-wrecking as it gets. Throw into the mix being at a new school and having joined halfway through the year and knowing everyone is talking about you and you've got the perfect storm of utter crapness.

Best case scenario is that everyone is too busy and wrapped up in themselves to give you a second glance, you find a spot on a table with people who you vaguely know and are vaguely decent, make small talk, eat quickly then get out of there. Worst case scenario is that people are watching you, there's nowhere to sit near people you know, you end up plonking yourself on a table with randoms, blushing furiously, eating in silence then practically running away.

And then, apparently, there's an even worser case scenario.

I was doing my usual about-to-be-fed-to-sharks plank walk through the middle of the canteen with a particularly unappealing and pale slice of pizza sitting limply on my plate, like it had just lost the will. I hear ya, Pizza.

For some unexplained reason, the canteen was busier than usual – fit to burst, need-ear-defenders-it's-so-loud type full. There were hardly any spaces. I looked to the outer-rim seats which are my favourites – all full. I looked at the undesirable tables closest to the food bins – also full. I could feel my heart picking up the pace. Was it too late to just dump my lunch and leg it out altogether?

Then I saw a space. Four girls, Year Sevens I reckoned – they had a similar nervy and unsure aura to me – were leaving their table. I walked quickly, while also trying not to look too super keen, and put my tray down, just as two other girls did too.

It was Tabitha and a girl I hadn't seen before. This other girl was wearing her uniform in a way that was clearly not school rule-book standard and yet also didn't technically break any rules. It actually looked cool, despite the fact that the law of physics says that it is impossible to look good in a bottle green jumper and green piped shirt. She had blonde, tousled, shoulder-length hair, with the kind of natural wave that people spend hours trying to recreate, a slight tan (in March?!), and freakily bright, sharp blue eyes. I accidentally made eye contact as I was giving her the once-over, and had to swiftly avert my eyes and pretend to be fascinated by my pizza.

'How was Maths?' she asked Tabitha. and I instantly recognised the voice. Badass! It was Badass from the bathroom.

'Not great,' she replied. 'Callum was back, in full force. And I could tell everyone was talking about me.'

I stared intently at my pizza, trying not to look like I was listening.

'Of course they were – it's the most interesting thing to happen in this place since Mr Wright's braces broke and his trousers fell down in Year Seven. But they eventually stopped talking about that. This too . . .'

'Shall pass. Yeah, yeah, I know.'

'And years from now, you'll be sat there polishing your Nobel Prize for literature and they'll still be giving each other wedgies and scoring their wives – if anyone was enough of a sucker enough to marry them – and we'll laugh about what losers they are.'

Tabitha half-smiled, nodding.

'Talking of your Nobel Prize – have you heard anything back from that magazine about your short story yet?'

'No, still waiting.'

'Keep the faith, mate. Your writing is amazing, I know they're going to love it.'

There was a pause and I could feel them both look at me. I wondered if Tabitha realised I was in her Maths class. I needed to say something. Otherwise I would look strange. Now would be a good time to come out with some weak small talk. Maybe something like, 'Ah, that Maths lesson yesterday was a weird one, wasn't it?' Though that might seem like I was accusing *her* of being weird. Maybe just a more open-ended, 'That Maths lesson, hey?'

Just as I was about to pluck up the courage, a mass of shouts and guffaws and general noise made us turn. A group of boys sitting at the table the other side of the aisle from us were turfing some unsuspecting Year Sevens out of the way. I realised, with a sinking stomach, it was all the usuals – Marcus, Eli, Freddie and, of course, Callum. Libby and Sadie, her lapdog, were there too, doing their usual puppy-dog act. The boys were in football kit. I could practically feel Tabitha flinch next to me. I started to speed-eat my pizza.

'Quick lunch, team, then out at the minibus by 12.45,' Coach said, walking over. As usual, he was tracksuited and whistled to the max. Coach – real name Mr Bowd – insisted on being called 'Coach' because he imagined himself in some kind of

American high school. 'Ready to slay!' he said, causing the boys to whoop like a pack of dogs as he walked away.

'This'll be a walkover,' Callum said loudly. 'Newtown are a bunch of pussies. Coach reckons we could manage at least four–nil, easy.'

'We just need Marcus to grow a pair and play less like a girl this time and we'll be fine,' Freddie added, to much laughter.

'My problem wasn't the lack of balls, Freddie,' a floppy-haired boy I recognised from Media Studies said. 'It was that they were knackered.'

As if, I thought to myself. He looked like he'd only just hit puberty and was still working out what a girl was, let alone done anything with one. Typical boy bragging. I wished there was something obvious that happened when boys lied, like a full-on Pinocchio nose-grow, so they couldn't tell a lie without being called out.

'More like they were blue,' Callum said. 'I heard Nicola turned you down.'

A combined response of 'oooh's and chuckles and 'yeah's echoed around their table.

'She was just embarrassed because she was a rubbish kisser,' Marcus said, beginning to look nervous.

Just then, as I chewed my way through a forkful of tepid fruit crumble, I was hit by a wave of seriously bad, had-to-suck-air-through-my-teeth-to-ride-it-out period pains.

'Not again,' I hissed.

'I had to dump *her*, she was so bad,' Marcus was saying. Around him, there was a rising ripple of noise and commotion. A few people started laughing. A fizz of excitement worked its way through the whole canteen. I looked over, like everyone else.

Something strange was happening to his face.

I did a double take.

It couldn't be. No way.

'And don't get me started on what she couldn't do with her hands,' Marcus carried on, gaining confidence from the laughter, thinking everyone was finding him hilarious.

They were, but not for the reason he thought.

'What?' he said, frowning.

'Your nose, man,' Callum said, in between choking laugh-cries.

Marcus grabbed at his nose, feeling how it had swollen and lengthened. His face dropped, the comically oversized outline of his nose standing loud and proud and prominent. He burst into confused tears and ran out of the canteen, his tray crashing to the floor, spilling its contents as he went.

I put my head down, trying to control the spiralling thoughts whirring round my brain. This was weirder – and worse – than the rash yesterday. That had seemed random, a freak incident. This . . . this seemed . . . deliberate. Like someone had made it happen.

Someone like . . . me.

But it couldn't be. I grabbed my tray and made as swift an exit as I could manage, feeling Badass's bright blue, all-knowing eyes watching me as I went.

CHAPTER FIVE

The rest of the day – History and French – passed in a blur. Total exhaustion mixed with a thumping panic mixed with a cotton-wool, can't-think-clearly blur. Once again, the school was a hotbed of whispered rumours and gossip carried along on a general tidal wave of excitement.

I legged it as soon as last bell went, walking fast, trying to put as much distance between me and the school gates as I could. I took the small coastal path down into town to break away from the bottle green mass. It had started out as one of those gorgeous, bitingly cold but sunny winter days, though now the skies were definitely darkening. I loosened my scarf, trying to encourage the icy wind to clear away the fogginess of my mind. The sea churned at me as I rounded the corner. It felt good to be out of the school confines, but as hard as I tried to push them away, I kept getting flashbacks to Marcus's nose, growing, and growing. And Callum's rash, blooming suddenly over his face.

A dawning worry was creeping in at me from the corners, getting louder. I pushed it away. Tabitha had been sat right next to me. It could have been her; after all, everyone else thought it was. *Except Tabitha wasn't the one who explicitly wished boys' noses would grow when they were lying.*

Yep, that had been me.

But it couldn't have been me.

Could it?

Maybe I was experiencing some kind of episode brought on by intense period pains. That must be it. I was delusional from loss of blood. But everyone else had seen it too, both things – the rash and the nose. Surely a *mass* delusion was a bit much? Maybe the whole thing was a dream and I would wake up any minute, safe in our plush and warm Manchester apartment.

I pinched myself to test that theory, but it bloody hurt.

One thing was for sure, this island was weird. With a capital W. In fact, caps lock WEIRD.

Nothing like this had happened in Manchester – or anywhere else for that matter. No sudden rashes, no growing noses, no intense period pains. An overwhelming urge to be back there – where it was familiar, safe – washed over me. *Deep breaths*, I thought. Deep breaths.

I made my way down the uneven path and along the seafront. Our house was at the other end, perched halfway up the big hill, watching wearily out towards the sea, looking like it belonged in a horror film. Apparently this house, this ancient, run-down, seventies-décored, rickety former hotel was the one we *had* to have. When Mum was growing up on the island, she used to gaze at it, adoringly, every day, wishing she could live there, fantasising about what it was like inside (though I bet avocado bathroom suites and poo-coloured wallpaper never featured in her fantasies). So, when the house being up for sale coincided with her mid-life crisis, she saw it as a sign (from who, exactly, I don't know).

I couldn't quite stomach going home yet, especially as Nonna and her freaky powers of perception would likely lead to a ton of questions, so I sat myself down on the so-cold-it-felt-wet sand, my back leaning against the even-colder-it-felt-wetter sea-wall. I ran my hand over the cool shingles of the beach, searching for the green and blue translucent gems of seaglass, the hidden treasure I used to spend hours raking for when I was visiting Nonna in the summer holidays. My mind was spinning like a tumble dryer and I had a sinking feeling in the pit of my stomach, like my ship had hit an iceberg. The sea glared at me, salty and fierce and churning as wildly as my insides.

***

By the time I had wound my way home to the monster mansion I had deep-breathed my way into a resolution. Clearly something was wrong with me and I needed to see a doctor. I wasn't well. Maybe I was dying. Do people who are dying hallucinate rashes and growing noses? We'd had a fire safety talk in Year Four and I'm sure they'd said something about hallucinations being a sign of carbon monoxide poisoning, which would totally make sense with our rickety old house. And I'd read somewhere about a woman who had a brain tumour and hallucinated an Edwardian lady sitting on her bed. Maybe *that* was it, a brain tumour.

I kicked the heavy front door open – that was just the only way to unstick it – rehearsing my announcement and readying myself for the onslaught of questions it would prompt. I could hear a murmur of voices coming from the kitchen.

'Hello?' I called out. Dave came trotting through, rubbing against my leg.

'In here, Jessie,' Mum replied.

They were all sat round the kitchen table: Nonna, Mum and Bella. The usual pile of random house detritus was pushed to the far end. They were nursing cups of tea and looking surprisingly serious. Bella gave me a sincere smile, which freaked me out a bit.

I figured I just needed to pull the band-aid off, come straight out with it and hope they took me at least a little bit seriously.

'Hi, darling,' Mum said. 'Sit down for a minute, will you? We need to have a chat.'

'Actually, I really need to talk to you about something first,' I said, wanting to get it over with.

'Is it about what happened at school today?' Mum asked.

'What? What happened?' I said, panicking. How could she know already?

'My thing,' Bella said.

'*You* had a thing? What thing?'

'So, *not* my thing?' Bella said, perking up.

'I don't know anything about your thing!'

'So you have your own thing?' Nonna asked.

They'd got me all confused now. What thing did Bella have? Should I even bother with mine? What was I even going to say again? All eyes were on me.

'OK, so,' I said, trying to work out the best way to phrase it. 'Lately I've been getting really bad period pains and ... well, weird things have been happening. I think I'm hallucinating ... and, maybe I have a brain tumour? Basically, I might be dying and I need to see a doctor. Straight away.'

They all just looked at me.

Saying it out loud, I realised how totally ridiculous I sounded.

'Or I'm going mad,' I added. That was totally another option, to be sure.

Silence.

'What was *your* thing?' I asked Bella, seeing as no one seemed to be responding to mine.

'Uh, what? Oh, I . . .'

'She turned a frog purple,' Nonna answered, chuckling.

'Mum! It's not funny,' Mum reprimanded.

'It's a bit funny,' Nonna said, still chuckling, which got Mum laughing too.

Bella and I looked at each other, over at them, and back at each other in horror. This was madness. We were all mad. It must be the water. The sea-salt-contaminated Island water.

'You'd better sit down,' Mum said, eventually managing to stifle her giggles enough to speak. 'Sorry, we're not laughing at you, it's just . . .'

'I did say, Allegra, you should've told them before it got to this point,' Nonna said.

'Told us *what* exactly?' Bella asked.

'You're being really weird,' I added.

'Do not use that word.' Mum turned stern, her smile dropping. 'That is not a word we use in this family.'

I stared at her. 'Between the two of us we've caused a rash, a nose growth, and a frog to change colour and you've laughed in our faces – what would *you* call it?'

Nonna reached over and put her hand on Mum's.

'She's just confused,' she said, like 'she' wasn't standing right there.

'We'll explain,' said Mum. 'But please sit down, Jessie, you're making me nervous.'

I was making *her* nervous?

I dragged a chair out from under the table and sat down, even though I desperately wanted to remain standing, ready to run at any point.

'So,' said Mum. 'We have something we need to tell you. I've been trying to find a way . . . The thing is, I'm not really sure how best to explain this . . . A long time ago . . . No that's not right. OK, so . . . there's something you need—'

'You're both witches,' Nonna said, matter-of-factly.

'Mum!' said Mum.

'There's no other way to say it, love,' Nonna said.

Bella started laughing. I sat there with my mouth open. Mum and Nonna looked back at us, deadly serious.

'I don't think they're joking,' I said, elbowing Bella, who stopped laughing abruptly.

'What do you mean, "witches"?' she asked. 'That's silly. Witches don't exist.'

'They most certainly do,' Nonna said. 'Who else do you think keeps the Earth in its natural order?'

I could see Bella wanting to laugh again, but this suddenly seemed very, very not funny to me. My head reeled, a tumble dryer on a speed cycle.

'So, you're saying that *I* gave Callum a rash and made Marcus's nose grow because I'm a witch? I mean, a) that's ridiculous, and b) I didn't cast a spell or a hex or anything, I was literally just sat there, minding my own business.'

'And I definitely didn't tell that frog to turn purple,' Bella added.

'What were you thinking at the time those things happened?' Mum asked.

I thought back to that Maths class, to Tabitha walking in, Callum writing that note with the awful picture of her, with a pizza for a face. I never explicitly wished he would develop a rash . . . but I had thought, *if only he knew what it was like.* And in the canteen . . . I had definitely wished Marcus's nose would show if he was lying . . .

My mouth dropped open again. My expression du jour.

Bella let out a little gasp.

'Oh my God! I *did* think the frog was a really ugly green and that purple would be a more flattering shade for the poor thing.'

'You see?' Mum asked.

My heart was beginning to hammer-thump, and – was that a pain in my chest? Oh God, on top of everything else I was having a heart attack?

'You're talking rubbish. None of this makes sense,' I said.

'I think you know it does,' Mum said, gently.

'But . . . none of this makes sense,' I repeated, the words on a loop on my head.

'Your mother and I are witches,' Nonna said, booming and proud, waving her bangled arms in the air like a master of ceremonies. 'It's been in our family for generations. You're juvenile witches and your powers have only just come in. You can't control them yet, but when you want something particularly badly . . .' She trailed her fingers through the air mysteriously, like she was conducting an invisible orchestra. 'Well, then you can make it happen.'

I stared at her. At them. I felt numb.

'Remember all those stories about Great-Great Mad Auntie Alice? She wasn't mad, she was a witch – a very powerful one,' Nonna continued.

I did remember the stories of Great-Great Mad Auntie Alice – her house full of strange animals, hair that went down to the floor, a cottage in the middle of the woods. Also, housebound, friendless, isolated and mumbling to herself until she died.

'So you're both witches?' Bella asked. 'What sort of magic do you do?' She sounded cool and calm – like she hadn't just heard the newsflash that we were WITCHES who came from a long line of MORE WITCHES.

'Not much really, just bits here and there . . .' Mum began.

'That dinner! The other night!' I practically shouted.

Nonna grinned cheekily.

'Well, yes,' Mum said, giving Nonna a disapproving look. 'That was naughty.'

'Bloody necessary though!' Nonna added.

'But why didn't we know? *How* didn't we know?' asked Bella.

'You didn't need to know – you were too young to understand, and I wanted you to have a normal childhood.'

Nonna did a loud splutter-cough at that.

'And in terms of *how* didn't you know – I kept it from you as best I could, I hardly ever practised magic myself – especially not when I was around you girls.'

'I did,' Nonna said, defiantly. 'You just weren't very observant.'

Another glare from Mum. 'We can talk you through everything. Maybe once you've had a chance to . . . process.'

Another image of Great-Great Mad Auntie Alice flashed in my head – not the stooped, white-haired lady I knew from family photos, but a wrinkled hag covered in warts, with a big gnarly nose and an evil cackle. Going mad all alone in a cottage that looked like the one from Hansel and Gretel. Oh God, maybe she even cooked children – do witches cook children? Would *I* have to cook children? I shook my head to dislodge the image. I couldn't let my mind go into the intricacies of our crazy family history and its legacy. If this was true, if this was actually happening, what did it mean for *me*, now?

'Hang on,' I said, my voice smaller than I meant it to be. 'What does this mean for us? Are we going to be causing health conditions and accidentally changing animals into different colours with our thoughts from here on out?'

'No, no, no, not at all,' Mum said.

'You'll learn how to control your powers, to harness them,' Nonna said. 'We'll teach you.'

Mum reached her hands out over the table to take both of ours.

'I know this feels big and scary and overwhelming right now, but trust me, it's a great thing and you will, over time, realise how special and unique it makes you.'

'I don't want to be special and unique!' I said, standing up, my chair hitting the floor behind me. 'I want to be middle-of-the-road and under-the-radar and NORMAL! Isn't that what you've always told us – *It's never a good thing to draw attention to yourself, keep your head down, blend in.* How the hell are we supposed to *blend in* if we're accidentally hexing people all over the place?'

Nonna shot Mum a glare.

'Darling, that was ... *before* ... I wasn't ...' she stuttered, breaking eye contact.

'Why is this happening now, specifically?' Bella asked, still sounding annoyingly calm.

'Ah, well ...' Mum said, shifting even more uncomfortably, staring at the floor like she was hoping it might swallow her up.

'Because you're on the Island,' she said, tentatively.

'So if we hadn't moved here we wouldn't have developed these super helpful 'powers' we now have?' I asked.

'Yes, it's the Island that sets off the transition.'

'Fabulous! Another thing to add to the Why Moving Here Was The Worst Idea Ever list.'

'But now that we have them, will we have powers even if we're not on the Island?' Bella asked.

'You will, eventually, like your mum and I do,' Nonna said. 'But at the moment your powers aren't strong enough to work anywhere else. You still need the Island and its life force. You're like baby deer stumbling up on to your wobbly legs, you can't go far – think of it like that.'

Baby deer felt *way* too pleasant an analogy for whatever exactly this was.

'And ...' Nonna nodded at Mum. 'Tell them the rest.'

'And,' Mum said, slowly, reluctantly, 'the reason you have them right now, is because it's the right time of the month. But that's only for now. Once you develop your powers enough, like me and Nonna, you will always have them and—'

'What do you mean the right time of the month?' Bella interrupted, confused.

Mum did the biggest, most uncomfortable shift in her chair yet, looking at the floor.

'When you're menstruating.'

CHAPTER SIX

'Is Dave a witch's cat?' I asked, striding back into the kitchen, where Mum and Nonna were still sat, hunched over, talking in hushed, serious tones.

It was an hour or so after their bombshell. I'd been silently seething and fretting and generally having an existential crisis, mixed with nervous breakdown, mixed with total, absolute spin-out. Dave was on my lap. And she was being all attentive and cuddly and I was telling her everything, and as I was talking to her it occurred to me that she might be a witch's cat and I knew that if she spoke back I would absolutely freak and that would be the end of me. So I needed to check, urgently.

'No, darling.' Mum said. 'She's just a regular, slightly annoying household cat. Please, come and sit down and we can chat.'

'But she's black. And witch's cats are normally black. In books and stuff.'

'I promise you she's not. Please, Jessie, sit down, let's talk.'

'I could *make* her talk to you if you want,' Nonna said, grinning.

'Not helpful,' Mum snapped.

'And she always seems to know when I'm sad,' I said, ignoring Nonna.

'Jessie!' Mum said, all doe-eyed and imploring. 'Please, come and talk.'

No way. She was out of her mind if she thought I was about to sit down and have a witch story time with her any time soon. After today's witch-bomb revelations, it was clear she'd been lying to me my entire life. I still had my Dave suspicions, but I had no other option than to believe her for now.

'Fine. Just checking,' I said, stomping back up the stairs.

CHAPTER SEVEN

I woke up stupidly early the next morning, though I wasn't sure I'd actually slept at all, what with the new-found megawatt period pains and the squawking seagulls and rampant witch nightmares (featuring thousands of purple frogs and rashes and boils and noses and cottages where children were being cooked).

The morning didn't bring relief from the full-on front and back period ache, in fact it was worse. I wanted to nestle under the duvet with a hot water bottle, but also felt an overwhelming urge to be out of the house. I couldn't face seeing Mum or Nonna, but it was way too early to head to school. My stomach rumbled at me aggressively. I'd missed dinner last night, having barricaded myself in my room after the Dave chat. Someone had left some toast outside my room, which I hadn't been able to stomach at the time and when I opened the door to glance at it now I saw was rock hard and congealed, with suspiciously Dave-like tongue grooves over it.

I threw on my discarded uniform from the day before, catching sight of myself in the mirror. Did I look witchy?

Five Possibly True Facts About Witches, Collated From My Basic Knowledge of Witchy Books and Movies:

1. They have warts.

2. They fly on broomsticks.
3. They stand over boiling cauldrons, cackling and stirring potions made from things like newts' eyes and frogs' hearts.
4. They cook children (TBC).
5. They're ostracised and unloved and unliked and live lonely, isolated lives.

'Witch.' I said the word out loud, feeling the shape of it in my mouth. Me, a witch? I moved closer to the mirror, examining my reflection. Same flat mousy hair, same dull brown eyes, same pale skin. No warts on my nose, that was something, at least. It was hard to reconcile all the witch talk last night with the same old, unremarkable, unhappy me in the mirror. I in no way looked like a witch. Or felt like a witch. Whatever a witch even is. My mother, a witch? *Surely* I'd have noticed something. There hadn't been any unexplained broomsticks or cauldrons lying around, no potions or frogs and newts. Does she do that stuff – the *hubble, bubble, toil and trouble*? Does she hex people? What powers does she actually have – do *we* actually have? What can we do, besides inflicting rashes and ailments on sexist boys and performing cooking wizardry? Do we only have our powers when we're on? And if so, WHY THE ACTUAL? And if it is all period-related, how come Nonna still had powers? I was pretty sure that ship had sailed . . .

I felt dizzy with the thoughts. The swirling, whirling, witchy, periody thoughts. So many questions – *all* the questions. And yet there was no way I could face asking Mum any of them. I was too angry with her, and too confused. Distraction and being away from the house were definitely the way forward.

I scraped my hair back and crept down the stairs as silently as I could, grabbing my bag from the hallway. The door slammed closed behind me, but I didn't care by that point, as I'd already broken free. As soon as I stepped outside and the icy wind slapped me in the face I wished I'd thought to take my coat rather than my flimsy hoodie, but there was no way I was going back inside. I couldn't risk seeing any of the coven and having to actually speak about the End of Days horror they had just unleashed on me.

I picked up the pace, so as not to get frostbite, and stomped my way along the coast path. I was headed to my all-time favourite Isle of Wight place, Steephill Cove, where Nonna used to take us, back in the happy Island days. Whenever Bella and I came down for the summer we'd spend whole days here, jumping in and out of the water, climbing on the rocks, searching for crabs, stopping briefly to devour Nonna's picnic (always soggy cucumber and cheese sandwiches). We'd make Nonna stay until we were the only people left and we were shivering and slightly blue around the lips. It's always been my Island happy place, and it was totally what I needed right now.

It wasn't as sunny as it had been yesterday and the sea was more grey and angry than sparkly, but bright sunshine would've clashed with my mood. I always prefer the weather to mirror my mood. There's a word for that – Mrs Matthews was always boring on about it – pathetic something. Whatever it was called, the weather today felt right somehow. Although given last night's revelations, a thunderstorm or tsunami might have been more appropriate.

A boat bobbed on the water in the distance, on its way in or out; I couldn't tell. It made me think of fishing trips with Gramps – lovely Gramps – ruddy and pink-cheeked and smiling, always telling us some nautical tale of mermaids and monsters. Nonna made little captain's hats for us and sent me off with supplies of Diet Coke and salty crisps, apparently the best cure for my overwhelming seasickness. I stopped in my tracks – if witches are real, did that mean mermaids were too? I shuddered, vowing to never swim in the sea again.

As I rounded the corner, the cove came into view – a tiny, picture-perfect fishing bay, complete with lighthouse, beach shacks and boats. I felt a bit lighter just seeing it. My stomach rumbled hard. I needed food. And if I remembered correctly, there was a café here that would do the job perfectly. My feet moved faster at the thought of it. I might even go full English, treat myself, make up for a missed dinner and a freak family. I bowed my head down and pulled my hood strings tighter as the wind picked up a notch, already anticipating the warmth of the café. But when I reached the door and lifted my head, my stomach went from rumbling to distraught. The café was still there, but it was closed.

I wanted to fall to the floor wailing, have a full-on toddler tantrum – on top of everything – this?! Why was the universe punishing me? I could see someone around the side of the café, moving boxes. I walked over, jealous of the suitably thick and comfy coat they were wearing.

'Uh, hi?' I ventured. 'I don't suppose you're opening any time soon, are you?' Too late, I noticed the bottle green skirt.

The girl turned round.

Oh no.

It was Badass.

''Fraid not,' she said. 'We close over the winter. I'm just sorting some stuff ready for opening in a few weeks.'

I nodded and backed away. I hoped she wouldn't recognise me. *Oh no, what if I accidentally wished myself invisible?* That would be totally unsubtle and definitely not normal. *Think of nice, non-witchy things. Fluffy clouds. Unicorns. Oh no, not unicorns, what if one appeared?*

'I'm Summer by the way,' she said, those piercing eyes of hers looking me up and down suspiciously. 'We kind of sat together at lunch the other day, with my friend Tabitha – you guys have Maths together.'

'Uh, yeah,' I mumbled, edging away. 'I'm Jessie.'

'I know,' she said, still dissecting me with her eyes. 'You know that school is in the other direction, right?'

'I, uh . . . yeah, needed some air,' I muttered.

'Where did you move down from?' I felt like I was being interrogated.

'Uh, Manchester. But my mum's from here.'

Why did I add that detail? I was trying to prove I was 'allowed' and not just some random outsider, but all I'd done was open up the conversation and made escape more awkward and less likely.

'Yeah, my folks knew your mum from school apparently. You've bought the old Beachview Hotel on the hill haven't you?'

'Yeah,' I said shortly, not enjoying the reminder that everyone knew everything here.

Summer seemed to know exactly what I was thinking. 'It's a

small island,' she said, looking at me for too long, like I was a stray dog that she wasn't sure whether to befriend or shoo away. 'Listen, I'm about to make myself a bacon sandwich if you fancy one too – my Friday treat for completing my endless chores. I've just got to finish moving these boxes first.'

My stomach did a back-flip at the mention of a bacon sandwich, but I didn't have the energy to make the required small talk.

'I'm fine thanks, I need to head to school.'

She looked at me, her blue eyes cutting straight through my crap. 'Ah, bummer, I could really use a hand. Could you maybe spare a few minutes? I mean, unless you particularly need to be an hour and a half early for school?' she said, the edges of a knowing smile forming.

I blushed under my hood. There was nothing for it.

'Sure. What are we doing with them?'

'Well, I've done all the hard work, lugging them down the hill. Now I just need to move them into the storage room.'

She unlocked a small shed round the back of the café and we moved the boxes, me carrying them to her, her arranging them inside the shed. My insides were squirming, and rumbling still. I tried to keep my brain focused on fluffy clouds and exotic beaches (unicorn replacement) in my head, desperate not to accidentally hex her. Not that there was a reason to – but I couldn't be too careful.

'So you work here then? At the café?' I asked, when the awkward silence became too much to bear.

'Yeah, the café and the restaurant,' she said. 'My family owns them – and a bunch of holiday lets. And a bunch of kids. Not that they own the children, they've just had a lot of them. And I get left holding the baby, literally.'

'Wow. Do you live down here?'

'Sure do – that house over there.' She pointed to a double-fronted white house at the far end of the bay. 'I'll give you the not-so-grand tour. Guessing Manchester must've been a bit different to the Island then?'

'Just a bit,' I replied, trying not to sound too acidic.

'Visiting a cousin in Milton Keynes is about as far north as I've ever got.'

'Really?'

'Yep. We're not much for travelling in our family. Mum says why would we bother leaving the Island when everything you could want is here. I have mentioned rainforests and mountains and—'

'Culture,' I added and then immediately wished I hadn't.

'Ha!' she said, laughing, to my relief.

'I didn't mean . . . sorry. That was rude.'

'It's fine, you're not wrong. Though, we do have a fair bit happening on the Island – a fringe festival and everything, I'll have you know.'

'Well, I take it back then. It's a proper cultural hot spot.'

'I wouldn't go that far, but you know, we're getting there.'

I handed Summer the last box, which she put neatly in place.

'Thanks for the help,' she said, closing and locking the shed. 'Now you have to accept my bacon sandwich as repayment. Fact.'

At the thought of food, my stomach went from back-flip to somersault. I really did need to eat. And, it had kind of been nice, chatting to another human being my own age – and *not* thinking about my Problem That Shall Not Be Named. Plus she hadn't broken out into a rash or had any facial features disrupted, so it seemed like that side of things was all under control . . . for the moment at least.

'OK,' I said. 'If you're sure.'

Just then, a little girl with wild blonde hair came running up to us, arms full of rocks.

'Rock,' she said, passing an unremarkable one to me.

'Sorry, this is my sister, Autumn. I know – don't say anything about the names – my mum's a hippy.'

'I wasn't going to say anything. I think they're both beautiful names.'

Summer rolled her eyes at me.

'Thanks for the rock,' I said. 'How old are you, Autumn?'

The girl didn't answer, just passed me another rock, eyes on the ground.

'Rock,' she said.

Summer squatted down next to her, making eye contact.

'Autumn, this is Jessie. Say hello, please.' She signed as she talked. Reluctantly, Autumn looked up and said hello to me. Before passing me another rock.

'When she gets on a rock vibe, there's no distracting her. Or a crab vibe, or a shell vibe. She's seven. God, you're shivering,' she said, turning to me. 'Here, come inside, I'll get you a cup of hot chocolate – and a blanket.'

Summer led me through the bright blue front door and into a huge, light-filled living room. Two identical blonde-haired children, around five or six, were sat on the sofa in pyjamas, plates of toast and precariously placed plastic cups of juice next to them, eyes fixed on the TV.

'Reigne, Topaz, this is Jessie,' Summer said, getting no reaction whatsoever. 'Ugh, they're TV zombies, sorry.'

There was a driftwood coffee table in front of the sofa and bold, colourful paintings of seascapes and boats above it. On the other side of the room, there was a cushioned reading nook nestled in the bay window, with built-in bookshelves running around it. A thin wedge of winter sun was streaming in through the big window, its rays making the room look like something from an interiors magazine for 'beach chic'.

'I'll put the kettle on,' Summer said, heading into the kitchen. 'Make yourself at home.'

Autumn came in through the front door, took a brief, unimpressed look at me and padded through to the kitchen, arms still full of beach treasure. I tucked myself away on the window seat, not wanting to disturb the twins, and took in the room in more detail.

There was a wall of photos by the arch, leading through to the second half of the living room – I'm guessing where a wall had been knocked through. Not stiff, professional photos like Mum used to insist we have done every year; these were candid photos – shared glances, generous laughs, knowing smiles – all caught while the subjects were unaware. I could see Autumn on there, and Reigne and Topaz, Summer, and others (quite a few others by the looks of it) all with bright blonde hair, all with big smiles. The backdrop was always the same – the beach. This beach, Steephill.

I heard banging and cooking noises and soon the smell of bacon wafted through. After what seemed like an eternity,

Summer came back in, carrying a tray carefully balanced with two big mugs of steaming hot chocolate piled high with cream, and a plate of bacon sandwiches. The TV programme finished and the loud, energetic theme tune of the next episode started, the twins still transfixed.

'One more then no more,' Summer said to them, sternly. 'Time to get ready soon.' They ignored her. 'Reigne, Topaz! Recognition please – one more then no more.' They nodded in unison. 'Warmed up a bit?' she asked, carefully handing a mug over to me.

'Yes, thank you,' I said, shuffling myself forward, cradling the hot chocolate like it was my precious newborn. I reached out and took a sandwich with my other hand, not able to wait a second longer. 'So, how many of you are there?' I asked, looking towards the photos and biting into my sandwich, which was, in fact, by far the best bacon sandwich of my life. I could easily have had ten.

'Ah, the wall of shame. Seven. There's seven of us kids.'

'Seven? Wow. What's that like?' I asked, blowing on my hot chocolate.

'Like a constant theme park. No, that sounds too fun – like constantly being in a *queue* at a theme park. No, that sounds too calm – like an overbooked, understaffed, too-loud crèche,' she said. There was a bang and shout from upstairs as if to prove the point.

We both took careful sips of our hot chocolates. It tasted divine – a duvet in a mug. I burned my tongue slightly, but I didn't care.

'That's a bit harsh,' Summer said. 'There are nice things about it. And when it gets too much, I go surfing to escape.'

'You surf?' I asked, impressed.

'Hell, yeah. It keeps me sane. I take it you don't?'

'Never tried it.'

'Ah, standard city girl. We are SO getting you out on a surfboard.' She leaned forward on the sofa, her eyes twinkling.

'I don't know . . .' I said. 'I'm not really . . . outdoorsy.'

'What does that even mean? You can't not be outdoorsy here – that's the best bit of the Island. Promise me you'll try it – just once.'

'I get seasick. Does that matter on a surfboard?'

Summer laughed. 'Promise? Just once? Even Tabs has come out with me, you've got to try it once.'

'OK then,' I said, knowing it was the only way to move the subject on, but also slightly infected by her enthusiasm. Maybe I *could* try surfing.

'MUMMMM! He's got my shoe!' a different blonde-haired child shouted as she stormed into the living room. 'MUM? Where are you?'

'She's doing the B&B breakfasts,' Summer said. 'Tell Jonah I'll take ten minutes of his screen time away after school if he doesn't give it back.' The new blonde-haired child grinned at this and went pounding back up the stairs. 'Sorry, told you – mad house. Where were we? Ah yeah, surfing. Surfing is one of the Seven Wonders of the Isle of Wight.'

I couldn't help but let out a snort.

'Oh, I take it you're not loving it here then?' Summer asked, eyebrows raised.

'I didn't say that, I just . . . what are the six other wonders anyway?'

'I'll show you one day.'

'Does that mean the six other wonders are all surfing too?'

'No, it does not!' she said, unconvincingly. 'Well. Maybe three of them are.'

We both took a sip of our hot chocolates, the cream leaving a slim moustache on my upper lip. A loud bang came from the kitchen.

'Autumn?' Summer called. There was no response. 'I better go and check on her.'

She pushed herself up from the seat, carefully cradling her hot chocolate and headed into the kitchen. I had another sip of my own, appreciating how warm I was. It had worked wonders and I could now feel all my limbs again. My attention was caught by one of the paintings on the wall, the smallest one – a little rectangular frame not much bigger than a book. I stood up to get a closer look, careful not to obstruct any TV viewing. It was of the tiny, perfectly formed cove that stood right outside the house. The thickly painted blues and whites of the sea and sky were mesmerising and dreamy.

'Oh, hello,' said a woman, as she walked through the front door, smiling. She was holding a chubby, red-cheeked baby who had a small tuft of the family's distinctive blonde hair. I could tell straight away, from having seen the photos, but also by the long blonde hair and bright blue eyes that were exactly like Summer's, that it was her mum. I felt like an intruder and instantly, annoyingly, blushed. She stared at me a bit too long.

'Oh hi, I . . . I'm Jessie, Summer's friend. She's just . . .' I stammered, pointing to the back of the house, nearly spilling my hot chocolate.

'Mum, is that you?' Summer called.

'I'm Kate, so nice to meet you,' the woman said, still looking intently at me, walking closer and holding out her free hand.

I shook it. 'I love these paintings,' I blurted out, wishing Summer would come back.

I seem to have a thing about other people's parents, almost like an allergic reaction. It makes no sense; they're just normal adults and it's not like I'm five and can't talk to grown-ups, but whenever a parent is around, I freeze and turn into a total, flustered, monosyllabic idiot.

'Oh, thank you,' Kate said, the baby grabbing at fistfuls of her hair. 'I don't get much time any more, but I like painting when I can.' She was still looking fixedly at me. I felt so uncomfortable it was like my whole body was itching.

'Mum, stop staring at Jessie, you're being weird,' Summer said, finally coming back in.

'Sorry, sorry,' Kate said. 'I just . . . you're Allegra's daughter, aren't you?'

'That's me,' I said, wanting to disappear.

'I used to know your mum. You have her eyes,' she said. 'I heard she'd moved back. She's bought Beachview, hasn't she?'

'Yeah,' I said.

Kate came closer. She put a hand on my shoulder, her bright blue eyes on mine. I felt like I was being lasered. 'Please say hello to her from me,' she said. 'Kate Crowley, I was then. I would really love to see her again.'

'Mum!' Summer came over. 'Don't scare my friends.'

'Sorry, sorry,' Kate said, laughing and slipping an arm around her daughter. Autumn came running through then, full speed, and rammed herself straight into her mum, nearly sending her flying. The baby gave a happy giggle at the sight of her.

'Hey, nugget,' Kate said, 'have you been behaving for Summer?'

'Rock,' Autumn said, thrusting a fist, presumably containing a rock, in Kate's face.

'Oh, we're on a rock vibe today, are we?'

'Sure are,' Summer said.

'Well, you've got your physio session with Kelly, little lady. Daddy's going to take you.' Autumn didn't respond; she was staring at her rock, deep in thought. Kate squatted down next to her, expertly balancing the baby and managing to get eye contact. 'Nugget, it's Kelly time. Go with Daddy to see Kelly.'

'Kelly!' Autumn shouted, jumping up and down.

'The girl loves physio,' Summer said, smiling.

'So how are you settling in, Jessie?' Kate asked.

'Um. Fine, thanks,' I said.

'School sounds like it's been a bit dramatic this last week. Summer was telling me about Callum breaking into a rash and—'

'Mum,' Summer said. 'Jessie's new, she doesn't even know anyone's name yet. Don't interrogate her.'

'And what else was it? That boy's nose?'

I felt a sudden, familiar twinge in my abdomen. *Oh no. No. Not this.*

The room grew darker, suddenly, as clouds rolled in over the sun. Through the window, a boat in the distance went from bobbing to roiling. A wave crashed onto the beach out of nowhere.

No no no.

'Yeah, really weird. I have to go now,' I said, putting my mug on the coffee table. 'School . . .'

'It looks like it might be about to rain though,' Kate said, glancing out at the now-grey skies. 'Are you sure you don't want a lift? I'll be driving this lot in – we have space.'

'No, I'm good, thanks. I've got to . . . grab something from home first,' I said, trying to style out my abruptness. I turned to Summer. 'Thanks for the sandwich, and the hot chocolate.'

There was an awkward pause. I could feel the cramps worsening and, as they did, the skies were darkening, dramatically. I needed to get out of there before there was a full-blown natural disaster. I gave a big smiling sigh, the kind that signifies, *that was nice, but let's move on* and headed to the door at speed.

'Are you sure you don't want a lift?' Summer said as she followed me outside, the wind whipping my hair in front of my eyes. 'It's full on with all the kids, but better than getting wet.'

'No honestly, I'm good.' I was eyeing the sea nervously. The waves were getting higher.

'Sorry about my mum,' Summer said. 'She can be a bit extra sometimes. It's the artist in her. She's actually pretty cool, when she's behaving like a normal human being.'

'No, no, I liked her,' I said, distracted. 'Thanks again for breakfast! See you at school!'

I walked away quickly, my feet crunching on the path, the afterglow of the hot chocolate and my chat with Summer already fading as my stomach churned, my head pounded, and a massive fork of lightening lit up the sky, narrowly missing the boat bobbing in the roiling sea.

CHAPTER EIGHT

The Queen Vic rumour mill screamed into action in registration. Everyone was already overexcited by the prospect of a party at Sonny Patterson's house later; little pockets of animated chats were happening in cliques all round the classroom. I slumped over my bag, hardly able to keep my eyes open, my sleep-deprived night of horrors and the early morning catching up with me. I tried to drown out the incessant buzz of gossip, which was actually pretty hard as I was sitting next to the beating heart of it (Marcus). I'd never wished for a pair of headphones and some ear-splitting death metal music more in my life.

'At Sonny's last party Jenny Goldsmith hooked up with Layla Ross in the bathroom,' Marcus said, with an unnecessary level of glee in his voice. 'Girl on girl! It got them both two extra points.'

'Was that before or after she barfed and blocked the sink?'

'Wasn't that Hayden?'

'Yes, boi! What a legend!'

'And Hannah Wade had on THE shortest skirt ever, practically gagging for it, luckily Chris here obliged – isn't that right, Chris?'

Chris stayed quiet, though from the backslaps and high fives happening around him, I imagined his expression was confirming it. An eyebrow lift, a nod so subtle that if the confirmation ever came back to bite him, he'd be able to insist, truthfully, that he had never *said* anything.

Honestly it was like looking at a pack of chimps. It wouldn't have surprised me if they'd started pulling fleas off each other and sniffing each other's arses. 'Gagging for it'? Really? So, if we want to wear anything longer than knee-length we're tight-arse prudes and shorter than knee-length we're gagging for it. So where does that leave us? *Ugh*, I thought. *They're the hormone-ridden dogs in heat gagging for it.*

'Maybe she'll—' Marcus started, then he broke off. He was trying to get the rest of the sentence out, but he seemed to be choking on something. No, not choking . . . *gagging*. Every time he went to speak, he retched. Big, loud, about-to-be-sick type retching.

Oh no. Not again.

I tried to think of calm, sunny beaches. I wished Ms Simmons would appear. Everyone was crowding round Marcus now, the boys laughing hysterically, thinking it was all a big joke, the girls looking curious. Now would be a good time, Ms Simmons . . .

'Good morning, 10S!' she said, finally arriving, looking impeccably awesome in a sharp trouser suit and red heels.

The class reluctantly tore their attention from Marcus, who had started breathing normally again, and faced the front. As Ms Simmons put down her bag, a low wolf-whistle echoed through the room as one of the boys noticed her outfit. She froze, then straightened up, glaring at the back of the class – a proper effective teacher look which had everyone falling silent instantly.

Ms Simmons was young and attractive and fashionable which, for boys who were used to Mr Anstead's BO and Mrs Hermitage's saggy tights, I guess meant she was basically a supermodel. And apparently fair game.

'Some of you appear to think we're in the 1950s,' she said icily. 'Where that kind of behaviour might have been acceptable.' There was a pause. The class held its breath. I grinned. 'That kind of behaviour is not acceptable *anywhere*, and if I hear it again you will go straight to the Head's office.'

Ah. The disappointment of an empty threat, after it had started off so well. Everyone knew that the Headteacher, Mr Harlston, was about as effective as a chocolate teapot (as Mum would say). Or a holey condom (as Nonna would). Useless, in other words.

***

'Ah, Jessie,' Mr Anstead said, later that morning, as he handed our tests back in Maths. His rank coffee breath wafted over me. I'm pretty sure my eyes had been closed and I'd been technically asleep; this was not a pleasant awakening. He lowered his voice slightly. 'You may want to ask a knowledgeable friend to help catch you up. Clearly, there are some gaps from your last school.'

I glanced at the worksheet and tried not to laugh. I could do this with my eyes shut. Obviously I'd gone too far with the intentional mistakes. Rookie error.

'I can help this lunchtime if you want,' Callum said, turning round from his seat in front of me.

'He's not the model student in class,' Mr Anstead said, chuckling, 'but he's surprisingly capable.'

58

I'd rather stick needles in my eyes, repeatedly, while sat in an ice bath, thanks all the same, I imagined saying.

'Thanks, but don't worry, I'll look it up on the internet,' is what I actually said, wishing Callum would swivel back round and leave me alone.

'It's no problem,' he said, giving me a nausea-inducing wink.

Having one-on-one time with Callum Henderson was, in addition to being stomach-churningly awful, likely to attract attention. As much attention as being super-smart would have. So much for flying under the radar.

'Half one in the library then?' Callum said.

'Start slowly with her, Callum, it's tricky stuff,' Mr Anstead said.

Just then, a twinge of cramp struck me, and the big pile of papers Mr Anstead was carrying dropped in a splayed heap all over the floor. Oops.

***

The second the bell rang for break, I stuffed my books in my bag and exited the classroom, determined not to get cornered by Callum and risk another incident. I headed straight to the toilet and locked myself in a cubicle.

It would be fine, I told myself. One maths tutoring session with Callum over a lunchtime wasn't a major disaster. I was sure I could concentrate enough on the maths to not do any damage. No rashes or nose traumas. I'd nod my way through it and be done. End of story. I left the cubicle full of resolve.

Libby was at the mirrors, reapplying foundation – or whatever girls who wear make-up do in front of mirrors. I gave her the polite, vague head nod that I thought was appropriate in these kind of situations.

'Hi,' she said, still looking in the mirror.

'Hi,' I replied, washing my hands as fast as possible.

'Jessie, isn't it? You joined a few weeks ago. I think we have PE together. I'm Libby.'

Oh yes, we do. PE. My weakest, most hated subject.

'I heard on the grapevine you were getting a bit cosy with Callum in Maths today,' she said, turning away from the mirror and facing me head-on.

Getting a bit cosy? I'm not sure I would have called it getting *cosy*. Exchanging a few words – unenthusiastic on my part – more like. And how did she find out so fast – does she have spies? Her eyes, long-lashed and wide, were staring straight at me. She did not look all that welcoming or friendly. Probably not the best time to add that Callum was going to tutor me.

'You're new,' she said. 'So in case you don't know, Callum is my boyfriend.'

I stared at the floor and felt a furious blush creeping up on me – FOR NO REASON. I hadn't done anything wrong. It's so me, blushing and squirming at the slightest hint of confrontation. I felt a twinge in my stomach and panic rose in my chest. *Please don't do anything weird,* I told my uterus. *Think of a beach,* I told my brain. *Think of a nice warm sea and a sunny day.*

'I know,' I said, in a way smaller voice than intended.

Suddenly, the tap nearest me came on, of its own accord. And then the middle one, and the one in front of Libby, some of the water splattering on to her skirt.

'What the?!' She flinched, surprised, and jerked away, wiping her skirt with her hand, glancing at the tap, which had now stopped.

'I swear this school is haunted,' she said, more to herself than to me. 'Anyway, what were we saying?' Her face morphed from a terrifying scowl to an only-slightly-less-scary smile. 'So yes, Callum is my boyfriend, and as long as we're clear on that, any friend of Callum's is a friend of mine. So, are you coming to Sonny's party tonight?'

She went back to looking in the mirror and applying her make-up. I wasn't even sure if she was waiting for an answer.

'Uh, I . . . haven't . . .'

'I'll DM you the details,' she said. 'It'll be fun. He has a massive house and his parents are cool with it all. And pre-drinks on the beach, as always. See you in PE.'

And with that, she turned on her heel and headed out of the bathroom leaving me standing there like a total lemon, head spinning, wondering what it was that had just happened, angry at myself for playing my cards so badly I'd ended up in the claws of the exact people I'd been trying to avoid.

CHAPTER NINE

'So basically, you have to take it back to the original expression, by moving this integer over here, you see. And now this needs to be balanced out,' Callum said, leaning in over my book. He smelt of too-strong Lynx, with an undertone of boy sweat and hair gel.

I nodded like one of those bulldog things in the back of cars, even though what he was explaining was so basic he may as well have been teaching me the alphabet.

'Ah OK, yeah. I think I get it,' I said. I filled in some numbers, correctly this time. The sooner this was over, the better.

'That's it!' He looked pleased with himself. 'I think you're ready to try one of the harder ones now.'

I made myself pause slightly looking at some of them. I even did a cartoon thinking face.

'So how are you finding it here?' he asked, edging closer to me.

'Yeah, good, thanks,' I lied.

'Your family's bought the old Beachview Hotel, haven't they?'

'Uh, yeah.'

'Bet that needs a lot of work. Apparently it's haunted – Mad Old Mrs Fletcher used to run it. Rumour is she killed her husband and buried him under the patio after he tried to leave her for a younger woman. They didn't have any hotel guests for years – too scared of the ghost. Have you seen it?'

'A ghost? No,' I said, not believing a word he said while also, annoyingly, feeling goosebumps creep down my spine.

'And you're a Downer, yeah?' he asked, eyes gleaming.

'My surname? Yeah. Well, I'm a Jones but my mum's maiden name is Downer. Why?'

'Oh nothing,' he said. Clearly he was desperate for me to ask more questions, so I ignored him and carried on with the work.

In a minute he carried on, just like I had known he would. 'Just, you know, it's a small island, stories do the rounds. The legend goes that Downers can be a bit of a handful – feisty women and all that. In a good way.' He winked again. A horrible, slimy, creepy-old-man wink that made me want to vomit in his face. I stared at my work so hard my eyes hurt.

'You should come and sit with us at lunch, you know,' he said. 'Make some decent friends. You might catch something sitting with those freaks.'

I paused, wanting so badly to tell him to stick it, but knew that would not be wise. *Blend in, Jessie.* 'Thanks,' I said weakly instead, thinking that no matter how desperate I got I would never sit with his bunch of Neanderthal boy-babies and their groupies.

'Are you coming to Sonny's? Libby said she invited you.'

Great, they'd been talking about me.

'Maybe. I'll have to check with my mum. We might have plans,' I muttered. 'Right, I'm done,' I said, finishing off the last equation.

He looked surprised. Maybe I'd been so keen to get this over with I had done them a bit too fast. He checked over them all.

'All of them are right, too. Well done.' Cue patronising smile.

I started packing up my books, feeling mightily relieved. I had survived. All was fine. I had not accidentally revealed I was a maths genius and I had not accidentally, magically broken any of his limbs, much as I would have liked to.

'Let me know if you need any help again,' Callum said. 'I'm pretty good at maths.' His hand grazed my knee under the table and I felt my abdomen cramp. He yelped, snatching his hand away. 'Wow, think we had a little spark there,' he said, grinning and rubbing his hand.

'It must be static,' I said, standing up, cringing on the inside, blushing on the outside, and knowing I absolutely needed to leave. 'Thanks for all your help. I think that's done the trick.'

I grabbed my bag and headed for the door.

'I'll see you at Sonny's,' he called after me.

As if.

***

By PE that afternoon Libby had apparently decided we were new best friends. She sought me out in the changing room and refused to leave my side, despite my best efforts.

'Cal said the tutoring went well,' she said, linking arms with me as we walked to the pitch. I couldn't tell if she was being threatening or sarcastic or (God help me) genuine, but I didn't like it. 'But that you've got a lot to catch up on so you'll probably need more sessions.'

My heart sank all the way to my slightly wet trainers.

'I think I'll be OK, actually,' I said, trying to sound hopefully positive but not arrogantly confident – it's a fine line. 'I've got the hang of it now.'

'Sometimes I play dumb around him, you know, to get him to help me – and to help his ego. Typical boy!'

My heart started thumping – was that directed at me? Did she know I was playing dumb? Oh God – did she think I was doing it to get closer to Callum? Ugh!

'So what are you going to wear tonight?' she asked, completely changing the subject.

'Tonight?' I asked, stalling in the hope I could think of an ironclad get-out.

'To Sonny's, remember? You're definitely coming – you have to! His parties are always awesome. His parents have the best-stocked booze cupboard.'

'Oh, I realised I can't tonight . . . I have . . .'

'Come on, ladies!' Coach shouted, spinning a netball on his finger like he was some kind of low-rent Michael Jordan. 'Enough of the mothers' meetings! On the line please.'

I ran enthusiastically to the line and threw myself into the warm-up like never before, running through possible and immovable excuses as I did so for why I couldn't possibly go to this sodding party later. I was definitely not digging this sudden BFF vibe she was going for and it was putting me even more on edge – which I hadn't thought was possible.

After the near electrocution of Callum earlier, I had been feeling pretty shaky. I'd considered running home, getting into bed and locking myself away so that I wasn't a risk to myself or anyone else. But even though I had no idea what I was doing (or, more worryingly, what I was *capable* of doing) I was determined to persist with the normal-teenage-girl thing. If I could make it through this first day of being, well, magical – and I was so nearly there – that was a win. And when I got home, as long as I could avoid Mum and Nonna, I could maybe practise in the safe confines of my house, where no one could come to any harm.

As I'd arrived mid-year, they'd put me in a random PE set, until they could assess my ability. It just so happened that it was the top set and as my ability was absolutely non-existent, it wasn't the best result. I was praying for them to realise soon and put me in my rightful place with the other people who had no hand-eye co-ordination, couldn't remember the rules, and couldn't run to catch a bus.

When we were mid shoot practice (yawn), the top set boys' PE group walked past the court on their way back from whatever much better sport they'd been doing – basketball, I'd guess. They paused by the fence, watching. Perfect. If there was anything I loved more than doing sport inadequately, it was having people *watch me* doing sport inadequately. I looked back to the hoop, trying to ignore them, but then I heard the laughter. Loud, hooting boy laughter – the kind that's usually reserved for being mean or rude about people.

And sure enough, that was exactly what they were doing. Somehow, they'd managed to produce a pad of paper and a pen. They were holding up numbers. Scores.

They were pointing and calling out and laughing. It was hard to determine exactly who they were aiming the numbers at, but it didn't really matter. They were being dicks. Some of the girls were laughing nervously, some of them blushing furiously and looking angry. But no one was saying anything. I felt the anger building in me. I looked at Libby, hoping that, as gobby and direct as she seemed to be, maybe she'd say something. She looked mildly pissed off, but not like she was about to stand up to anyone. Of course not; the main culprits were Callum and Marcus. Her boyfriend and his best friend.

Cramps pinched. Oh man. This wasn't what I needed. I took some deep breaths, tried to turn away – maybe if I didn't see it, it wouldn't rile me quite so much. I couldn't risk whatever I might accidentally do. But I could still hear them, clear as day. The numbers being shouted out, the laughter that followed . . .

No. Please no, deep breaths.

Maybe if I could deal with it in an official, totally non-witchy way, the cramps would go away. But it was so not my place to kick off. I'd only just got here. It's a well-known truth that complaining to teachers about annoying boys does not help keep you under the radar. Though maybe it was a better alternative to raining down some kind of unexplained magical hellfire on them. I suddenly wished that Summer was here; I was pretty sure she wouldn't be holding back. But she wasn't, and no one else was saying or doing anything. I had no choice. The cramps were getting worse.

'Sir,' I said, walking over to Mr Bowd – I refused to buy into his fantasy and call him Coach. 'Those boys over there, I don't know if you've seen them, but they're scoring us.'

He glanced over disinterestedly. Of course he'd seen them; everyone had. 'It's just a joke,' he said, smiling.

'I don't find it very funny,' I said, not quite believing his response, while also, sadly, very much believing it. 'And I don't think they're scoring us on our shooting abilities.'

'Well, maybe you need to develop more of a sense of humour to get by in this school, Ms Jones,' he said. 'Anyway, it's the end of the lesson now. C'mon, ladies!' he shouted. 'Time to go in.'

Everyone else started walking in. I stood there in disbelief, daggering Coach and the boys, who were clattering away in a flurry of guffaws and high fives. Suddenly a cramp came, big and sharp. I looked away, hoping that I could prevent whatever witch retribution my ovaries wanted to exact.

'AGH!' There was a pained shout from behind me. I glanced back. Marcus was on the floor, the rest of the boys standing round laughing at him, in proper fits of hysterics, a lone netball next to him on the grass.

'Who threw that?' Coach asked.

Now he was outraged.

CHAPTER TEN

The house was thankfully silent and empty when I got in, which was absolute bliss. There was no way in hell I wanted any kind of a conversation – or eye contact – with Mum or Nonna yet. My head felt ready to implode, pounding with the events of today. Callum and Libby and Marcus – gagging and netballs and electric shocks. I wanted to get under my duvet and bury my head in the sand of Kardashian repeats, but I knew that my sacred alone time was limited and I needed to make the most of it.

There was no denying I had some freak powers and also no denying that I was liable to do some serious damage if I wasn't careful. And, as much as I would dearly have loved to send Callum up in flames, that would probably have caused unwanted questions and attention. My powers didn't really fit with my staying-under-the-radar master plan – but it was clear I needed to learn how to *not* use them. I needed to learn control. Which I was very obviously lacking. If I could teach myself control, without the interfering help of Mum or Nonna, I would be home free and back on the normal, unfreaky, nothing-out-of-the-ordinary track.

How I was going to do this, I did not know. But I *did* know that I was starving and another advantage of no one being around was that there was no one to restrict my crap food intake. I dumped my bag in the hallway, and made my way through what had once been the hotel lobby, complete with reception desk and old-skool pigeonholes for keys (currently being used for shoe storage) and into the kitchen.

I rummaged through the fridge – or rather, cast a quick glance over its scant contents. There wasn't really enough food for a true rummage. Eggs. At least there were eggs. A quick check of the bread bin revealed a few mould-free slices at the end of a loaf. Bingo.

I looked around the kitchen with its bright orange pine units and floral wallpaper, probably the height of fashion back in the seventies. The cooker was a big industrial one, I guess for catering meals back when the building was a hotel. Everything had a slimy layer of oil on it and a musty, deeply embedded smell of grease and guests and gross. The smell lingered on all my clothes, and in my hair, no matter how much I tried to wash it out with strong-smelling shampoos. A constant, foul reminder. It almost made me want to cry. Why on earth had Mum done this to us? Brought us here, to this dive house on this dive Island, knowing full well it would spark up our powers, making us outcasts. My upset turned to rage.

Deep breaths.

I stared at the egg I'd got out.

And started to wonder . . .

Mum and Nonna said these powers were good, and helpful, and made us special. *Let's see, shall we?*

I focused on the egg. Really hard. I imagined a chick emerging from the egg. A cute little yellow fluffy chick, fluffing about, as chicks do.

Nothing.

I tried holding the egg and thinking it.

Nothing.

I moved it closer to my womb – it seemed to make sense, seeing as that was where all my 'power' was coming from.

Nothing.

Clearly, magicking an actual living, breathing chick out of an egg was beyond my limited skill set, which was fair enough. Maybe I should try something simpler, more straightforward, less God-like than creating life. I dug out a (miraculously) clean frying pan , cracked the egg into it and tried accessing my fickle magic one last time. I focused on the raw, runny egg so hard my eyeballs nearly popped out, imagining it cooking, the heat, the white actually turning white, the taste of a freshly fried egg. I closed my eyes, put my hand on my abdomen, desperately trying to channel all my magical period-based witchiness into creating a tasty fried snack.

A ripple of cramp; that was good.

A teeny-tiny chirrup; that was bad.

I opened my eyes.

Standing in the middle of the frying pan, all yellow and fresh and fluffy, was a teeny-tiny chick.

It looked at me like I was its mother, its shiny black eyes cute and searching, its little beak chirruping, opening wide.

Arse. This was not ideal. My magic had its wires seriously crossed – or was on a delay. I had been thinking of fried egg! Delicious, fresh, tasty fried egg with a lush, runny yolk. Oh man, I'd better not let that cross my mind again – who knew what could happen? I definitely didn't want to accidentally cook my newborn chick. That I had created. My skin rippled – I felt powerful and panicky.

I had not thought this through. What the hell was I supposed to do with a chick? A magical chick who was clearly hungry and wanting its mum. It carried on cheeping at me, more insistently now.

'Come here then, Chicky,' I said, gingerly holding out my hand to it.

It paused, seeming to think about it, then climbed on board. It felt warm and surprisingly light in my palm.

'You're actually kind of cute,' I said, bringing it slowly up to my face.

I wondered for a moment whether it might answer back.

It didn't.

My time was running out – someone would be home soon and I needed to get the evidence of my magical balls-up out of the house. With my stomach still rumbling, I looked up how the holy hell to keep Chicky alive.

There were some conflicting pieces of advice, including one website saying to give it cold coffee, which didn't seem right, and another advising to feed it cut-up hard-boiled egg, which seemed even less right. In the end I put Chicky in a cardboard box up in my room, locking a very curious Dave out, and went digging in the garden for worms, which are harder to come by than you'd think.

It took me ages. In the end, I found a measly two to offer up to Chicky, who sniffed at them, then retreated into a corner of the box. At that point I heard Mum's car pull up so I quickly changed out of my uniform, threw on some jeans and a jumper and, once I knew Mum was safely in the kitchen, tiptoed out of the front door like some ridiculous stealth ninja, leaving Chicky and her worm dinner behind.

CHAPTER ELEVEN

It felt good to shake off the musty old house, even though it was icy cold and windy outside. Fresh air was good, violent salty fresh air even better in some ways – perfect for clearing away the cobwebs and all that. My mind still wandered though, to the cobweb-strewn places I was trying to avoid thinking about.

Like the not-so-glorious events of the day and the underlying rage that was apparently now my foundation. I hated that we'd moved *again*, I hated that we'd moved *here*, I hated the house, I hated that everyone knew our business. Mum had always told us to fit in as best we could – every new school we started, every event, every school production, every place or situation there were other people – blending in was basically the family motto. And yet she'd knowingly brought us to the one place where blending in would be thoroughly, totally, one hundred per cent impossible. I didn't have a fighting chance of being normal and fading into the background here.

One of the things I loved about Manchester was that it was easy to be anonymous. That's the thing with all the big cities we'd lived in actually; they're so full to bursting with all kinds of shapes and sizes and personalities that you can always find your people – or not, if you don't want to. Don't get me wrong, a school is a school is a school anywhere – they're all a cesspit of popularity contests and overt and covert bullying – but in a city school, not everyone knows your business before you've even introduced yourself.

I'd lived in small places before – one of Mum's out of the blue moves (this one because 'she felt like being in the countryside might suit us') had seen us end up in a tiny village on the outskirts of the Lake District. But that had felt different. Maybe it was because it was primary school, before the full force of peer judgement, ostracisation and stupid, randy boys kicked in. Though, to be fair, stupid boys exist from reception; they just don't fully manifest until hormones Frankenstein them at around twelve.

The Island was small in a different way. Everyone knew everyone – and everyone knew everyone's children and uncles and aunts, half-brothers, step-siblings and second-cousins-once-removed too. Even Mum and Nonna. Every time I mentioned someone at school – which I did as little as possible and only accidentally – they would ask me their surname, which would normally be followed by either a shared look, a raised eyebrow of recognition or very occasionally a little 'ooh' or 'ah'. It was like living in a fishbowl. A small, slightly fetid fishbowl, where the other fish have been swimming in circles for centuries.

While I was festering, I'd wandered down to the seafront. I walked along the main strip now, which was completely deserted – not even dog walkers – heading for a little patch of beach I knew just round the corner of the headland. Out of sight, out of the way. I was too busy looking down, watching my footprints leave their marks in the sand and searching for glints of seaglass, to see the people ahead of me.

By the time I had, it was too late.

'Jessie!' Libby shrieked. 'Jessie!'

She came running across the sand to me, grinning like we were best mates reuniting after gap year travels.

'Oh, hi,' I said, rearranging my face so the dread wasn't apparent.

'I knew you'd come to the party!' she said.

Oh God. The party.

'Ah, I can't, I'm just on my way home . . .'

She raised her eyebrows questioningly. Clearly I wasn't going home – my home was in the other direction.

'Come on, I'm not taking no for an answer. Unless you're on your way to a hot date. Are you?'

I considered lying, but knew it would end up being too complicated, so I opted for a vague shrug. She grabbed my hand and pulled me along to where her friends were sitting huddled up on the steps leading to the observatory. There were three other girls, all versions of Libby but with slight differences. Same over-caked make-up (in varying shades), same puffa jackets (in varying colours), same potential for mean in their eyes (of varying ferocity).

'Everyone, this is Jessie. Jessie, you know Sadie already' – Libby gestured to the blonde wearing the green jacket – 'and this is Phoebe and Caz.'

They gave me the once-over, slightly raising their painted-on eyebrows as they took in my ripped jeans, stained jumper and scraped-back hair. I felt like Cinderella pre-Fairy Godmother makeover. Maybe I could magic up a fairy godmother to sort me out? I felt totally out of place and wrong, like a meerkat dropped into the monkey enclosure – or the shark tank. I wished I was hanging out with Summer instead. It hadn't felt like this with her.

'Jessie is HellaBella's sister,' Libby said proudly, as if presenting a prize boar at auction. The others gasped, clearly impressed.

Ah, now Libby's interest in me suddenly made a lot more sense.

'Oh my God, you're so lucky. Does she do your make-up for you?' Phoebe asked, frowning slightly at my face in its distinctly make-up-free glory.

'Is she really nice? She seems really nice?' Caz asked. 'And funny.'

'So funny,' Sadie said.

'If your idea of nice is being such a parental suck-up that I call her Henry,' I said.

Libby chuckled; the other three just looked confused.

'As in Henry Hoover?' I explained, though they still looked baffled. I sighed. 'Yeah, she's OK.'

'I saw you having lunch with the Weird Sisters at school the other day,' Sadie said. It took me a second to realise she meant Summer and Tabitha. 'You don't want to make a habit of that, hanging with Wannabe *Blue Crush* Surf Champ and Try-too-hard Jane Austen is not a good strategy if you want decent people to like you.'

I noticed Libby flinch slightly. 'Here, have some of my coffee,' she said, holding her eco cup out towards me.

'Uh, I'm good thanks,' I said, still reeling from Sadie's comment and not feeling we were at the coffee-sharing phase yet.

'Really, have some.' She thrust it closer.

I accepted the cup, took a nervous sip with everyone watching, then flinched. It was coffee – but not just coffee. It had been mixed with God knows what kind of strong alcohol. If they hadn't all been gawping at me I would've spat it out. I swallowed and offered the cup back to Libby.

'Have some more,' she urged. 'You need to catch up.'

I was about to refuse, make my excuses and run away. But as the alcohol made its way down the back of my throat and into my chest, leaving a warming trail, I realised there was nothing I was in a rush to get back to. Twenty minutes sitting with these Mean Girls and having a few sips of random liquor suddenly seemed like a much more attractive prospect than heading home and having Mum in my face trying to get me to open up and talk to her. Libby and alcohol or Mum and harsh reality? I'd go with Libby and alcohol, thanks. So, I had another sip.

**

'Truth,' I said, knowing I couldn't face a dare.

It was some time later, I don't know how much time specifically. Enough that it was starting to get dark and, I realised, very cold. I'd been mostly sitting back observing, trying to keep myself to myself, but I knew it would be my turn eventually.

'Boring,' Sadie said, rolling her eyes.

'OK, what's the furthest you've got with a boy?' Phoebe asked, rubbing her hands together – either in glee or to keep warm, I couldn't tell.

'You can't come up with anything more original?' Libby said.

'No, I can't. And don't act like you're not interested.'

I hated this question. Full on, squirm-in-my-seat, would-rather-eat-worms, hated it. How should I answer it? I'd only just met these people. I didn't want to admit I'd never kissed anyone properly and become a laughing stock already, but equally, what was their level of acceptable? I didn't want to seem like I was easy and out for all their boyfriends. I needed a safe middle ground – but one person's middle is another person's slut. I wondered if I should say I was one of those people who made a chastity pledge – I'd read somewhere they were the new cool thing.

'Well, I mean, a gentleman never tells,' I said, in what I hoped was an intriguing voice.

They just looked confused. 'But, you're not a gentleman,' Sadie said.

'Oh my God, have you gone all the way?' Caz said.

I thought of Pete Knowles, my boyfriend in Year Eight, trying to kiss me at the school gates and me freaking out and swerving my head so he ended up kissing the wall. No, I had definitely not gone all the way.

I heard footsteps crunching along the sand in our direction, along with shouting and guffawing and general boy-bants noises. All the girls looked over.

'Saved by the bell,' Libby said quietly to me, giving me a faint wink. She wasn't wrong though – I never thought I'd actually be pleased to see Callum and his band of merry men. I breathed again.

'What took you so long?' Libby asked.

'All right, all right, ball and chain. Don't nag,' Callum said, holding up two clinking carrier bags which, I presumed, contained alcohol.

There were three other boys with Callum – Marcus, Freddie

and Eli. They were all wrapped up in hoodies and jackets, which reminded me, again, that it was actually pretty freezing now. Everyone else was standing, so I eased myself up, my backside numb from sitting on the concrete steps, my vision wavy and unsure. I looked at the empty beach, at the sea, which was now a dark mass, the sky at that turning point, on the verge of dropping into proper night. I checked the time on my phone, surprised at how late it was. That alcohol had gone to my head way more than I'd realised, and I didn't like it. I could feel the beginning of a headache right at the base of my skull, like a small, hard nut.

'Well, whaddaya know, Jessie's here,' Callum said, looking directly at me.

'I told you I'd get her out somehow!' Libby said.

'Fresh meat,' he said, with a smirk I really didn't like that much.

The other boys sniggered.

'Play nice,' Libby said. 'She's my friend now.' She put her arm around me.

Suddenly all the unexpected joy at escaping from home and Mum dissipated. It was like a pack of hyenas were closing in on me. I was cold and felt very alone and out of my depth. The sea, so welcome and refreshing earlier, now felt threatening, its waves crashing chaotically too close to me, its salty tang burning the inside of my nostrils. Even Mum trying to talk to me or Nonna wafting some stinky herbs in my face and cleansing my aura would be better than this. I felt an overwhelming desire to be home, in my attic icebox, cuddling Dave.

'Right then, who's having what?' Callum asked, sitting down on the steps and reaching into the carrier bags.

'I've really got to go,' I said, slipping out from under Libby's arm and making my way towards the path and freedom.

'You can't go yet!' Libby said. 'We haven't even made it to the party.'

I had to stand firm. Walk firm. 'Sorry, my mum's expecting me.'

'It's fine, you texted your mum to say you were with friends. Text her again to say you're coming round to my house,' Libby said, insistent.

I only had a vague memory of texting Mum, which again reminded me that I'd had too much to drink. Libby started walking towards me. Should I run? That might look a tiny bit stupid, breaking into a Usain Bolt just to get away from the cool kids.

'Honestly, I totally forgot, we have a . . . a family thing tonight. She'll be fuming if I don't get home soon and then I'll be grounded and not allowed out at all,' I said, figuring this was a good bit of carrot-dangling, not that I ever planned on delivering said carrot. 'See you on Monday!' I said, finally managing to put what felt like a safe amount of distance between us.

'Bye, Party Pooper!' Libby called after me as I sped up the beach.

As I trudged back the road towards home I could feel the regret blossoming in my stomach, like in Biology when you squeeze a tiny drop of bacteria on to a petri dish and watch as it grows and spreads. I should have just made my excuses as soon as I'd seen Libby, gone home regardless, and ignored Mum as usual. Avoiding all conversation at home and locking myself in my room would have been better than hanging round with those brain-dead Barbies, who now – disaster – thought I was happy to play tag-along and be part of their gang of mean. I had a nasty taste in my mouth and it wasn't just from the alcoholic latte.

It was fine, I reasoned. I hadn't friend-committed so deeply that I was now bound to daily canteen time and sleepovers. It was a one-off and I could keep it that way, go back to being distant tomorrow.

I'd made it up the hill and was at the top of the high street. There was a slight Friday night buzz – couples dressed up heading out for dinner, pubs full of people laughing and drinking. I heard someone calling my name, and I instinctively looked behind me. Callum.

Callum? What was Callum doing chasing after me up a hill? My stomach dropped. I was so close to home. Maybe now *was* the time to run.

'Hey,' he said, catching up with me, hardly even out of breath after running up the hill. 'You left this,' he said, holding up a black beanie hat with a spider logo on it. I had never seen it before and it certainly wasn't mine. He took a step closer, edging me into the deep doorway of the post office.

'That's not mine,' I said, sidestepping away from him.

'What? I was sure it was,' he said. 'Aw, man, what a doofus!' He stepped closer again and my heart started pounding.

'What a gentleman I am though, hey?' he said. 'You should probably . . . reward me in some way.' His face looked different, smug and expectant as always, but now with an edge. The smell of stale beer and ripe alcopops hit me as he stepped closer still.

I backed up, until I had nowhere left to back up to, the wall of the post office cold and hard against my shoulders. I took a deep breath and tried to focus on my anger, my revulsion. I must have enough magic left in me, surely – it was only day three of my period. *Please let me have enough magic left in me . . .*

And then, before I had even felt the hint of a cramp, Callum leaned in and kissed me, his lips wet and uninvited.

'What are you doing?' I said loudly. 'Get off me!' I pushed him away, my only remaining option after my stupid, uncontrollable powers let me down.

His eyes flared in surprise for a split second, then filled with pure anger. 'Stupid cow,' he hissed. 'It was just a bit of fun. You were asking for it, you've been coming on to me since you got here.'

Then I did run.

CHAPTER TWELVE

I spent the weekend going through something like the seven stages of grief – headache, denial, disbelief, rage, more denial, more rage, fear.

Callum had kissed me.

My first sodding kiss and any agency had been taken from me by that greasy-haired bellend. I started to question myself – had I, like he'd said, been coming on to him? I thought back to our 'tutoring' session – had I done anything that would've given him the impression I liked him? I'd nearly electrocuted him when he accidentally-on-purpose touched me. Then I'd scarpered first chance I'd got. Not exactly giving off a 'take me to bed' vibe. Maybe he took that as me being coy, playing hard to get?

No. Absolutely no way. There was no subconscious part of me that was sending come-hither signals. Callum was entitled and arrogant and sly and mean and I'd known a hundred boys before with varying shades of Callum and they were not my kind of people. And how dare he make me question myself like this! This wasn't my fault. This was a stupid, full-of-himself boy, who was used to getting what he wanted, deciding, for a laugh, that he wanted a go at some fresh meat and not caring what the fresh meat thought about that. I mean, we'd literally just had a PSHE session about consent. They showed us that cup of tea video. If you offer someone a cup of tea, they may say 'yes please', they may say 'no', they may say 'yes' initially and then when the tea arrives they may have changed their mind and if so you shouldn't make them drink it. YOU MADE ME DRINK THE CUP OF TEA CALLUM AND I HATE TEA.

By Monday morning, I'd calmed down, with the help of serious and sustained Dave cuddles and chat. (Despite the fact the cat was in my bad books; when I'd come home on Friday night there had been no Chicky in my room, only Dave – who had somehow managed to break in – and a few fluffy feathers. The window had been open, so it wasn't conclusive, but I wasn't hopeful.)

Summer had DMed me over the weekend and we'd messaged a bit about random stuff – what the surf was like (she was on a mission to get me surfing), comparing notes on annoying sisters, that kind of thing – which felt good, if strangely nerve-wrecking. Part of me desperately wanted to open up and tell her about what had happened with Callum, but I talked myself down – I didn't know these people, and their friendships and history. Yes, she'd had a run-in with Libby in the toilets and they definitely hadn't sounded like best mates, but I was a total newbie, and in my experience, total newbies always come bottom of the heap, no matter what. I'd turned down her invitation on Saturday to go surfing and a second invitation on Sunday to go for lunch with her and Tabitha, citing a vague 'family things' excuse, but the thought of seeing them both today made me feel a whole lot better about going in. Not *good*, mind you, but better.

These were the facts:

1. Callum had kissed *me* – an important distinction.
2. It was without consent, without want and without provocation.
3. I had rejected him, making it clear how I felt.
4. Most importantly, knowing boys like Callum, he wouldn't ever want the fact that I had rejected him to be public knowledge, so it was actually extremely unlikely that anyone except for the two of us would ever know about it.

And that last fact was pretty much the only thing that got me out of bed on Monday morning. I didn't need to worry about people finding out, because there was no way he was going to tell anyone – it was hands down too embarrassing. Now I just needed to work out whether I owed it to Libby to tell her that her boyfriend had tried it on with me. Despite Girl Code, I was leaning towards *no*.

***

'Here she is,' Nonna said as I walked into the kitchen. 'We were just talking about you.'

I couldn't bear a deep and meaningful family summit this morning. My mind was in enough of a mess as it was without being reminded of the whole witch thing – the whole completely *useless* witch thing. What good was being a witch if your powers couldn't even fend off unwanted advances from a creepy boy? And on day three of my period – you'd think that would still be prime witching time!

I was period-free now though. And, thanks to my regular-as-clockwork twenty-eight day cycle, I knew I had twenty-two days of non-period, non-witch time ahead of me. I could push everything to the tiniest, never-visited corner of my mind – at least for a while.

Mum and Bella were at the table, Bella on her social media, as usual, Mum at her sewing machine, concentrating as she fed the fabric through.

'Great, always love to hear that people are talking about me behind my back.' I grabbed the last clean bowl from the cupboard and poured myself some cereal.

'Dave was telling me you've been a bit upset this weekend,' Nonna said.

I paused my milk-pouring to turn round and look at her. Dave was lying on the floor next to the chair, licking her privates. Had she betrayed me?

'Only kidding – just wanted to see the look on your face!' Nonna said, breaking into a big belly laugh. 'I figured it out myself.'

Ha bloody ha. Have a laugh at my expense, why not.

'Mum, that's not nice,' Mum said under her breath.

'She needs to find her sense of humour,' Nonna said. 'It's gone AWOL these last few weeks. Come here, petal.'

I wanted to resist as she'd annoyed me, but actually the sight of her standing there in her flowing flowery top with her freestyled hair and welcoming face, arms outstretched – I suddenly felt overwhelmingly like I needed a Nonna hug. I deserted my cereal and walked over to her, squashing my face into her chest, breathing in the familiar Nonna smell of patchouli and lavender.

'Are you doing something witchy to me? Because I'm feeling better already,' I muttered from somewhere next to her boobs.

'I'm just giving you a hug,' she said, releasing me back to my cereal.

'Finished!' Mum held up a mini pair of dungarees in a floral, Liberty-type print. 'What do you think?' she asked, a proud grin on her face.

'Mum! They're super cute,' Bella said.

Of course she'd say that.

'Who are they for?' I asked. 'Because in case you haven't noticed, none of us are toddlers.'

'Well, no one in particular,' Mum said, faltering. 'I just ... the last time I made anything was for you girls when you were little, so I thought ...'

Bella shot me a brief glare and mouthed something to me that I didn't catch.

'They're gorgeous, Mum. Well done,' she said.

'Thanks, darling. I might have a think about what else I could make,' Mum said. 'I've been so busy with it all – unpacking, sorting the building works – sorry the house is such a tip.'

'Always,' I muttered.

'This being a housewife thing isn't as easy as it looks.'

'Housework, shmousework,' Nonna said, flapping her hands. 'You do what makes your heart sing, love. We're all big girls, we can wash a few dishes.'

Speak for yourself, I thought.

'What do you reckon to this look?' Bella said, as a total non sequitur, showing me her phone screen. 'I'm thinking of doing a tutorial for something similar – a statement eye, that kind of thing. I've got some of the girls roped in for me to experiment on.'

The girls? She had girls already? Typical Bella, a girl gang at her fingertips within approximately five seconds of wherever we land. I looked at her screen. It was video from a catwalk, showing models with bright yellow eyeshadow swipes and nearly white lips. Apart from the fact I had zero interest in anything remotely to do with high fashion or make-up, they all looked bizarre. Why was Bella even showing me this and attempting to engage? This was not normal recent-Bella behaviour.

'Um, I mean, I wouldn't wear it, personally, but it's . . . interesting?'

'I'll pass that on to Versace – Jessie Jones thinks your looks are "interesting".'

'I'll email him directly, we're close friends,' I said.

'So close that you don't know she's a woman? How are we even sisters?' Bella laughed.

I glared at her.

I'd had enough. I'd get my breakfast to-go. I abandoned my bowl of cereal and made a beeline for the bread bin, wishing Mum hadn't banned our standard Pop-Tart breakfast in favour of wholemeal bread. Not that I was going to say anything about it to her now. Mum and I had barely spoken all weekend. She was treading on eggshells around me and I was avoiding her and the witch-shaped elephant in the room, determined to not be pinned down for that deep and meaningful I definitely wasn't ready for.

'Walk together?' Bella asked, as I was picking up my bag, mid shoving toast in my mouth.

'Fine,' I said, wanting to shake her off but not having the energy.

'Are you OK?' Bella asked, as we walked down the hill. 'You've been a bit of a zombie all weekend.'

'I had loads of homework to do.' My fail-safe excuse.

'I heard you crying on Friday night,' she said cautiously, like she was holding out a piece of raw meat to a lion that might bite her hand off.

How had she heard me? I had completely cocooned myself in my duvet, which I'd figured was safe enough soundproofing. I stared at her. There was a tiny part of me that desperately wanted to talk to her about it, about Callum, about the hideousness of Friday night. The need to say it out loud, to put it into words, and give it a form so I could make sense of it grew. I looked into her eyes and thought I saw a hint of the old Bella, the Bella who got me, who was on my side.

'Things seem weird between you and Mum. Weirder than normal. Is that why you were upset?' she went on, seemingly encouraged by my eye contact.

I made a non-committal sound.

'I really think you need to talk to her, properly,' she continued, unrelenting. 'Or listen to her, I guess – listen to what she has to say, don't push her away.'

And there she was, the new Bella, faux-wise and mature, always sticking up for Mum. I couldn't be bothered to have this conversation any more, I knew exactly where it would go. The green-clad bodies were amassing as we got closer to school. I picked up my pace.

'No more than usual. I'm fine. I'd just had a bad day,' I said, resorting to the sullen, sulky me that now seemed to be my default.

CHAPTER THIRTEEN

I was convinced Callum wouldn't have told anyone about the events of Friday night.

I was wrong.

And I knew I was wrong from the minute I walked into school.

It was like a scene from one of those American high school movies, where everyone is clustered in huddles around lockers – jocks in letterman jackets and girls all sparkly and beautiful à la old-skool Lindsay Lohan – and the main character enters and everyone falls silent and then starts whispering and pointing as they make their way down the gleaming corridor. Like that, only a grotty Island version with threadbare office carpet and bottle green uniforms.

It wasn't a total, tumbleweed silence to begin with, more a change in the air. Some people, mainly in years above or below, were going about their business not paying me the slightest bit of attention. But as I got to the Year Ten corridor, it hit – a pregnant pause, the stares, followed by a buzz that came at me like a swarm of wasps. I put my head down and marched as fast as possible to registration, thinking it couldn't be about me, about *that*. Surely plenty more gossip-worthy things had happened over the weekend?

'*Bitch*,' I heard someone hiss at me as I walked into our classroom.

OK, so maybe not. I felt a white heat surge through me. This was not supposed to happen. Why would Callum have told anyone? There's no way he'd want people to know he was rejected. It didn't make sense.

'*Boyfriend-thief*,' another voice whispered.

Unless . . . unless he hadn't told them the full story.

Of course.

He hadn't told them the full story.

Why would he, when he could make up any old bullshit and they'd believe him?

I wondered what he'd said – that *I'd* come on to *him*, probably.

How stupid could I be?

Did Libby know? It seemed everyone else did, so more than likely. Not good, not good, not good.

'Good morning, everyone,' Ms Simmons (early today, thank God) said.

I took my seat and tried to steady my nerves, grateful for small mercies like the fact that neither Callum nor Libby were in my form. Then I remembered, with a stomach dive, that I had both Maths and PE later in the day. There were murmurs and whispers and stifled laughs coming at me from all sides. I tuned them out where I could, but voices broke through:

'*Libby is fuming.*'

'*What a back-stabber.*'

'*As if Callum would go there.*'

I wanted to scream. Or run out of the door. Or cry. Part of me wished I still had my period and my erratic powers so I could make them shut up, while the other part was grateful I didn't, on the off-chance I'd accidentally do something dramatic, like permanently zip their mouths closed.

'Settle down, settle down, that was second bell,' Ms Simmons shouted above the noise.

I spent registration in a state of heart-pounding, ear-ringing blind panic, so that when people got up and started filing out of the room and a new set of students came in, I hardly noticed.

'Quickly, come in, get seated,' Ms Simmons said. 'We've got a lot to get through today.'

It was Media Studies, usually my favourite subject, but today I couldn't find the love for any lesson. Today, I would rather have been cleaning out toilets with my bare hands than be anywhere near this school building. I wondered if it would make things worse if I were to take to the floor, adopt the foetal position and start rocking myself while gently weeping. Probably.

'As you know,' said Ms Simmons, 'we're coming to the end of our module on documentaries, and all that remains is for you to work on your final films, which will be a group project. In our sessions this week, you will be planning your masterpieces.'

She put a planning sheet up on the whiteboard. I'd been really looking forward to this project, to actually getting stuck in and doing some filming, putting all that theory to the test. But now the thought of having to work in a group made me want to throw up.

'I've put you into groups and unless there is a major issue – as in a threat to your health or safety – there will be no movement on those groups.' There were the expected groans from some people. 'I don't want to hear any moaning – getting along with people who aren't necessarily your BFFs is a life skill that I promise you you'll be needing in the future.'

I readied myself.

'Group One – Freddie, Sadie, Hayden, Tara and Oscar. Group Two – Marcus, Harry, Tabitha, Tom and Jessie.'

'Careful, guys, she'll try and pounce on you,' someone said under their breath.

Ms Simmons paused to glare and then carried on, but I'd zoned out. I was in a group with Marcus, aka Brainless Henchman No 1. Not to mention two of his other cronies from the football team (Media Studies was considered a doss subject, hence the heavy sport-type quota). This was not good. Nothing about this day was good. Nothing about this year was good, come to think of it – and we weren't even halfway into it.

'I've taken the effort to type up a handy reminder of the brief at the top here – you will be making a film about an issue that is relevant to you, as today's youth. You will need to expand on this in the supporting piece so make sure you choose something appropriate. You will not be allowed to start filming until I have signed off on your topic.'

'How young people need more porn,' Marcus shouted out, much to everyone's delight.

'It also needs to be PG – thank you for the reminder, Marcus – and, as I said earlier, I will need to sign off on it. So try not to waste my time or yours on something ridiculous. Off you go.'

Feeling like I was facing the firing squad, I dragged my chair over to where our group was forming – around Marcus, obviously. It's not like he'd move for anyone.

'Hold on to your boyfriend, Tabitha,' Sadie said as she walked past. 'Oh, wait. You don't have one.' Marcus laughed, as did Tom and Harry.

'Callum tells me you've been a naughty girl,' Marcus said. 'And here I was thinking you'd sloped off home like a regular party pooper on Friday.'

Tabitha caught my eye and gave me the faintest sympathetic smile.

'Focus on the work, please,' Ms Simmons said, as she handed out the sheets.

'Sorry, miss,' Marcus said. 'Just catching up on the weekend.'

'Not in my class, thank you.'

He saluted her, winking at the boys as he did so.

'Right then, what do we reckon – other than my brilliant porn idea, which I don't think will get through.'

'There's been a big debate going on recently about building a bridge to the mainland,' Tabitha said. 'It's kicked off again as that MP took a petition to Parliament.'

'Boring,' Tom said.

'Thank you, next,' Marcus said, fist-bumping Tom.

Tabitha rolled her eyes in frustration and opened her mouth again to speak.

'I've got it.' Marcus practically shoved his palm into Tabitha's face to shut her up. 'We're all sporty.' *Uh, no.* 'And sport is the future.' *No again.* 'So, how about something about the success of the school sports teams?'

'I'm not sure that's particularly all-encompassing, shows us using our voice, as the youth of today, or is even an issue actually.'

It came out of my mouth before I had the chance to stop it. They all looked at me, Tabitha nodding, the boys staring. Marcus with a glint in his eye.

'It speaks,' he said.

'Not just kisses people,' Tom added, winking, 'without consent.'

I tried to keep eye contact with Marcus, not wanting to let him win, but I could feel my cheeks burning hot and the tears biting at my throat again.

'What about climate change?' Tabitha said, clearly trying to dissipate the tension. 'That's just about the biggest problem our generation faces. We could give it an Island-specific slant, what initiatives are happening here to make the Island as sustainable as it can be, and what more we can do.'

I wanted to be supportive and say that it was a great idea (which it was), but my voice had disappeared somewhere into the black hole of my soul.

'OK,' Harry said, as if Tabitha hadn't spoken. 'If we need something wider-ranging – sports initiatives on the Island and how they're contributing to the sports scene in the country. And we could get the school sports teams in there somehow, get ourselves a bit of glory.'

'I like it,' Marcus said. 'Let's vote. All those in favour, raise your hand.'

Of course, all three of them raised their hands, and of course, Tabitha and I didn't as her idea had been much better. I knew I should protest, I knew I should carry on the good fight, but I didn't have the energy to, and, by the gloomy look on her face, neither did Tabitha.

'At least we've got each other,' she said, quietly.

***

The day got worse, as all days on the Island tended to, and in Maths there was no escape. The slimeball himself was there, with a smug grin and a twinkle in his eye. Man, I wanted to have it out with him, there and then, in front of everyone – my head was throbbing with all the things I would have liked to say to him. But of course, I didn't say anything. What good would it have done? It would be his word (star football player, Mr Popular) against mine (strange, quiet new girl with the weird family who doesn't really talk to anyone). There was no point in even trying.

I sat down quickly, managing a weak smile in response to Tabitha's. I was actually looking forward to switching off and zoning into the Maths, something straightforward and easy and logical and devoid of emotions. It was just a shame about the slicked-back douche sitting in front of me, who, when Mr Anstead started writing on the whiteboard, passed a very obvious note, specifically angled in my direction, to Freddie.

JJ

-1

Definitely wouldn't. Too easy.

CHAPTER FOURTEEN

A netball in my face. That was the first I saw of Libby that day.

I'd ignored Summer's messages saying to meet in the canteen and hid in the toilet cubicle all lunch break, digging out the remnants of a Twix and a pack of raisins from the depths of my bag for nourishment. I knew that Libby would be looking for me, I could feel it in my bones, and I also knew I was not up for a public showdown. I was hoping that if I went to change early, I could avoid any locker-room mishaps and once we were in PE I would be safe.

I'd forgotten to factor in Coach and his now-apparent hatred for me. There was no safe space to be had. He didn't even blink as Libby threw the ball directly at my face.

'Sorry, slipped.' Libby glared at me as I held my nose in pain.

The play went down the other end of the court. I watched as she ran down, the other girls laughing with her, and the injustice of the whole situation overcame me. I ran after her, suddenly determined.

'Libby, can we talk please?' I asked, panting from the thirty-second run, wishing once again that they'd move me into the lower set.

'I have nothing to say to you, bitch,' she hissed.

'I don't think you've been told the full story,' I tried.

She caught the ball and swivelled to face me, her eyes blazing so strongly I half-expected lasers to come out of them and fry me. If she threw the ball in my face from this distance, she would probably break my nose. She paused, eventually deciding against permanently maiming me, and threw it over my head.

'Oh, I've been told the full, desperate story – he went after you to return your hat and you cornered him in the post office doorway and tried to kiss him. He said he had to fend you off.'

'That's one hundred per cent not what happened.'

'So, first you pretend to be my friend, then you come on to my boyfriend and now you're calling him a liar? Classy.'

'I didn't come on to him. Absolutely in no way did I come on to him. Why would I?' And there I went again, speaking my mind without thinking. Libby's glare was now nuclear.

'Oh really? You're too good for him, are you? Too good for this Island with your blogger sister and your trendy city ways? You and your family are all weird, outcast freaks. I know for a fact Callum wouldn't ever stoop so low as you. Why have cod when you can have caviar?'

So much for Girl Code. I wished she could have believed me, woman to woman, barely getting by girl to seemingly together girl – trusted me, rather than a boy who she must have realised was sketchy. But she'd been clear as crystal: we were done, my life was now even more of a living hell than it had been previously.

And with a final glare she ran off and rejoined the game, leaving me, quite literally, out in the cold.

CHAPTER FIFTEEN

Scrolling through social media when you're feeling low is never a good idea. I knew this, everyone knows this – it's Mental Health 101 – and yet, there I was, deep in my funk, scrolling through social media. It was almost time to head to school and I was still in bed, putting off the inevitable, the seagulls screeching angrily at me, Dave nudging my phone for attention. I knew I had to face the outside world, but I just couldn't make my body acknowledge the fact.

It had been a week – a full week of me keeping my head well and truly down, weathering the storm, ignoring everything that was thrown my way. And boy was stuff thrown my way, constantly. Whispers, sneers, snide grins, notes, comments, death stares from Libby that outshone the most evil of evil Disney villains.

It would blow over, I told myself – or rather, Summer told me, repeatedly. I'd confided in her and Tabitha about what had really happened, though they'd already guessed the minute they heard the rumour. Summer had used every swear word and synonym for sleazebag she could find about Callum, while Tabs had referenced Michelle Obama and encouraged me to take the high road. And they'd both repeated, as mantras, 'This too shall pass', 'Ignore them', 'They'll find a new target soon'. I got the impression Tabitha was speaking from experience. They were probably right; these people would find a new target eventually. But in the meantime, they were very much enjoying targeting me.

I had wallowed hard, locking myself away when I was home, responding with only the briefest of non-committal grunts to Mum's attempts at conversation, and basically becoming a total social recluse. The one positive, as I had to keep reminding myself, was that at least my period was still two weeks away, which meant at least I didn't have to factor that extra whirling witch tornado into the overall shitstorm.

I scrolled through pictures on Shireen and Nadia's Instagram from a party up in Manchester. Everyone looked happy and smiley and chummy. It made my stomach hurt, even though I knew that if I had still been up there, I probably wouldn't have gone. Shireen and Nadia were my friends, but only very loosely – we would walk to classes together and sometimes sit together at lunch. I think Shireen had been to my flat once to pick up a textbook. We hadn't been close; but then again, they hadn't hated me. I felt a yearning.

Then I did something even more stupid and bad for my mental health: I looked up Libby's Instagram. There was a photo of her and Callum. He was attempting to look all cool and aloof, turning to the side, staring into the distance, his arm round Libby like he was using her as a leaning post; and she, super filtered, was planting a kiss on his cheek, marking her territory. The caption read, *'Stronger than ever, nothing (no one) will tear us apart'*. I nearly vommed in my mouth.

If I couldn't escape from the Island, then I at least needed to escape my head. I couldn't face Mum, or anyone here, but I needed the familiar.

Dad.

Five Things About Dad:
1. He makes up silly names for things – like 'washdisher' for dishwasher, and 'snausages' for sausages.
2. He's a lawyer, like Mum. They met at university, their eyes locking at some dull Law Society quiz.
3. Dad sent Mum a quiz question every day until she agreed to go out with him, which he says he thought was romantic at the time, but now realises was harassment and apologises for profusely.
4. They split up because . . . actually, I don't know why they split up. I just know it went from there being lots of laughing to shouting to a Cold War scenario to him moving out.
5. He moved to Dubai for his new wife's job four years ago. (I've never been.)

It had been a while since we'd spoken. What with the time difference and his job plus the kids, he didn't get round to calling much, more the odd WhatsApp with a silly meme (cat ones were his favourite) or a motivational quote. I did a quick time check and FaceTimed. It rang out the first time. I tried again. Four rings in and he picked up. His pixelated face, with a bright blue pool in the background, came up.

'Dad? Can you hear me?'

'Hey, JJ. How are you doing?' he said.

The weight of the question and the sound of his voice nearly made me cry. How *was* I doing? I debated whether to be honest, and if so, *how* honest.

'Well, actually . . .' I started, not entirely sure where I was going with it. 'I . . .'

'Daddy! Your turn, your turn!' a little voice said in the background.

'I'll be there in a minute, sweetie, just talking to JJ,' he called back.

'JJ!' the voice said. Darcey came waddling over with her armbands on, her *Frozen* swimsuit stretched over her toddler tummy.

'It's JJ?' another voice, Dashel, asked from out of shot. 'I wanna say hi!'

They crowded into the frame, talking excitedly to me at the same time, hanging off Dad with that little-kid intimacy that made me sad.

'Hey, JJ,' his wife Pippa said, kissing the top of Dad's head. She was tanned and toned and wearing designer sunglasses.

'Sorry,' Dad said, 'we were in the middle of a game of Marco Polo. Can I call you another time? Was it something important?'

I looked at the four of them, a picture-perfect family straight from a shop-bought photo frame. I swallowed down my feelings, pushing the tip of my tongue against the roof of my mouth to stop myself crying.

'No, don't worry,' I said, aiming for light and breezy. 'Enjoy the Marco Polo.'

'Love you,' Dad said, everyone else echoing him.

'Love you more,' I said, repeating our usual refrain.

Then I threw my phone across the room, startling poor Dave, and sunk into a deep pit of self-loathing. Of everyone-loathing.

***

I wasn't allowed to sink for long. Mum practically forced me out of the door to school. I was tired. Couldn't feel my face, jet-lagged type TIRED, the events of the last week weighing heavy on every atom of my mind and body. I hadn't really been sleeping, just frantically sweating the nights away, chaotic, bite-sized fragments of dreams swirling in my head. My brain felt like it had been on a rollercoaster and was still reeling from it.

The one benefit of this was that I gave less of a rat's arse about what the school day was likely to bring. It was like my censorship chip, the tiny filter in your brain that makes you care what people think, hadn't been switched on.

Which was just as well, because it started the minute I got in. I could see there was something different about my locker from the far end of the corridor, which was confirmed by the amount of people milling around it laughing and taking selfies. As I got closer a 'shush' did the rounds and everyone looked at me. Some had the decency to move away, but most stayed to watch the show.

It was pretty pathetic, to be honest. Lots of Post-Its stuck on it with '-1' written on them and one torn page from a planner with BOYFRIEND THIEF penned in clear, colourful bubble letters. As I inched closer still, I saw another one, longer this time, neat handwriting arranged in neat lines:

104

Jessie is a little ho,
Who has a big fat butt,
She tries it on with every boy,
Because she is a slut

That was the one that made me feel sad, and not because I was concerned about the size of my backside. It would've taken a long time – the idea, the rhyming, the calligrapher-level hand-writing. Someone had really invested in that one.

'Oh my God, *really*?' I heard Summer say, barging her way towards me, Tabitha in tow. 'Sod off all of you,' she hissed, causing the stragglers to tut and disperse. 'It's hardly Shakespeare, is it? Not that any of that lot could understand Shakespeare.'

I felt a wave of relief seeing them there.

'Hey,' I said, starting to pull the notes off.

'Wait!' Summer stopped me. 'Photo evidence.' She got her phone out and took photos of the locker, including close-ups of each Post-It. 'People can't get away with this,' she said. 'It's got to stop.'

'You OK?' Tabitha asked, taking the notes off with me, looking as downcast as I felt.

'Not great,' I said.

'I tried to find you yesterday but you disappeared, did you not get my messages?' Summer asked.

'I did a cubicle lunch,' I said.

'I looked in there! That was my first port of call.'

'I went to the Year Seven block – safer option.'

Tabitha nodded, like she knew it well. Summer looked at me

with a mixture of disappointment and pity. I had to look away. I couldn't bear seeing myself in her eyes like that.

'What is it with you girls, hiding away?' she said, sounding parental. Tabitha and I both blushed and looked to the floor, like guilty children being reprimanded. 'Dude, come and find me when you feel like that. Don't let them drive you to the Year Seven block – those animals don't even flush half the time.'

We laughed. Then the bell went and my heart sank. I wanted to stay with them. I felt stronger standing next to them, like I had a vague chance of making it through the day.

'At least it's a Drop-down Day today,' said Summer. 'So at least no having to deal with Sleazebag of the Century in Maths, We'll try and save you a place in the hall.'

***

When Dante wrote about the Nine Circles of Hell he missed out Drop-down Days.

They are concentrated, whole-school PSHE days and the freshest hell of them all. The only vaguely redeeming feature of this particular one was that at least it was without the boys, who, without fail, raise their idiot game fifty per cent on Drop-down Days.

After the period talk at my school in Year Six, the boys managed to get their hands on some of the tampons the girls had been given and accordingly covered them in red felt-tip pen, strategically placing them in prime positions all over school, including Mrs Wilson's chair, Lucy Morton's bag and even the front of the lectern in the hall. It was stuck there for whole-school assembly.

Now, the girls in our form shuffled into the hall. Ms Simmons ushered us into our seats row by row, with no room for movement. I looked around for Summer. If I timed it right, in a millisecond that Ms Simmons wasn't watching, maybe I could make a break for it. But Summer's form wasn't in yet, and Ms Simmons is one of those teachers who doesn't have a millisecond when she's not watching. I manoeuvred myself to the back of the line, just in case. I was wedged between Lily Ross and Caitlyn Havers. No sign of Summer but it could have been worse.

And just as I thought that, it got worse.

Libby's form were next in and, because I'd obviously pissed the gods off, she ended up sitting right behind me. I could sense everyone around me relishing the placement, the potential drama. Heads were turning, whispers were spreading. I played dead, like the mice that Dave brings in – I didn't turn around, I didn't move a muscle, hardly breathed.

'Slut,' Sadie coughed, pretty ineptly – there's an art to the slut-cough and you'd think she'd have had practice, the amount of general terrorising she does.

There were sniggers. I tried to focus on my breathing and mentally remove myself from the situation, but it was hard. Impossible even. I was an injured gazelle and the lions were closing in. Meditation was not going to save me now.

'Good afternoon, girls,' Mrs Metcalfe finally shouted, way too loudly, into the microphone. 'Thank you for being prompt. Today's session is about . . . We'll be looking at . . .' She trailed off, fussed with the top button of her done-up-all-the-way-to-the-top stiff blouse and blushed. 'Well, I'll hand you over to our guest speakers from Care Aware.'

She left the stage like a rocket – a prim and flustered one. The lights dimmed slightly, and we sat waiting, wondering what insight and excitement would be coming.

Someone shuffled on to the stage. A woman dressed as a schoolboy in a uniform, rucksack hanging off one shoulder, wearing a baseball cap and pretending to chew gum and look at a phone while shuffling along. From the other side of the stage, another person appeared – this time a woman dressed as a schoolgirl, also walking along, looking at a phone. They both paused on different sides of the stage, and faced the front, still on their phones. The 'boy' pretended to type a message that came up, projected, on to the big screen behind them.

> Hey, Gorgeous. Fun date. Miss you.

The girl, supposedly receiving this message, smiled and clutched her phone to her chest, then typed back.

> You too.

Suddenly, a sound effect kicked in over the speakers, a bunch of rowdy boys, all with lairy voices:

'You texting Lover Girl?'

'You done it yet?'

'What base?'

'Is she frigid?'

'Get her to send a pic!'

'Yeah, go on!'

The 'boy' pulled an 'uncomfortable but trying to be cool'

expression. More jeering. And then, more overly dramatic pretend-typing.

> What are you up to?

> > Just arrived home.

> Thinking of you.

> > You too.

> You looked so pretty today.

> > ♥ 😄

> Your figure is so gorgeous.

> > Do you really think so?

> Totally! I'd love to see more of it . . . ☺

> Maybe a little sneak peek?

> But no worries, just because my exes sent me pics, doesn't mean you have to.

> Maybe just one?

A dramatic pause.

'Jessie would be all over that,' Sadie said, not even attempting to be quiet, causing an outburst of giggles.

I was glad the lights were off so no one could see me turn fuchsia. The 'girl' on stage looked up to the audience, scared, questioning, finger on her chin like she was seriously thinking. There was a sudden sound effect – a crash of lightning? And then a very loud voice shouted 'STOP'. And then ... oh no, God no ... music started playing and the pair on stage took off their uniforms to reveal T-shirts with a camera icon with a stop sign through it. And then (horror upon horror) they started singing.

He seems way too into your boobs,
You don't have to show him your boobs,
You think he's being nice and sweet,
He's not, he's just being rude.

It was to the tune of Stormzy's 'Big For Your Boots'.

There was a silence as everyone tried to work out if what we thought was happening was actually happening, then a ripple of laughter began as the women bounced around on stage, earnestly, heartfelt and we realised that yes, yes it was. I had a twinge of feeling sorry for them, but really they were grown women, they should've known better.

I saw Mrs Metcalfe at the side of the stage, looking equal parts confused and perplexed and Ms Simmons next to her, head in her hands. The whole hall was in total meltdown now, not that the performers seemed to notice. Perhaps they were used to it. We were laughing so hard we were struggling for breath. And still, they continued all the way through to the final verse, which had some serious lyrical issues.

> *Don't let him get too near your boobs,*
> *Your body is yours, and your boobs,*
> *Your vagina, and everything between,*
> *It might end up on YouTube.*

CHAPTER SIXTEEN

'The cringe of it!' Summer said, pushing her way through the throng to find me afterwards. The sea of green was moving us along, like turtles in a slipstream. 'My cheeks hurt from laughing. If Stormzy were dead and had a grave, he would be turning in it.'

It felt so good to see her smiling, genuine face again – a safe harbour in a shitstorm – but I didn't want to be too needy, to attach myself to her like a barnacle that she couldn't shake off, much as I was desperate to. It did feel amazing to have actually laughed for the first time in what seemed like forever though.

'Just remember, Summer, you never have to show him your boobs.'

'Sorry I couldn't save you a place. That Libby placement was full suckage. Did she hassle you?'

'It was more Sadie who was being a snide bitch, but whatever, I'll live,' I said, finding some mock bravado from somewhere.

'She's a snake. I mean, a total no-brain sheep, but also a snake.' Something caught her eye and she paused, checking me over, then reached out her hand and touched my hair. 'What the—! Come with me.' She grabbed my hand and pulled me out of the stream, marching me into a bathroom on the quad.

'What is it?' I asked, confused.

'Those stupid-arse girls. Honestly, they wouldn't know Girl Code if it swung a used tampon in their face.'

'What is it, Summer?' I asked, this time more forcefully.

She took a deep breath. 'Some bitch has stuck gum in your hair.'

I gave an open-mouthed gasp, my hand instinctively reaching back to feel it. My fingers hit on the still-warm gooey lump buried beneath wads of my hair. Tears pinched at my eyes.

'It's fine, we can fix it,' Summer said, not entirely convincingly. 'Here.' She shook her hair free and handed me her hair tie. 'Put the rest of it up, then let's run it through with hot water.'

She eased my head into the sink. The tap was one of those you have to push down every ten seconds to get a spurt of hot water, so she had to juggle jabbing the tap and working the water through my hair. I closed my eyes, not wanting to examine the sink scum too closely.

'Honestly, it's like they're five years old. They have hair. You'd think they'd realise how much of a giant pain in the backside it is to sort this crap out.'

I didn't mention that that's exactly why they would've done it.

'It's a low blow,' she said, frantically scrubbing at my hair.

The water was becoming too hot to handle. I knew it was a lost cause, and I also knew Summer would never give up. The bell had gone at least five minutes ago. I told her I needed a break and inched my head up, wringing out the clump of wet hair.

'No joy?' I asked, trying to keep my voice level.

'I think if I keep trying . . .'

My fingers felt for it again, reluctantly. It felt just as stuck as before, only more solid.

'You need to get off to class,' I said. 'I can sort this.'

'How? It's definitely a two-woman job.'

'I think my mum has a magic-formula spray thing at home,' I said, a complete lie and also ironic given the 'magic' aspect. I knew I was going to have to cut it out and I felt sick at the thought.

'Honestly, you go. I'll come find you at lunch,' I said, another lie.

'You sure?' she asked, torn.

'Positive, I'm fine. If I tie it up, you can't really tell, no one will see.'

'OK. But come find me if you need me at all – make up some random excuse if you need to get me from class. Your dog's died or something, whatever, I don't mind.' She picked up her bag and gave me a quick power hug. 'You really should report them for this, you know. If you let them get away with this stuff, they'll keep on doing it.'

'Yeah, I might,' I said, the lies collecting like charms on an unwieldy necklace, hanging heavy round my neck.

CHAPTER SEVENTEEN

There was no way in holy hell and all that's wrong in the world that I was going back to the hall, or sessions or anything that involved being seen by other people. Those disgustingly mean girls would be waiting for me to appear with a chunk of gum covered in someone else's spit thoroughly wedged to a point of no return in my hair. Eagerly anticipating seeing my distraught, red-eyed face, my hair dishevelled from desperate attempts to retrieve it, my spirit broken. I wouldn't give them the satisfaction.

I snuck out through the staff car park gate. I'd realised in my first week this was a good escape route; one of the teachers was always forgetting their key card so it was often left off the latch. I headed home. I knew Mum was out and I was hoping Nonna would either be in her potting shed working on some miracle cures or with a client. She had an uncanny sixth sense, but she also had crap hearing so if I was quiet enough I might just manage to avoid interrogation. Plus, I could handle an interrogation if it meant not having to go back to school to face my execution. It's all very well weathering the storm, but that relies on the storm actually passing – my storm seemed to still be gathering strength, hurricane-like, and there was no solution other than to take myself out of its path. If I wasn't there, they couldn't do anything to me.

I crept in the front door and, not hearing any voices, made my way upstairs. The giant landing was a mess. Strips of textured wallpaper had been torn off, revealing other textured, flowery wallpaper underneath, and test patches of wildly different colours were painted all over the place. They all looked bad to me – I couldn't imagine this house looking anything other than bad.

I passed Bella's slightly ajar door, glimpsing her perfectly organised, fairy-lit room through the gap. Her bed made, her floor clean, her dressing table laid out with perfect rows of brushes and neat, labelled stacks of make-up. It was strange how different we were – like, proper chalk-and-cheese different. Did we even still have anything in common, besides our parents?

Finally, I made it to the sweet release of my bed. Dave was already curled up on my duvet, a fluffy, warm ball of relaxation. I snuggled in next to her, burying my head in her fur, letting myself dissolve into sobs. She made a lazy half-meow and stretched her legs out in appreciation, not even remotely interested in my outburst.

I tentatively felt at the back of my hair, my fingers brushing against the solid clump of hair in which the gum was buried. I wanted, more than anything, to ignore it. To stay here with Dave and forget everything. But I knew I had to deal with it sooner rather than later.

***

Turns out that getting chewing gum out of hair is impossible. Over an hour later and I was still locked in the bathroom. I had tried everything – washing it, half a bottle of conditioner in the area, careful combing. Nothing had worked and now I had greasy hair, a sore head and severe arm ache (it's practically a gym session reaching round the back for that long). It didn't help that I couldn't really *see* it, no matter how I angled myself to peer into the various mirrors I'd stolen from Bella's room. I was getting more and more worked up and was at the point of reconciling myself to a pixie cut, when there was a knock on the door.

'Jessie? Are you in there?' Bella asked.

Arse. I'd forgotten she had free periods. I considered ignoring her, but figured it was obvious someone was in the bathroom and since Mum and Nonna both had their own, if I didn't acknowledge her she might think I was some kind of toiletry burglar.

'I'll be out in a minute,' I answered.

'What are you doing home?'

'I'm ill,' I said, adding a little croak to my voice for effect.

There was no response.

'Go away, I'm busy,' I said.

'Have you taken all the mirrors from my room?' she asked, sounding annoyed.

'I was just . . . borrowing them.'

'Well, I need them, I'm about to shoot a video.'

Now? She *had* to shoot a video now?

'Can it wait? I'll be out in a minute.'

'Not really, no. What are you doing with them anyway?'

'None of your business,' I snapped, feeling trapped and stupid. 'I'll . . . pass them out to you.'

I opened the door tentatively, as small a crack as I could manage to fit my hand and a mirror through, keeping my head tucked away behind the door.

'What's going on?' she asked, suspiciously.

'Nothing. Take your mirror.'

'And the other one?' she asked.

In a rookie move, I stepped away, briefly, to get the other mirror from the shelf and she used the opportunity to step inside the bathroom. Her gaze swept around the detritus of the bathroom – a full-on, searching, Columbo-style examination. She looked at me and her eyes narrowed.

'What's going on with your hair? Are you doing a mask treatment?'

I instinctively clutched the back of my head. 'Nothing.'

'Wait – is that gum?' she asked, coming closer.

'No, it's nothing, it's . . .' I trailed off. There was no reasonable explanation for the disgusting mass in my hair.

'What happened?' she asked, her tone changing from annoying to annoyingly sympathetic.

'I leaned my head against a . . . wall. Where there was gum.'

She gave me a disbelieving look.

'Do you want some help getting it out?'

My instinct was to herd her and her pitying, patronising look and her perfect, problem-free life out of the room and slam the door closed. But another part of me was screaming, *Yes, I SO want help*. I wanted someone to scoop me up and sort me out, to wrap me up in a cuddle, to tell me it was all going to be OK, to fix me – and to get the sodding gum out of my hair.

'Come on,' she said, as if sensing my internal scream. 'Sit on the side of the bath.'

I did as I was told, happy to hand over responsibility. I felt her fingers gently working through and around the clump.

'Wow, it's quite a mess,' she said.

'I'm aware,' I snapped.

'We could ask Nonna to help? I'm sure she could magic it away in about thirty seconds flat.'

'No!'

She took a step back, taking me in. 'I don't know why you're being so weird about it all. You'll have to talk to them about it some time – fairly soon too. Ticking menstrual clock and all that.'

I scoffed. There were still fifteen days until my next period. Plenty of time.

'I said "no". I'm not ready to . . . talk about it. And if you're not going to help me with the gum, then I'll just deal with it myself.'

'Because that's working out well for you,' she said, smiling. 'I'll help. Just stay there, I'll be back in a minute.'

'No Nonna though,' I said, panicking.

'No Nonna.'

She was back a couple of minutes later, proudly brandishing a jar of peanut butter.

'Ta da!' she said. 'Secret weapon.'

'Uh, what? There's no way you're putting peanut butter in my hair!'

'Trust me,' she said, rummaging through the bathroom cupboard, her voice muffled. 'According to YouTube, this is the way.' She emerged holding a box-fresh toothbrush.

'Because YouTube is the font of all knowledge.'

'Well, it's not like we have any other options, given your refusal to take the easy route. So, bite your tongue and let me get on with it.'

There wasn't a lot I could say to that, so I shut my mouth and turned my head round for her. Soon the smell of Skippy wafted my way.

'Are you going to tell me what *really* happened?' Bella asked, as she gently worked the peanut butter into my matted hair.

I considered it. It might feel good to get it off my chest. But she would only overreact. Plus, I didn't really want to think about it, let alone say it out loud. I wanted to pretend it had never even happened.

'I'd rather not, if that's OK,' I said.

'I know you've been getting a bit of stick at school,' Bella said, quietly. 'And I know you well enough to know that what I've heard isn't true.'

'It's not,' I snapped. The thought of gossip about me making it to the sixth form made me feel sick.

'That sucks,' she went on. 'I'm sorry I'm not around to . . .'

'To what? Fight off my bullies with your make-up knowledge?' I snapped, like a wounded animal lashing out. She didn't say anything and I felt a pang of guilt. 'You can't help that sixth form is in a different block. Anyway, it's not your fault that we moved to this hole. It's not *you* who needs to be sorry. It's Mum.'

Bella started filling the sink with hot water and then came and sat on the toilet seat, facing me. 'We need to leave it for a few minutes,' she said. 'You really should talk to Mum, you know.'

'I'm too angry with her still.'

Silence.

'I just don't get it,' I said. 'Why would she drag us here, especially knowing what would happen? We were perfectly fine before.'

120

'That's why you should talk to her,' Bella said, still in that annoyingly gentle voice. 'You need to ask her that yourself. She didn't think we *were* perfectly fine, any of us. And you know what? I kind of agree.'

'Of course you do,' I muttered.

'Don't be a brat,' she said.

ARGH. Is there anything worse and more likely to make you behave badly than someone *telling* you that you're behaving badly? Don't be grumpy, don't be sulky, don't be a brat. I looked at Bella sitting there, all fake-mature and wise. I missed the old Bella.

'Right, let's have a go at this now,' she said, holding up the toothbrush and coming to sit beside me.

'This whole witch thing is just crazy,' I muttered, as she worked away at my hair with the toothbrush.

'I get it,' she said. 'I really do. And I'll say it again, speak to Mum. Hear her reasons, let her know how you're feeling.' She paused, rinsing the toothbrush. 'You know we're from a long line of Island witches? It's kind of cool. The Downer women are pretty kickass.'

'Great. So you've been having a nice cosy witchy chinwag with Mum and I'm left out in the cold, again.'

'Jessie Jones! Don't you dare!' she said, flicking me with the peanut butter water. 'That was entirely your choice – don't even bother being all hard-done-by about it.'

She had a point. Not that I had any intention of letting her know that.

'OK, I think you're clear.' She stood back and took in her

handiwork. 'You'll need to give it a good wash and you might smell a bit peanutty for a day or two, but the gum is out.'

I put my fingers to my hair, feeling smooth – if greasy – hair, rather than a hard, angry wad. I felt a surge of gratitude and sisterly love and turned to hug her.

'You know you can always come to me for anything, right?' Bella said, all serious and heartfelt. 'I know we're not the best of friends . . . any more . . . but I'm always here for you. Just so you know.'

'It was just a hug, don't get carried away,' I said, smiling. 'Can you do me a favour though?'

'Go on,' she said, suspiciously.

'Can you tell them I'm not well and don't want any dinner?'

She opened her mouth to say something, but I got there first. 'I will talk to Mum, I promise. I just can't face them today.' I did my best meaningful and earnest grin, which seemed to work.

'Fine,' Bella said. 'But promise me you will talk to her.'

'Promise,' I said, pleased with myself. 'And one last thing. Can you bring me up some crisps?'

'Jessie!'

CHAPTER EIGHTEEN

I had planned to go into school the next morning. But when morning came, I couldn't make myself move. The thought of putting that horrible uniform on and walking through the gates, of making my way to my locker, not knowing what fresh hell awaited me – I just couldn't do it. This was me weathering the storm – by removing myself from its path. And I planned to do it for a while.

'Sweetheart, it's me,' Mum said, knocking on the door. 'Can I come in?'

I'd texted her to say I was ill, precisely because I didn't want to see her in person. Seemed it hadn't worked.

'I'd rather you didn't,' I called back.

She opened the door anyway. I retreated further into my duvet.

'I said, "I'd rather you didn't."'

'Yes, I heard, but you know, I'm your mother and I need to at least see for myself that you're still alive.'

'I'm talking, aren't I?'

She put her hand on my forehead, despite me turning my head away. 'You haven't got a temperature, that's good. Can I get you anything? Ice water? Toast? Where does it hurt?'

'Everywhere,' I said, not lying. 'Everything hurts.'

I could feel her staring at me closely, no doubt wanting to say something heartfelt, but eventually deciding to keep things practical. 'Nonna and I are going out, she's got a hospital appointment and then we're off to meet a builder.'

'Off to cast some spells, more like,' I muttered. You know when you say a stupid thing you don't necessarily mean and it makes you sound like a five-year-old? Yeah, that.

'Pardon, darling? I can't really hear you from under the duvet.'

I didn't repeat it. Eventually, she carried on.

'I've called the school for you. I know you've had a lot to deal with so I'm letting you have today in bed. But I'm *certain* you'll be fit and well tomorrow.'

Silence. I could tell she was still hovering though.

'I'm absolutely here if you need me – for Lemsip or dry toast. Or talking.'

I still didn't respond.

'Make some kind of confirmation gesture, please – a kick, a grunt, whatever.'

'OK,' I said, loud enough to make it through the duvet.

'Good. Goodbye, I love you, please open a window.'

***

One day off school turned into two, as I knew it would, and then three, until I'd managed to blag the whole week off. One of Mum's good points is her consistently soft parenting and Mum Guilt, which she has overspilling barrels of.

I did a fair amount of proper-feeling-sorry-for-myself, hating-the-world, watching-all-the-crap-reality-TV wallowing, which, honestly, felt incredible. Shutting out the world and concentrating on other people's dramas was just what I needed.

I felt vaguely bad about fobbing off concerned texts and calls from Summer and Tabs with a fake-flu card, but mostly I was happy in my solitary bubble of denial.

Or I thought I was, until a tiny little niggling voice started whispering.

A long line of Island witches?

The Downer women are pretty kickass?

I tried to shut the voice up – I didn't want anything to do with this madness. I would take the contraceptive pill back-to-back and use them to skip my periods if it meant not having to accept the fact there was something freaky about me. But as much as I tried to ignore it, the damn voice wouldn't shut up. I couldn't face asking Mum or Nonna about it though. That would be giving in. I didn't want to admit curiosity and have to engage with them about the bombshell they had dropped.

But . . . I could look into it myself. Maybe even venture out of my self-imposed prison and go and do some research in the library. I've seen people in TV shows go to libraries and look through old newspaper articles on those special machines. I could do that. Except . . . I had no library card and no idea where the library was. My laptop stared at me from my bedside table, offended I'd even considered another option.

Once I opened this magical can of worms, there would be no closing it again. But the curiosity, the nagging voice, was too insistent. And besides, looking into our history didn't mean I was signing up for witch school.

'Let's do this then,' I said to Dave, picking up my laptop and propping myself up on some pillows. She gave me a disinterested half head raise.

I pulled up Google and typed, *'Downer Witches Isle of Wight'*. 49,600 entries came up. OK, so, definitely a thing.

One name was at the top of the entries: Molly Downer. I clicked on the Wikipedia link.

Molly Downer – reportedly the last witch on the Isle of Wight.

Ha! Incorrect so far. I read on.

Illegitimate daughter of a local vicar.

Jesus, how disappointingly standard.

Downer would entice customs men in order to get free alcohol.

Some strong slut-shaming there.

She did not marry, and became a recluse. Local people considered her a witch and one woman called Harriet began to taunt and harass her, resulting in Molly cursing her that 'should any good fortune fall upon her, she would die before possession', which duly happened in 1847.

Wow, OK. It was a bit confusing with the language but I think I got it. A woman, snubbed by her can't-keep-his-dick-in-his-pants vicar father, lives alone and doesn't like any of the probably substandard husband options the village has to offer. So the men and their egos get annoyed at the rejection, another woman gets jealous that Molly is getting all the attention (even though Molly wants none of it), so she starts being mean to her and turning other people against her. Makes up some crap about Molly cursing her and, unfortunately for Molly, the woman dies as she's about to come into some money which makes it look like the curse is true. And just like that, a woman is ostracised and bullied for essentially choosing to live alone and not marry. Tale as old as time – basically an early incel incident, before we started calling men who don't get laid incels.

Many local people attested to her curative powers as a 'charmer' against minor illnesses. Eventually she was found dead by a woman who lent her books, and was buried without rites in Brading Churchyard.

So Molly Downer was a healer, like Nonna. I know not everyone believes what Nonna does with her herbs and natural remedies works, but, at worst, people think she's a slightly crazy old bird. Back then though – what a different story. Molly was completely alone, tormented for being different, for not being 'normal'.

I slammed my laptop shut and pushed it away from me, burrowing back under the safety of my duvet. It felt like too much to take in. It was a weight – the legacy, the power, the ancestors. It wasn't something I'd asked for and I wanted to just ignore it.

But there was a part of me, that whispering voice, that felt like I was betraying Molly by turning away from my witchiness.

Mum has always told me and Bella how important it will be for us, as women, to vote. How not voting is disrespecting the efforts and the lives lost of all the women who fought for our right to vote – it's practically spitting on their graves, she says. This felt the same. Molly Downer, my great-great-great-great (however many times) grandmother was an actual real-life person. Bullied, tormented and isolated. She's lying in an unmarked grave somewhere, ostracised for her powers, and here I am denying mine and wanting nothing to do with them.

Maybe Molly had felt like me? Who's to say she enjoyed her powers and liked healing people? Maybe she hated it and saw it as a curse. Maybe if she could speak to me from beyond the grave – and I pray to God she can't – she'd tell me to run away from it all. Or maybe she'd tell me to embrace it. Either way, learning about Molly had made it all seem less like some suspect weirdness from Mum and Nonna, and more real.

Too real.

CHAPTER NINETEEN

'Knock knock,' Bella said, walking into my room, carrying her laptop.

I glared at her from the bed. 'I think the idea is that you knock *before* you enter,' I snapped. It had been so long since I'd spoken that my jaw felt creaky.

'Hey, sis,' she said. 'What's going on?'

She came and sat on the edge of my bed, placing her laptop carefully on the covers and putting a hand on my leg.

'Nothing. I'm fine,' I said.

'You don't look fine. Oh my God, are you *actually* ill? I thought you were just, you know, avoiding.' She sighed. 'It's been over a week now, Jessie. Is your plan to stay in your room for ever?'

'One hundred per cent, yes. I'm down a rabbit hole. An Island, school bullies, witch rabbit hole. And no, I don't want to talk about it.'

'Ah,' she said, edging closer.

'What do you want, anyway? You never come up here.'

'Now that I'm here I remember why – it's bloody freezing. And a safety hazard. I can't even see the floor beneath all your crap. You could have whole families of mice living under there.'

'Well, feel free to bugger off again then. No one's keeping you here.'

'It's fine, I'll be brave,' she said, scooting up next to me, leaning back against the headboard. 'So, just hear me out before you say anything.'

'Mmmm,' I said, suspicious.

'Promise?'

'Whatever. Just speak.'

'It's not that long now until we both have our next period.'

I let out a long, hollow groan.

'You promised you'd listen.'

'"Whatever" does not constitute a promise. The law courts would agree.'

'Please, Jessie,' she said, her voice serious. 'This is important. We really haven't got that long. I thought we could do a bit of research.'

'I'm not ready yet. And I don't want to talk to Mum about it.'

'I'm not Mum! I'm *me*, your sister, who is in the same situation as you and is having a mild freak-out. And you happen to be the only person going through the exact same thing.'

I turned round to face her. To be fair, there was fear in her eyes. I couldn't remember the last time I'd seen her look anything other than completely together and composed.

'Look, I know I'm not your favourite person – and trust me, you're not mine a lot of the time either – but, whether we like it or not, we are in this together and I'd feel a whole lot better if we tackled it together too.'

She had a point. And it did feel nice to have someone vaguely on my side, or with the same interests, for once.

'I've given myself till Saturday,' I said. 'I'm ignoring it until then, which still gives me four days to prepare.'

'Uh, no. We've got about *two* days from now, maybe a few more if we're lucky,' Bella said. 'I thought you were supposed to be a secret maths genius.'

'I am, and I know how to count to twenty-eight.'

'Except *my* period is every three weeks, usually. And sometimes I get a mini-period within a cycle – which is super fun. So it really could basically be any day now ...'

'Sucks for you, but I've still got at least another week,' I said smugly. *Or did I?* A horrible thought was forming. I'm usually clockwork regular – except for last time. Last time I wasn't. Last time I was early. Which would mean ...

'Sorry,' Bella said, offering me a weak smile. 'We're in sync now. Like the band. Mum said it's a powerful moon cycle witch thing.' She attempted a laugh. 'I mean, they say it happens to most females living together after a while, but witches being all about nature and moons and cycles makes it even more likely. And I guess it has bigger consequences for us too. I thought you knew.'

I was supposed to have more than a week left. And now ...

'No!' I wailed. 'No no no no no! You and your stupid irregular periods! I should have more time!'

This was possibly the worst time for me to get my uncontrollable witch powers. With things as they were at the moment, if I went back to school I was likely to explode Callum and turn Libby into a diseased toad. This was not good.

'Sorry,' Bella said again, quietly. 'It's super annoying for me too. Trust me, I'd rather be regular. If that's any consolation.'

'It's not.'

She rested her hand tentatively on my arm.

131

'Did you have any good news along with that Doomsday clanger of bad?' I asked at last.

'No. But I've come up with a plan.'

'Hmmm.'

'I've downloaded as much witchy stuff as I could dig out – I've got it all: *Sabrina* (the old one and the new one), *Bewitched*, *Charmed*, *The Witches*, *The Craft* and some other really freaky looking nineties films . . . I just figured it might be a fun, gentle way in. We can watch, make some notes and then when we sit down with Mum and Nonna we'll have a starting point. We'll have some firm questions. "Can we do this or that?" "Do we have a portal to another realm in our laundry cupboard?" That kind of thing. What do you think?'

I thought I wanted to throw myself in the sea, I thought I wanted to run away back up to Manchester, I thought this whole thing seemed like a nightmare I was hoping I'd wake up from.

'Honestly, Jess, I think this might be a fun way to start!' Bella saw my expression. 'OK, maybe *fun* is the wrong word . . .'

At least it was a plan, which was more than I had.

'Fine,' I said reluctantly, propping myself up on the pillows. 'But I can't promise I'll stomach it for long – it may just freak me out more.'

'Understood,' she said, beaming, opening up the laptop and pulling out a notebook (of course she had a notebook).

'Actually I have done a bit of research on my own,' I said, pleased with myself.

She grinned, obviously impressed.

'Let me tell you all about Molly Downer.' For once I had something to bring to the party.

I filled her in on everything I'd found out about Molly and we watched some films and Nonna brought us up dinner, and later hot chocolates and homemade monkey bread. We watched films about witches with talking cats and resurrected boyfriends and serious Dark Magic issues and spell mishaps and (always) too much eyeliner and we chatted and had a few mild freak-out moments together and all the while Bella made notes. Eventually, the seagulls stopped squawking and Mum came up to tell us we really did need to go to bed.

That night, I couldn't sleep for all the witchiness whirring round my brain: Sabrina (the first), dealing with her witchy heritage, two weird but lovable aunts, a talking cat and comic capers at school – not to mention the school bitch, Libby (aptly named). Sabrina (the second), fighting against a way darker magical world and, you know, the actual Devil. Willow in *Buffy*, living in a world where witches exist alongside vampires and demons and all kinds of scary, otherworldly, please-God-don't-let-any-of-them-be-real creations.

Watching all these films, and knowing that everything I'd thought was pure fiction may actually have had some aspect of truth to it, was mind-blowing. Mind-blowing – but also, in some ways, even more enjoyable. Like knowing a very special secret.

CHAPTER TWENTY

'I don't understand why you need me to come,' I said, slamming the car door with more force than intended, then trying to style out my own surprise. 'I'm ill!'

Mum rolled her eyes at that. 'You're looking so much better,' she said. 'And if you're off school, at least you can be doing something constructive. And I told you, I'd appreciate your advice – you have such good taste.'

We both knew that was not true. I am not known for my taste. In anything – TV shows, music, clothes, soft furnishings, friends – anything at all. No one who knows me at all would say, 'Oh let's ask Jessie, she's got good taste'. Mum was obviously up to something.

I could sense I was in a precarious position though. It was clear to everyone I wasn't actually ill and I was on the verge of pushing my luck. Mum can be lenient and a soft touch, but even she has her limit and I knew I was fast approaching it.

We sat in silence as she reversed the car out of the drive and navigated the seafront. We weren't in tourist season yet, but with Easter approaching there were noticeably more people with each passing weekend. Some of the cafés that close over the winter were starting to open now, and there were a few brave people sat on outside tables, wrapped up in big padded coats, making the most of the sunshine. There were dog walkers and families strolling along the promenade, the wind lashing their hair in their faces. I wound down the window and stared out at the sea below as we turned on to the open cliff road. The air was cool, but fresh and welcome.

'What exactly are we doing?' I asked at last.

'I told you. The builder I'm thinking of hiring for the renovation wants us to see this project he's just finished,' Mum said. 'It's in Freshwater. We can stop and get a coffee on the way if you want.'

'Freshwater! That's miles away!'

When you live on the mainland, and you say something is 'miles away', you generally mean more than about three hours. When you live on the Island, where nowhere is more than forty-five minutes away from anywhere else, 'miles away' means anything more than twenty minutes. And boy, are people reluctant to travel more than that twenty minutes. It's amazing how quickly your state of mind – your perception of time and distance – changes.

'It'll be a nice drive. Quality time together,' Mum said.

I didn't even bother answering that.

'So,' she persisted. 'How are you feeling?'

'Not great.'

'You've been off for a long time. The school has been calling. Do you think you'll be ready to go back soon?'

As ready as I'll be to stick pins in my eyes, I wanted to say.

'I'm still not feeling totally right,' I tried.

'How were things at school before you got ... ill?' Mum asked, drawing out the 'ill'. 'Were you finding the work OK?

Don't feel like you've missed out on too much, transferring halfway through the year?'

'*Again*,' I muttered, making a point. 'It was fine.'

'And how are you finding it making new friends?'

'Fine.'

Fine, if by 'friends' she meant people who wrote nasty things on my locker and put gum in my hair. I thought of Summer, who had been texting me and asking if she could pop by to check I'm all right. I'd put her off, again, and again. I wasn't sure why. Maybe I was embarrassed by the gum episode, maybe I thought if she met my family she'd run a mile, or maybe I didn't want to start actually liking someone and risk losing them if and when my hidden 'talents' came to light.

Silence. I watched a bird hovering over the hedge by the roadside, stalking its prey.

'Jessie, you've got to do better than "fine",' Mum said. 'I'm trying here. Trying to be more involved, trying to be more present. *Fine* doesn't cut it any more.'

I sighed, glancing over at her. What did she expect from me? It's not like I was going to launch into the ins and outs of Shitsville High and wasn't it better for her that I didn't? Did she honestly want to open that can of worms? It was all her fault anyway, this mess, and it wasn't like there was anything she could do, or undo, about it now.

'It is genuinely fine,' I said firmly. 'When I say fine, I mean it. It's school – it's not like I'm going to be hopping and skipping and praising the joys. Moving halfway through the year wasn't great, but I'm *fine* with the work. Like I said, all fine. Anyway,' I said, taking another tack, 'how's your sewing going?'

Mum beamed. 'Very well actually. I found this gorgeous vintage fabric . . .'

Bingo. Off she went with sewing chat which morphed into house plans chat and I was covered all the way there.

Fabric-based distraction. A fail-safe move.

**

'Right then, I think this is it,' Mum said, as we turned into a gravel driveway.

The house in front of us looked like a converted barn – a long, stone building with a fresh timber extension on the side and massive bifold doors opening out onto a front courtyard, where there was an outdoor seating area around a sunken firepit. It actually looked pretty nice. There was a transit van parked in the driveway with 'Handy Andy's Building Services' emblazoned on the side and a smaller sticker underneath: 'I came, I saw, I nailed it.' I grimaced.

Mum glanced in the rearview mirror and adjusted her hair before getting out. Wait. Was she wearing lipstick? She couldn't be, Mum never wore lipstick these days. Now that she didn't need to power dress and sock it to the Man in board meetings every other day she had stopped, embracing the au naturel, Earth Mother look instead. How had I not noticed for the whole journey?

Just then, a man (Handy Andy himself, I guessed) exited the barn building and walked towards Mum, hand outstretched, smiling.

I wondered if I could get away with staying in the car for this totally unnecessary exercise, but before I'd even finished the thought Mum tugged me out.

'This is my daughter, Jessie,' Mum said. 'I thought I'd bring her along, she has a good eye for these things.'

CAN WE PLEASE STOP THIS CHARADE OF PRETENDING I HAVE ANY KIND OF AN EYE FOR ANY KIND OF THINGS?

'Hi,' I muttered, giving him my hand, which he shook profusely.

Andy was tall and gangly with a little protruding beer belly that looked totally out of place on him, as if it had grown on the wrong body. He had a receding hairline he was obviously trying to cover up and the ruddy, weathered face of someone who spends a lot of time working outdoors.

'Well then, shall we?' he said, gesturing to the house. 'After you, ladies.'

I trudged after Mum, Handy Andy behind us, which seemed a bit stupid to me seeing as we didn't know where we were going.

'Take a left in the hallway,' he instructed, as we walked through the front door. 'The kitchen is straight ahead there.'

We emerged into a gorgeous open-plan kitchen, exposed stone wall along one side, built-in seating and chunky wooden table along another. There was a huge kitchen island in the middle and a conservatory roof flooding the room with light. The bifold doors I'd seen from the car led out into the courtyard.

'Wow!' Mum said, looking around. 'It's beautiful!'

Handy Andy grinned.

'Not bad, hey?'

'Not bad! It's gorgeous,' Mum said. 'What do you think, Jessie?'

What did she think I thought? Of course it was bloody gorgeous. You didn't need my apparently impeccable taste to see that.

'Lovely,' I dead-panned.

'So, previously the house ended over there,' Handy Andy said, pointing to a thick stone wall. 'We built the whole of this structure, knocking through the wall. The exposed brickwork, the vaulted ceiling . . .'

I zoned out. He went on and on and on. Tiles, brickwork, slate floor, ground source heat pump, fitted this, fitted that, blah, blah, whatever. It was a beautiful room, but I really didn't need to be there, even when Mum cracked out the plans and her vision board and tile samples she'd retrieved from the car and pretended she wanted my input. I still couldn't work out why she'd brought me – if it was quality time she wanted, there were surely less painful options.

With Mum and Handy Andy engrossed in a particularly passionate conversation about sinks, I managed to inch my way out on to the courtyard and lowered myself onto the sofa. I closed my eyes and lifted my face to the sun.

The tinkling of Mum's laugh floated through from the kitchen. I glanced back inside. I was sure they were sitting a bit closer than seemed strictly necessary. Was she *flirting* with Handy Andy? Mum had dated a few men after Dad, but the few we'd seen (or at least seen the profiles of) had all been gorgeous and successful and . . . with decent heads of hair. This mid-life crisis was getting out of control.

I tried to zone out, to focus on the birdsong and my breathing, but my mind couldn't help itself – it was having a dark disco. Molly, the randy reverend, bitchy Harriet, Libby, Callum – it was covering all the grim bases. I knew I was going to have to go back to school at some point, and the thought of it, of walking though those gates and down those corridors, made my stomach clench.

I wished we'd never left Manchester. I wished that Mum had never quit her job and bought the draughty old house. More than anything I wanted to go back to normal. Before the Island. Before the witch bombshell.

If we hadn't moved to the Island, my powers would never have emerged. And there was only one person to blame for that.

'Well thank you so much for that, Andy, I really appreciate it,' I heard Mum saying. 'I'll firm up those plans and get back to you by Tuesday. We're very keen to get started, as you can imagine.' She let out what appeared to be a little giggle and shook his hand. Finally, we could leave.

'Right you are,' he said, walking her out into the courtyard. 'Nice to meet you too, Jessie,' he said, turning his attention to me. 'Are you settling in OK down here?'

'Yeah, fine thanks,' I said, not keen on the small talk.

'The kids here are generally a good bunch. I should put you in touch with my three. They're around your age, I reckon. My ex-wife has them most of the time' – total emphasis on the ex part, for Mum's sake no doubt – 'but we could arrange something.'

I shuffled uncomfortably.

'That sounds great, what a lovely idea,' Mum pitched in, overcompensating for my lack of enthusiasm.

He turned back to Mum. 'Brilliant, we'll sort something out. And I look forward to hearing from you about the work.' Then he winked. An actual wink.

Gross.

***

'Andy seems nice,' Mum said as we pulled out of the drive.

'In a Basic Bob, probably-still-lives-with-his-Mum way,' I said.

'Jessie! That's not nice. He was very helpful, and funny – and I thought it was kind of him to suggest getting you together with his kids.'

'Mum, I don't know what's happened to your man-radar since the move, but he is so not your type.'

We sat in silence for a minute, me wondering if I had actually been too mean, her probably fantasising about romantic micro-wave dinners staring at his bald patch.

'So, I think we need to talk,' Mum said, eventually.

'I was just joking,' I said.

'It's not that,' she said. 'About this whole . . . witch revelation.'

Suddenly I realised this had been the whole point of the trip; I was cornered, with no chance of escape other than doing an action-film roll out of the moving car.

'I read in one of my parenting books that—'

'*Parenting books*?' I said, viciously, not able to keep the anger from my voice. 'Isn't it a bit late in the day for that?'

Mum flushed. 'That hurts, Jessie. I know I've been absent in many ways these last ten years but part of the reason for this move was to change that. I'm trying to do better. So yes, parenting books.'

I glared at my reflection in the side mirror, startled by the ferocity of my scowl.

'So I read in one of my *parenting books* that a good way to approach a difficult conversation is to have it side by side, so you don't need to make eye contact. Walking, or driving, for instance. It can encourage a more open line of communication.'

141

Silence.

We turned the bend in the road, the long beach and white cliff edges coming into view. A few rogue cars and campers were parked up on the grass verge, wet-suited surfers heading to and from the beach carrying boards.

'The fact is, your next period is approaching. And you need to dig yourself out of this pit of denial you've buried yourself in.'

I could feel my heart start beating faster, fury ringing in my ears. *Was she actually kidding?*

'Denial?' I spat. '*Me?* I've got nothing to do with this mess! This is all you. ALL YOU. We'd finally found somewhere that could've worked – I had people I could almost call friends, you had a great job, Bella . . . well, she's always fine. I would've been perfectly fine if we'd stayed up in Manchester – completely oblivious, living my life as a normal teenage girl. NORMAL. And now? Now, because *you* selfishly decided *you* wanted to move back, knowing full well what would happen, I'm in the middle of a witchy shitstorm nightmare that I can't escape. I think I'm entitled to a little bit of denial.'

'Watch your language, Jessie. And your tone.'

'Or what? Are you going to hex me?'

Mum visibly flinched. I hadn't meant for that to come out, or for it to come out how it had, like a weapon. I was losing control. My fists were clenched, nails digging into my palms.

'No. As much I might want to, I'm not going to hex you,' she said, quietly. 'Can we please try and discuss this like grown-ups?'

I had turned away from her, staring out of the window. My eyes fixed on a point on the horizon, a distant cliff, I concentrated on trying not to cry.

'Why did you do it?' I asked, when I'd managed get my voice under control. 'Why move us back?'

She sighed.

I carried on staring at the cliff, using it as my talisman.

'You might have thought we were fine, but we weren't,' she said softly. 'I was running away, living in denial – and denying you girls your true selves. I hadn't been fine for a long while – never feeling quite right every place, or job or relationship I tried, always thinking the next thing I changed might fix it. I just didn't realise it until I found that lump.'

'That lump that turned out to be nothing,' I interjected.

'And thank God it was nothing. But when I thought it might be something, well, it put things into perspective.'

'So you were thinking of yourself?' I asked, bitterly.

'No, Jessie,' she sighed. 'I was thinking of *all of us*, as a family. Suddenly I was forced to see the bigger picture. I had a clearer view of what was important. I had been so consumed with running away from myself – from my true self – that I hadn't stopped to consider what that was doing to me. And by extension, what it was doing to you girls. I was denying you the chance to know yourself. Denying your true nature – what makes you *you*. I know it's hard for you to understand, but you have to take my word for it. It's better for all of us to be back on the Island.'

'Take your word for it? So, by "talk about this like grown-ups", what you mean is, you're the grown-up and I have no say. I just have to take your word for it. I'm good, thanks.'

I was done. The car had started to feel like a prison. I needed air. Not just air through the window. Proper, gusty sea air.

'Can you drop me at Steephill?' I said. 'I want to walk home.'

'No,' she said. 'I'm pulling rank. We need to talk.'

We came up to a red light. Now or never. I checked in the mirror, then tried to open the door. It wouldn't budge.

'Are you kidding me?' I said, pulling harder on the handle. 'You're keeping me prisoner with your magic? This is insane. I'll report you to social services.'

I could see her stifle a smile, which made me even more furious. There was *nothing* about this that was funny.

'I'm keeping you prisoner with central lock,' she said, calmly. 'And you're being ridiculous, but report me if you want. Good luck with that.'

I pulled my legs up to the seat, hugging them tight to me. I felt tears prickle behind my eyes, but I refused to cry, especially in front of her.

'I just want us to talk, Jessie,' she said, gently.

I didn't answer. I was worried my voice would crack. The light turned green, she indicated right, down the road to Steephill, the relief washing over me. She pulled the car over and stopped, I felt her turn and look at me, letting out a big sigh.

'You can go. But please, think about what I said. Your next period is not that far away and I really do think we should talk before then. And I love you. So much.'

Whatever. I was already half out of the door and had to use every ounce of self control not to slam it shut as hard as I wanted to.

'And you're going back to school tomorrow,' she called after me as I walked away. 'You can't run for ever. Take it from someone who tried.'

CHAPTER TWENTY-ONE

I didn't actually go to Steephill. I had changed my mind about wanting the sea. I felt annoyed at it today, with all its whirling and churning. Like it was responsible somehow for my current position, like it had carried me here on a wave and left me, defenceless, to deal with the madness.

I walked upwards instead. Up through the fields, past the neat stone houses to the coast path. The wind had got stronger, whipping my hair into my face, pushing me up and away.

My thoughts were vicious, like endless rounds of poisoned arrows. I was so angry with Mum. She was selfish and wrong. But . . . did she also have a point? My next period was approaching and, annoyingly, it's not like I could run away from it.

If Bella was right, and I was now tied to her stupid erratic cycle, I had much less time than I had thought to get a handle on this thing. And I definitely did not want a repeat of the random acts of destruction of last time. But I also wasn't totally ready to wrap my head around the ins and outs of this unfathomable legacy I'd been handed.

UGH. I didn't know what to do. I wanted to be like a flamingo and bury my head in the sand. (Wait, is that a flamingo? An ostrich, maybe. Whatever big bird in denial it was, I wanted to be like it.) Just for one more day. Then I would deal with it. One last day of relative, unwitchy peace.

When I reached the highest point on the path I snapped out of my trance, stopping, feeling my muscles burn. I looked out over the sea below, spotting a few people, small and ant-like, going about their business, completely oblivious to the girl with special powers and a black hole in her stomach above them. The sea, in all its grey, endless glory rolled back and forth below me, a double-edged sword. The façade of freedom and yet the thing, or one of the things, that was effectively keeping me prisoner.

Beyond it, I wondered, were there girls like me, having these same thoughts, this same anger and quicksand confusion? In Bolton maybe? Or Skegness? Abu Dhabi or Azerbaijan even? Obviously, there are girls all over the world being harassed and worn down every day by ignorant boys, but were there also some who were waiting, terrified, for uncontrollable witch powers to arrive along with their period? Super Plus Tampax and a side order of hexing?

'Kimye! Kimye! Come back!' I heard a voice shout as a small dog, black and white with a scrunched-up face, ran up to me and leaped at my leg. I knelt down to give it my hand to sniff and a figure ran up behind it.

'I'm so sorry, she's a bit over-friendly,' he said, as she rolled over for me to stroke her tummy.

'It's fine, she's gorgeous,' I said.

'See, she's your best friend now.'

I glanced up and my stomach dropped.

'Oh hey, Jessie,' the boy – Freddie – said, looking

uncomfortable. 'You're alive! We thought you might have left. How come you're not at school?'

Perfect, because what I absolutely needed today was one of Callum Henderson's minions in my face. I remembered Callum passing him that note about Tabitha, Freddie giving a stupid chuckle in response.

'I could ask you the same thing,' I said, focusing on Kimye.

'I've uh, injured my shoulder.' He gave an awkward, caught-out smile. 'I mean, it's much better now, but to be safe I thought I should . . .' He trailed off.

I must've looked intrigued because he felt the need to add, 'Please don't tell anyone that you've seen me, there's a big match later and I won't hear the end of it from Callum if he knows I was skiving. Sometimes I just need—'

'He won't hear anything from me,' I said quickly, wanting the encounter over.

Kimye was sitting at my feet, looking up at me longingly.

'She's wanting another stroke.' Freddie was visibly more relaxed now. 'She *really* likes you. Kimye! Come here, leave Jessie alone.' He patted his legs.

Kimye nudged her head more determinedly against me. I gave her a quick pat and edged away.

'It wasn't my choice by the way,' Freddie said. 'The name, I mean.'

I looked at him, risking eye contact. He was taller than he seemed at school, his shoulders just broad enough to balance the height. His eyes were a striking hazel colour, or the one I could see was, the other was hidden by his dark hair flopping over it. He had a small mole just above his lip, in a perfect

Marilyn Monroe placement that, for some reason, softened his face a bit.

'Full disclosure – I'm not totally averse to a spot of Kardashians,' he continued, pushing his hair out of his eyes, 'but I wouldn't have chosen to name the poor dog after them. That was down to my mum and little sister. And yet I'm the one who does most of the walking and I feel like a right tool calling out to her – which I always have to do as she's constantly befriending randoms and refusing to come back to me.'

I raised my eyebrows.

'Sorry! Not that you're a random or anything. Argh, digging myself a hole. We were heading up that way' – he gestured to the right – 'if you fancy joining?'

My initial reaction was to run in the other direction – I did not want to make small talk with a Callum Henderson groupie who would probably report back anything I said. But Freddie seemed different out here – the way he looked, the way he carried himself. Less bravado, less regular jock. I found myself drawn to him, with his floppy hair and stupidly named but super-cute dog. A quick mental scroll through my Hideous Times Highlights showed that while he *had* laughed at Callum's note, he hadn't done anything horrible to me himself. Before I knew it, we were traipsing along the coast path, Kimye bouncing along by our feet.

'So, why are you skiving?' he asked.

'No comment,' I said. He must have an inkling that his consistently cruel buddies were part of the reason I was skiving.

'OK, fair do's.'

We walked a bit further in silence.

'How are you finding it on the Island?' he said eventually. 'It's a pretty big change from Manchester.'

I glanced at him, trying to work out if he was being intentionally mean or clueless. He must have seen the way I'd been treated. His face gave nothing away. 'Umm,' I said, wondering how honest to be. Obviously not totally honest. 'I mean, it's never great starting at a new school mid-year.'

'You sound like you've done it before.'

'Oh, yeah. A few times. It's my mum's thing, to move.' I flinched, remembering the conversation with Mum in the car.

'Why do you move so much? Is it to do with her work?'

'Kind of,' I said, not being able to answer that myself, doing a mental checklist of reasons she'd given in the past: 'being in the countryside might suit us', 'a great job opportunity', 'more diversity in a city' all sprang to mind.

'Ah, so this might be temporary.'

'I was hoping so, but I'm not so sure this time,' I said, thinking back to all Mum's declarations of how she'd found her roots, and felt whole again. Barf.

'How come you moved *here*?' he asked, producing a ball for Kimye and throwing it into the long grass by the path. She started running after it, then paused, seemed to think about it, and decided against, trotting back and looking at him hopefully.

'Every time,' he said, chuckling and running off to get the ball. 'You need some dog school!' He ran back, ball in hand. 'Sorry, carry on. Why here?'

Did I want to go into this? I felt too tired to come up with a fake cheery story. And he had asked. Twice.

'My mum had a bit of a health scare – I mean, she's fine, nothing was wrong, it was just a lump, but it kind of cascaded her into a mid-life crisis and she decided she wanted to "reassess her priorities". And apparently the only way she could do that was to move back down here, where she grew up. And instating family dinners and girls' nights and talking about feelings.'

I took a breath. I hadn't meant to launch into a full-on rant.

'Wow. OK. That's pretty big.'

'I don't know about "big". Annoying, definitely.'

'I'm a grockle too,' he said, 'if it's any consolation.'

'Grockle?'

'Someone not from the Island. Not Island born and bred – I think it used to be used for tourists, but now it just applies to anyone not originally from here. But at least you're not a DFL.'

'DFL?'

'Down From London – here for the weekend with their fancy coffees and fancy cars and red trousers. They're the lowest of the low.'

'So when did you move here?' I asked, taking my eyes off the path for once and glancing at him. He swept his hair out of his face, or tried to; the wind wasn't letting up much.

'Year Seven. Long story, but my mum needed to get away and I guess she thought the Island seemed like a safe and wholesome place.'

We carried on walking, his words floating in the air like balloons ready to pop. 'Safe' and 'wholesome'. They seemed so ridiculous I almost wanted to laugh. There was a pause, and I sensed he wanted to say something else.

'It gets better,' he said, eventually. 'It doesn't feel like it ever will, but it does. It's a bit like the Hunger Games; you just have to find a way to survive.'

'By killing everyone who stands in your way?' I asked.

He laughed. I laughed too, hoping it wouldn't come to that.

CHAPTER TWENTY-TWO

The next morning, I woke up feeling like Katniss – game face on, ready to brave my enemies. Seeing Freddie and realising there was some decent in him had given me a sprinkling of hope – maybe not all of them were as bad as they seemed. Maybe the storm had passed. Either way, I had to go back – Mum had washed my uniform and laid it out on my bed, making it very clear she was serious about me returning to school.

I had gotten up early and tidied away the piles of clothes from my floor while listening to nineties indie as loud as my ears could stand it and reciting positive mantras in the mirror. 'I am strong', 'I am loved', 'I do not need anyone else's approval', 'I am enough'. Repeating them twenty-seven times each made them at least register, if not settle.

I would ride it out. Eventually, they would get bored of me, if they weren't already. They were one chewing-gum-in-my-hair and twenty-seven Post-its-on-my-locker into their campaign – I knew there would probably be more coming my way, but I also knew it was survivable. They wouldn't beat me up, or burn me at the stake – it wouldn't be life-threatening. It was petty words and gestures, sticks and stones, and I could ride those out. The Easter break wasn't far off, I could definitely last till then, and by the time we got back they'd definitely have forgotten all about me.

My phone beeped with a message from Summer:

Looking forward to seeing you, stranger.

I am strong, I am strong, I am thick-skinned like a rhino.

I told myself that as I looked in the mirror, trying to trick myself into believing that the tired-eyed mouse staring back was hiding some deep pools of resilience.

I told myself that as I pounded the street on the way to school.

I told myself that when I found more notes stuck to my locker. I repeated it again when I heard the whispers start up in the hallway. When Callum smirked at me repeatedly in maths. I recited it like a mantra in my head, gritting my teeth so hard I'm pretty sure I wore them down a layer. I was counting the days until the holidays, while pushing thoughts away of the other thing I was on a countdown to, which (in hindsight) was pretty stupid.

***

'There she is!' Summer said, sweeping up behind me in the corridor at break, Tabitha falling into step the other side of me. 'We've missed you.'

I smiled, calling on my inner rhino, trying to be strong and bright and breezy. 'I was so ill,' I lied. 'Sorry I didn't take your calls or anything, I was bedridden. Flu is not fun.'

The blue of Summer's eyes flashed at me, scanning to see if I was telling the truth.

'Well you didn't miss much in Media,' Tabitha said. 'Just the usual Marcus fun and games and finishing off the doc theory – I can lend you my notes.'

'Thanks,' I said.

'And tell her your news, Tabs,' Summer prompted, nudging Tabitha.

'Oh yeah.' A wide grin lit up her face. 'I don't know if you remember but I submitted one of my short stories to a magazine and I heard the other day they've accepted it! It's going to be published.' It was the most animated I'd seen her.

'That's amazing!' I said. 'Well done. We should celebrate!'

'Totally,' Summer said, as the bell rang.

'Limp pizza celebration at lunch?' I said. 'If you're not too busy being a professional author, that is.'

'Ah, I've got Model UN,' Tabitha said, 'and Summer has the paper on a Friday.'

'Oh, totally too busy then,' I managed, my disappointment tinged with terror.

'After school, though,' Summer said. 'For sure.'

***

Friday lunchtime was the holy grail of lunchtimes for anyone in Year Nine or above, as we had the privilege of being allowed to leave the school grounds for lunch. This mostly constituted about three hundred students descending on the Broad Street chippy, but for me it was escape. I couldn't make it all the way home and back in time, but I could find a quiet spot where I could eat on my own that wasn't a toilet cubicle.

I'd made it as far as the front car park and the gate was in sight – I'd specifically left early to be in with a chance of a hassle-free exit – when I felt the first one. A sharp scratch to my head followed by sniggers as something fell on the floor by my feet. A paper aeroplane, with '*For Jessie*' written on it. I stooped to pick it up, hoping that doing so would be enough to make them stop. It had fallen part-way open, the word 'SLUT' written in big, bold, letters, taunting me. My heart thumped, a blush bloomed from my neck upwards. I carried on walking.

Then another one came, and another, and another one. They were coming at me quick-fire, the aim getting better, the laughs louder, the planes pooling at my feet. I glimpsed the odd word scrawled onto the planes. 'DESPERATE', 'FREAK', 'SLAG'.

'Open them!' someone called out. 'Don't be shy. You weren't the other night, were you?'

I finally turned and glanced over to where the noise was coming from. The football team, fully kitted out, were waiting by a minibus as Coach packed up equipment. Callum stood in the middle, arms folded, leaning against the minibus like a dictator surveying his kingdom.

I kept on walking and they all started booing. More people had come out on their way to lunch now, gathering in groups and cliques, looking on with interest. A few with a front-row view, including Sadie, had got their phones out and were recording, in the hope of some social-media-worthy drama. I burned with embarrassment, like my skin was on fire.

'Come on now, boys,' Coach said light-heartedly, taking a smiling bite of his apple. 'We've got more important things to do, like beating New Hampton!'

And that was what did it. Something inside of me snapped. *More important things to do?* He was an adult. He was standing right there. He had witnessed them throwing paper aeroplanes at my head and *that* was his response? Before I could even process the decision, I was turning around and walking over to him, glaring, furious, electric, so angry my eyesight was blurry.

'Oooooh, watch out, boys,' Callum said, to much laughter and hooting.

'They've just been throwing paper planes at my head,' I said, stopping in front of Coach. 'With things written on them, like this.' I held the note up to his face, close. He flinched.

'I am aware, Ms Jones, and I instructed them to stop.'

'Actually, you didn't instruct them to stop, you told them there are more important things to do,' I said, waving the paper angrily. I didn't feel like I was in my body. I was watching from outside myself.

'I will remind you, you are talking to a teacher, Ms Jones,' Coach said, lowering his voice and leaning forward, the smile on his face disappearing. 'And this is not appropriate behaviour. You are clearly emotional.'

'Appropriate behaviour? Are you kidding me?' I asked, my voice rising. 'Was what they were doing "appropriate behaviour"?'

I felt a surge. A wave of fury and something else, something unstoppable. Something familiar. A shooting, crippling pain. For once though, I was pleased. *Perfect timing, Period, let's teach this misogynist arsewipe a lesson.*

I concentrated, bearing into the pain, trying to summon

whatever magic it was that my period had brought with it last time. I stared at Coach, with his carefully styled hair and perma-tracksuit, the whistle round his neck on some festival lanyard tie, intended to be both a sign of coolness and a badge of authority. I hated him. I refused to break eye contact, willing something, anything, bad to happen to him.

'If you feel I have . . .' He began, then stopped suddenly. He stumbled on a word, coughed. Was this it? Was he about to cough up worms? Or a torrent of spiders? A swollen tongue so he couldn't speak for a few days? Any of them would be good. I watched, eager to know what my magic had conjured up this time.

His face was turning beetroot red, his veins popping out of his forehead. With a final, deep, grotesque cough, a lump of chewed-up apple came flying out of his mouth at full speed, spit-covered flecks of it landing on my cheek. The football team burst into stifled laughter, slapping Coach on the back to get any last bits out. I felt the burn spread over me, a blush so fierce I could pass for a tomato.

'Uh, Jessie,' Freddie said quietly, taking a step towards me. I followed his eyes to where a dark bloom was starting to spread around the crotch of my light grey trousers, clocking it at about the same time as everyone else did.

No.

NO NO NO.

What had I done to the universe that I was being punished so badly for?

'Ugh!' I heard one of them shout. 'Gross!'

157

'Dirty cow.'

'No wonder she's so crazy.'

'Time of the month, much?'

Not knowing what else to do, I turned round, focused on putting one foot in front of the other and got out of there as fast as possible.

CHAPTER TWENTY-THREE

Five Things About Being A Witch So Far:
1. IT SUCKS.
2. IT SUCKS.
3. IT SUCKS.
4. IT SUCKS.
5. IT SUCKS.

'MUM!' I shouted, forcing open the door, which today had put up even more of a fight than usual. I felt like I was on the run from an angry pitchfork-wielding mob. I'll teach them, every single one of those laughing, stupid, single-brain-celled buffoons. Starting with Coach. I'll magic that stupid whistle so far up his ...

'MUUUUUM!' I shouted again, rage surging through every part of my body. I heard her voice coming from the kitchen, so I stomped in that direction. 'Mum, I need those witch lessons! Now!'

I'd stopped off at the public toilets in the high street and, half a loo roll later, had vaguely sorted myself out – inasmuch as there was no longer any blood gushing out of me and I'd managed to blot some of the stain away, tying my jumper round my waist to disguise the rest. I knew I should go upstairs first and finish the job, but I wanted to maximise on my rage and take the plunge before I lost momentum and chickened out.

I pushed through the kitchen door, red-faced and sweaty, feeling like I was on the verge of either keeling over or spontaneously combusting.

Mum was standing by the sink, looking flustered and twitchy. 'Jessie, hello, darling,' she said, in what Bella and I call her estate agent voice (cheery, fake, overly high-pitched). I stopped. She was widening her eyes meaningfully in the direction of the kitchen table.

I turned. Handy Bloody Andy sat at the kitchen table with a cup of tea, looking slightly bemused.

'Hi, Jessie,' he said. I clocked his T-shirt, a picture of a screwdriver and 'If Dad can't do it, we're all screwed.' I shuddered and made a mental note to never meet his children if they gave him gifts like that.

'Witch lessons! You're such a joker,' Mum said, doing a fake laugh that made me want to barf.

Handy Andy picked up on the cue and joined in with the laugh, in that annoyingly fake way grown-ups do in social situations, even when they don't get the joke.

'Witch lessons!' Nonna said, striding in from her annexe, bangles clanging, big flowery top billowing. 'Are you finally ready to learn?'

'Mum,' Mum said, still in her fake voice, but this time more pointedly. 'Jessie was just joking. You know what she's like.'

Nonna looked from Mum to Andy to me, then back round at all of us again, spending an extra few seconds on me. Her eyes fell on my crotch. She knew. Somehow, she knew.

'You come with me, sweetcheeks,' Nonna said, taking my hand and leading me through to her annexe, giving Mum a parting glare as she went past.

***

Stepping into Nonna's annexe is like stepping through the wardrobe into Narnia. You know how at Christmas you get those Santa grottos at garden centres and you walk through a tunnel all covered in fake snow and fairy lights and there are little decorations scattered around everywhere and it feels totally magical – it's like that, but without the fake snow and Christmas decorations. Otherworldly, in a good way.

I remember her old house, on the other side of the Island, so clearly. A little stone cottage looking out over the beach with a thatched roof, twisty rose bushes arched over the doorway and a front garden full of beautiful flowers. She used to have one of those swinging benches out the front that looked out over the sea and she'd let Bella and I have our ice lollies there – ice lollies for pudding every night – we felt like queens!

Mum had said Nonna had moved in with us so we could look after her as she got older and so she wouldn't be on her own, but nothing about Nonna screamed 'in need' or 'lonely'. Maybe it was part of Mum going back to her roots, or maybe she needed some moral witch support dealing with us. Either way, as much as I missed the cottage, I did love Nonna being so close. Her annexe was that whole cottage crammed into a small living space and yet it didn't feel cramped or stifling, even next to Mum's attempted rustic minimalism in the main house. It felt homey and comfortable and safe – and it smelt like Nonna through and through.

'Do you need to go and get a tampon, petal?' she asked.

'I should be fine, I've got an industrial amount of toilet paper shoved in my pants.'

'Have a seat then,' she said, gesturing to one side of her bright yellow sofa and sitting herself down on the other. 'Now then, tell me what's the matter.' Her blue eyes twinkled with concern, the wrinkles at their corners deep and familiar.

I had to play this right – not that I was 'playing' Nonna, I told myself. That made it sound way more contrived than it was. Mum and Nonna had both been pestering me to accept my witchiness and to let them teach me about it and now I was finally ready. That was all true. I just might not mention that I wanted to learn about it in order to unleash the full potential of my powers on my enemies. So yeah, not 'playing' Nonna at all, just being selective.

'You can tell me,' she said, putting her hand on mine, her chunky rings cool against my skin.

'This is just all so rubbish,' I blurted out, the words getting caught in a sob. Because, while my insides were mainly a molten raging river of fury, I was also exhausted, drained, and apparently very sad.

After that, I was like a barrel going over Niagara Falls – not a chance in hell of going back. I ugly-cried and snotted, used up half a pack of tissues and, having eventually got the whole sorry story out, ended up burrowed into Nonna's chest, deep-breathing her patchouli and lavender essence. She rubbed my back, her rings and bangles rough and bumpy through my shirt.

We sat like that for a while, me just breathing her in, Nonna being all rhythmic and soothing.

'You are special, my darling girl,' she said eventually, tilting my head up. 'I know it's scary right now, and I know you've needed your time, but together we will get you through this. And you'll emerge from the chrysalis in your full, powerful, womanly glory, like a beautiful witch butterfly.'

I felt a pang of guilt, looking into those genuine eyes so full of love, but I reminded myself that I wasn't lying, not completely. I did need to embrace my witchery. And the thought of my full, powerful, womanly glory sounded right on track for what I had in mind.

'You make it sound like I'm going to have some kind of hardcore immersion therapy into the Occult.'

'Well . . .' she said, grinning cheekily.

'Oh, Jessie, I'm so sorry.' Mum hurried in, all flustered. 'I just didn't want Andy . . . It was bad timing, he was showing me some samples and . . . we got talking . . . I'm sorry, I'm here now and I'm all yours. Tell me everything.'

'You shouldn't have ignored her,' Nonna said, sternly. 'She needed you.'

'I know that Mum, but I couldn't exactly talk with Andy there.'

'Why not?'

'Mum, don't be stupid. It's not appropriate.'

'It doesn't need to be a secret any more, Allegra. They don't burn us at the stake nowadays.' Nonna was trying to put a light-hearted edge to her voice, but I could tell she was annoyed with Mum. All of a sudden, Mum seemed much younger. 'I thought you were done hiding,' Nonna added quietly.

'Mum! Please, not now,' Mum said, with a flash of anger.

'Darling, are you OK?' she asked, turning to me and taking my hand.

'She's ready,' Nonna said, and there was a shift in the air, a breathing out, a new energy.

Mum raised her eyebrows, questioning, her eyes brightening. 'Really, love?' They both looked at me, expectant.

I nodded, and I did actually feel a small seed of something like excitement. 'I'm ready to talk. And to have some lessons in how to manage these freaky powers I've inherited from you,' I said.

'Let's not use the word *freaky*, shall we?' Mum said. 'And good! I'm so pleased! Bella will be home in a bit. We wanted to wait until you were both ready, so you could learn together. We've got a lot to cover! Where to start though? Where to start . . .'

She stood up and started pacing, muttering to herself. She caught Nonna's eye and they smiled at each other. Then Mum held her hand out and a big, heavy, leatherbound book flew into it from Nonna's shelf. I gasped.

'Sorry,' Mum said. 'Too soon?'

CHAPTER TWENTY-FOUR

'Our family have been witches since time began,' Nonna said, her voice all serious and booming.

'Since time began? How do you know that?' Bella asked.

'Ssshh. Don't interrupt,' Mum said.

Once Bella had got back and was filled in on the plan, they'd rushed off to 'get ready'. I'd been expecting them to come down in some sort of flowing, black hooded capes with flower-threaded loose hair and broomstick accessories, but they both looked underwhelmingly normal – Mum kaftan-clad and Nonna wearing her usual billowy floral top. Though, with all the excitement, she *was* jangling more.

We were sat around the kitchen table, which was covered in all kinds of paraphernalia, making it look like a school project about witchcraft through the ages. I didn't know what half of it was, and the other half looked like tat from one of those alternative shops that smell of catch-at-the-back-of-your-throat incense in the market in Manchester. And there were candles. I'd never seen so many candles lit at once – I felt like I was in a romantic music video with some serious health and safety issues. Dave was curled up by my feet, purring softly, as if it was just a Friday like any other and she couldn't care less.

'Our powers have been passed from generation to generation.

From my mother to me, from me to your mother and now, from your mother to you,' Nonna continued.

I wanted to interject that I understood the concept and could we please get to the good stuff, but I sensed that wouldn't be well received. It was hard to take this seriously, when essentially it was just Nonna speaking in a slightly different voice with loads of random stuff on the table, but I kept reminding myself that it was real, and if I wanted to use my powers for revenge, I needed to pay attention.

'For generations, witches were persecuted, tortured, murdered and burned alive – because we were powerful, we were feared, we were women. Those were dark times and we were forced to hide our powers, deny our true selves.' Nonna couldn't resist a quick look at Mum at this point. Then she stood and raised her arms up in the air, bangles rattling. 'But we have always been here, and we will always be here. And from the ashes of those who came before us, we rise like phoenixes. We are survivors.'

At the mention of survivors, a vision of the four of us doing a Destiny's Child type dance routine in barely there outfits flitted across my mind and I had to stifle a giggle. I tried to catch Bella's eye, but she was rapt.

'OK,' Nonna said in her normal voice, sitting back down. 'So, let's start with the basics. What *is* magic?' This was clearly not a question we were expected to answer. 'Magic is a way of connecting with the energies of the universe. Its foundations are respect for the natural world and belief in beauty and goodness. All our powers start and end there – in the natural world, with nature's cycles—'

'Including menstrual cycles,' I interjected.

'It doesn't get more natural than that,' Bella said, always the know-it-all.

'She's absolutely right,' Nonna said. *Of course she is.* 'Where life begins.'

Ugh.

'Mother Nature at her finest.'

'So why do we get powers when we're having a period?' I refused to call it menstruating.

'Because that is when you are at your most powerful,' Mum said.

'It doesn't feel like that when I'm curled up in bed with a hot water bottle.'

'It is a thing of beauty,' Nonna said.

Hmm, not so sure about that.

'It is Mother Nature giving you the best, most powerful gift she could. The ability to give life.'

'I'm not sure that's always a good thing,' I said. I had a sense that childbirth was more of a punishment than a blessing. 'And, no offence, but I'm guessing you've stopped ... you know ... having periods. But you still have powers, right?'

Nonna smiled, and suddenly all the candles went out. Then they lit again. My eyes nearly popped out of my head. That was a firm *yes* then.

'Remember, it's only juvenile witches whose powers are limited to times they're menstruating,' Mum said. 'When your powers are strong enough, when *you* are strong enough, your powers will be with you constantly.'

Powers all the time – now *that* sounded promising. The period thing was a major pain in the arse.

'Ah, yes, but you didn't tell us when that would be,' Bella said.

'Yeah, when will that be?' I asked, keen to know if I could fast-track it somehow. It would be useful to have constant powers when dealing with Callum Henderson.

'Don't worry,' Mum said. 'It varies with every witch, but it's not likely to be for a while – unless you're really quite remarkable.'

Damn, that'd put me out of the equation then.

'And why do our powers only start when we're on the Island?' Bella asked.

'Because the Island is our coven's life force. It takes something strong to make your powers first appear. Being surrounded by water and by the souls of our ancestors who walk the Island . . . it calls to your power.'

'Sorry, what?' I said, my skin goosebumping at the thought of an army of dead Downers zombie-ing around Ventnor.

'What happens to your powers if you take the contraceptive pill?' Bella asked.

'And what about girls who are from a family of witches but don't get periods?' I added.

'Nature finds a way. Nature always finds a way. If you're a witch, you're a witch, you're a witch – through and through,' Nonna said. 'Now,' she continued, 'there are three parts to the Witch's Code – all are essential.'

'Wait, you mentioned our coven? Who, exactly, is in our coven? Is it just us? Are there more witches on the Island?' I needed more information.

'We, the four of us, are a coven. But there is also an Island coven,' Mum said.

'Wow, so, not just us. Are there many witches here on the Island?'

'There's a few,' Mum said. 'But we're a dying breed.'

'Will I get to meet them?' I asked, not sure if I was excited or nervous at that prospect.

'At some point. But let's not get ahead of ourselves.'

'And are there warlocks?' Bella asked, causing Mum and Nonna to do a proper LOL.

'Oh please!' Nonna said. 'Men have just spread that around to try and get in on the act! Now. Back to the Witch's Code.'

'Oh yeah, three parts,' I said, pushing the other billion questions I had lined up to one side.

'One,' Nonna boomed. 'Do what makes you happy, but not to the detriment of others. Two – the energies you give out will come back to you threefold. Three – everything must be balanced – nature must remain level.'

Sounded like a standard school motto. I was keen to get on to the good stuff.

'So, what kind of stuff can we, you know, actually *do* with our powers?' I asked, in the most innocent, not-remotely-out-for-revenge way I could manage. 'For good, I mean, obviously?'

'Well,' Nonna said, a full-on twinkle in her eye. 'Basically, anything and everything.'

The next instant, music started playing, the lights flashed, and all the objects from the table rose up and hovered in the air before swirling around us. Bella's hair turned red, Mum started croaking, and my fingernails grew two inches longer.

It was incredible. It was bizarre. It was too much to take in.

'What the—' Bella and I both said, staring at everything around us like we were gormless fish.

I felt like a toddler at a magic show. I had to remind myself that this wasn't sleight of hand or tricks; this was the real deal and it was Nonna – *my Nonna* – doing it.

'Ribbit.' Mum was flapping her arms at Nonna, I guess telling her to stop, but all that was coming out of her mouth were croaks, which obviously Bella and I found hysterically funny. Dave didn't stir.

'Sorry, darling,' Nonna said. 'I was just demonstrating.'

And just like that, in the time it took to blink, everything went back to normal – objects, music, nails, hair, Mum. I couldn't work out if I was relieved or disappointed.

'So you don't need to say incantations or anything?' Bella asked.

'For certain things, that are harder, you need spells. But for everyday things, the magic is within us.'

'Harder things like what?' I asked.

'Well, transformation, resurrection. That sort of thing. Nothing you need to concern yourselves with, certainly. Resurrection is Dark Magic, and we Downers have never been about that.'

I gulped, my throat feeling tight. *Dark Magic? Resurrection?* I didn't want to dwell on those clangers.

'So, if you guys have always had these powers, how come you haven't been using them?' Bella asked.

Nonna and Mum looked at each other and laughed, a secret little in-joke laugh.

'Oh, we've been using them,' Nonna said. 'Me, all the time, your mother only since she moved back here though. We've just been very careful to make sure you – and more importantly, other people – didn't notice.'

'What kind of stuff have you done?' Bella asked.

'Not cooking and cleaning, that's for sure,' I added.

'I suggested that,' Nonna said. 'But your mother insisted she needs to learn to do some things *authentically*.'

Mum rolled her eyes. 'Which is true!'

'Authentically?' I said. 'Is that code for badly?'

'Oi! Cheeky!' Mum laughed.

'Homework?' I asked, suddenly excited at the prospect of my essays magically writing themselves. 'Can I use magic to do my homework?'

'No, you cannot!' Mum said.

'Why? It wouldn't be harming anyone.'

'It would be harming yourself.'

'Interesting,' I said. 'So you're saying that in theory I *can*, but in practice I shouldn't.'

'Jessie,' Mum said, in her warning voice.

'Enough of this dilly-daddling,' Nonna said, standing up. 'Let's get our magic on! It's best if you learn your magic gradually and organically, establishing your own unique link and relationship with the universe. But you need to know some basics to start with. So let's begin with one of the easiest invocations – lighting a candle.'

As she spoke, two of the candles went out, then lifted up and zoomed across the table before settling themselves, one in front of Bella and one in front of me. It was freaky. And kind of thrilling.

'You have to feel the power, open yourself up to it – you think light, you will get light. Stay relaxed. Breathe in, channel, then release. It's easier in the beginning to close your eyes and visualise the energy coming through you.'

I was so ready for this. I closed my eyes, forcing the image of a candle into my head. My hand instinctively went to my abdomen, feeling for a relationship with my uterus. *Think light, Jessie, think light.* I opened my eyes. Nothing.

'Keep trying. It's virtually impossible to get direct magic first time. Try again. Don't force it,' Mum said, going for gently motivational.

It's much easier to *say* don't force it than it is to actually close your eyes and think of light, but not too much of light. Like, how is that even possible? It felt like my meditation efforts all over again. Relax, breathe in, channel, release. I opened my eyes – nothing. Again. My only consolation was that Bella wasn't having any luck either. I tried again.

And again.

And again – this time taking an extra deep breath, like I was about to dive under water. Then I heard Mum yelp and a chair scrape. I opened my eyes.

A candle over on the other side of the room had caught alight. And by 'alight', I mean there was a full-on blazing fire at its top and wax was melting and pooling in rivers over the sideboard it was sat on. Mum had instinctively stood up, ready to rush over to it, but before she had the chance Nonna had put it out with a glance. She looked at me with a flicker of excited interest I didn't know how to take.

'Well, well,' she said, her grin so big her wrinkles went double-depth. 'We have a live one.'

I felt Bella stiffen slightly beside me, her candle still decidedly unlit. I couldn't help but feel a tiny bit smug, even though my fire hazard wasn't exactly what you would call a success.

'Good work, Jessie,' Nonna said, eyes still twinkling. 'You just need direction.'

Story of my life.

'Bella, you'll get there. Let's go again!'

***

We practised lighting candles for hours, until the world outside had gone pitch black and silent and all I could see when I closed my eyes were wicks and floating flames.

Bella, of course, got there not long after my first misfire, creating a precise and controlled flame. Once she'd mastered it, she helped me in a surprisingly unpatronising way. It took me about five more attempts and some near misses before I managed to light the candle I was *intending* to light, but once I got it, the feeling was incredible – pure, focused, powerful. It felt good. *I* felt good. I felt like a goddess. Totally, bone-heavy exhausted, but exhilarated at the same time.

'Right then,' Mum said, pushing herself up from the table. She looked tired. 'It's late. You two need to get to bed and rest.'

'But we've only just started,' I said. I didn't have time to waste. Unless I could upgrade from lighting a candle to lighting a bonfire under Coach's arse, my new-found skill wasn't exactly going to teach anyone a lesson.

'Only just started? We've been going for hours!' Mum said.

'But we've only done one thing. Please, can we try something else?'

'Please,' Bella added, giving me some much-appreciated backup.

'Don't be such a stick in the mud, Allegra – they're keen, that's good!' Nonna said. 'They've not got school tomorrow. I'll make them a remedy to boost their strength and they'll be good as new.'

All three of us had our best puppy-dog faces on (except for Nonna, who was looking more bulldog). Mum was backed into a corner, and she knew it,

'Fine,' she said, reluctantly. '*One* more lesson, but after that, bed.'

'Yay! Thank you, Mum.' Bella and I crashed into her for a grateful hug.

'I'll get brewing,' Nonna said, actually rubbing her hands together in glee and shuffling off to her annexe.

'Mud and grass?' Bella asked.

'Agrimony and astragalus, actually,' Nonna called.

'But it tastes the same,' Mum whispered, laughing.

'Are you brewing it in a cauldron?' I joked.

'The cauldron is a pain in the arse. It needs three of us to lift it and take about an hour to boil, so I was going to use the kettle. But if you want me to I can,' Nonna called through.

Bella and I looked at each other, trying to work out if she was joking. An actual cauldron? Surely cauldrons and broomsticks were the stuff of cartoon, fantasy, made-up witches.

'Come and see it, if you don't believe me,' Nonna said.

Bella and I were there in an instant.

'In there,' Nonna said, pointing to the tall cupboard in the hallway, next to the back door. 'Open it, have a look.'

She stood back, hand on her hip, amusement in her eyes, while

I slowly opened the door. (I don't know what made me feel the need to do it slowly, it's not like the cauldron was about to fly out at me.) The cupboard was a typical Nonna-style mess – a hoover rammed in at an angle, a mop, excess toilet rolls, various cleaning products, a random shoe. No cauldron.

'Very funny,' I said. 'You had me for a minute there.'

'It's in there somewhere,' she said, frowning. 'Let me see.'

She bent down, with effort, and started rooting through the detritus, muttering. 'Come on you bugger, where are you hiding?' More rummaging. 'Aha, there she is.' She stood back, having cleared a path within the cupboard and, sure enough, there, right at the very back, was a big, black cauldron, looking exactly as you would expect a cauldron to look.

'Wow,' Bella said. 'It's . . . I mean . . .'

'It's been in our family for centuries,' Nonna said proudly. 'The spells that thing has boiled up, the magic it's worked, the naughty men it's made impotent. I tell you, it's incredible.'

'Can we use it?' I asked.

'Another time, love – she's heavy. But I promise, we'll crack her out and take her for a spin soon. Kettle for now.'

'Wait. Do you also have a broomstick?' I asked, excitement rising again. Was I going to get to fly on a broomstick one day? The thought of it made me tingle.

'I sure do,' Nonna said, grinning and rummaging in the cupboard again. 'Here it is!' she said, holding a standard Poundland red plastic broom in front of her and breaking into hysterical laughter.

'Nonna!'

'Sorry, I couldn't resist. No, we don't have broomsticks, not like the ones you mean. Don't believe everything you've heard about witches, petal. Now, tea!'

***

As suspected, the tea was revolting, but Nonna made us finish it and I had to admit, I did feel pretty restored afterwards. Mum had made us toasted cheese sandwiches too (her one fail-safe) and we devoured them sitting round the fire in the living room – the fire that Bella lit with magic!

'Right then,' Nonna said, edging herself forward on the sofa. 'Next up, moving things!'

'Telekinesis,' Bella said, matter-of-factly.

'Now that you've got the hang of fire, it shouldn't be hard. We're going to start with this,' Nonna said, draining her sherry glass and putting it on the coffee table. 'It's the same as before: you think the intention, stay relaxed, breathe in, channel, release. Jessie, you try first.'

I put my empty toastie plate to the side and moved down to the floor, crossing my legs and sitting, back straight, in some kind of serious, about-to-do-yoga pose. Mum gave me a little supportive shoulder squeeze and I could sense her anticipation. I looked at the glass, a lone drip of sherry making its way down the short stem.

I imagined the glass moving, I breathed in, I channelled, I released.

I felt the now-familiar cramp and tingle and something like a surge. The glass moved. Not a smooth, gentle glide across the coffee table though – oh no – it flew, full speed, into the wall and dramatically smashed, shards of glass scattering themselves all over the carpet.

176

There was silence. Mum looked horrified, Bella surprised and Nonna a little bit impressed.

'Are you OK?' Mum asked. I nodded, a bit stunned by the result of my efforts.

'Well, looks like we'll need more glasses,' Nonna said, grinning.

***

We did need more glasses. All of the trayful that Nonna brought back in and then some. Basically, all the glasses in the house, and most of them got smashed. But, as before, I got there in the end. Bella took a couple of attempts before anything happened, but when she got it, it was pretty much perfect.

And that was kind of the theme of the whole weekend. Whatever we did, I managed it first, but in a pretty disastrous, sometimes hazardous, way. Bella took a few more tries but was precise and grade-A standard when she got there.

I thought back to school. It was actually pretty lucky I hadn't done more harm. A random rash and a growing nose were nothing. I needed to up my game to be able to achieve the controlled, intentional revenge I was seeking – without burning down the whole school.

We were so tired that we didn't get up until the afternoon on Saturday, but when we did we were straight back on it. We magicked brunch – I couldn't believe Mum had been cooking food so badly all this time when she could have been serving actual, edible, nice food – and then (even better) we magicked the washing up.

We grew and shrunk things, froze things, melted things, suspended things, stirred things, multiplied things. We magicked up animals (I accidentally invoked a plague of locusts), we made wounds, we healed wounds, we grew hair, made hair disappear (a very useful skill), changed the colour of hair, made hair curly (who knew there was so much you could do with hair?). We magicked until we were aching all over and hardly able to keep our eyes open, until I was sure I actually heard my bed calling to me.

***

On the Sunday, they took us on a field trip at dawn. It was so early I felt like I was still dreaming, the bitter cold the only thing reminding me I definitely wasn't. They took us to the west side of the Island – the natural, less developed side. There's a big old chalky hill sticking out into the sea called Tennyson Down, named after some bearded Victorian poet who lived at the bottom somewhere. Nonna marched us all up to the top, huffing and puffing, the sky turning gradually from black to pink and purple, our breath frosty clouds in front of us.

'Here we are,' she said, when we'd finally reached the peak. A tall, dramatic stone monument towered above us, its edges tapering to a point where an intricately carved circle sat.

My chest was burning with the effort of the walk and I wasn't sure why we hadn't just magicked ourselves up here instead of making the giant schlep. But when I looked up (realising I'd spent most of the walk concentrating on the ground beneath me), it *was* quite a view. The whole Island was sprawled out below us, white cliffs and dusky bays, the grey sea making lazy, slurpy waves, like it was just waking up, not quite ready for the day yet.

'This is the most sacred place on the Island,' Nonna said. 'This is our foundation, our grounding, where we have our strongest connection to nature.'

Bella and I looked at each other. We'd learned not to doubt anything that Nonna said, no matter how crazy and ridiculous it sounded.

'But this has only been here since the Victorian times, hasn't it?' Bella asked.

'This particular piece, yes, as a monument to Alfred Lord Tennyson. But there has always been a witch's monument here,' Mum said.

'For centuries, our family has made our rituals here,' Nonna said. 'Our ancestors lie under this very earth.'

Oh man, not the ancestors again. I didn't like the idea of walking over dearly departed Great Aunty Alice and Molly Downer and whoever else might be lying there.

'Shall we?' Mum said, her eyes looking twinkly and alive for what felt like the first time in ages.

'Uh, shall we what?' I asked nervously.

'Let's!' Nonna said. 'It's time for you to meet the family.'

'Oh no. No, no, no!' I said, starting to back away.

'No way!' Bella said, doing the same.

Mum was laughing. 'She's just winding you up! We're not bringing anyone back from the dead. It's a ceremony, a way of cementing your relationship with our coven, with the Island.'

'It's either this or the full-blown naked ritual,' Nonna said.

'Yeah, I'm good thanks,' I said.

'Trust me,' Mum said, taking my hand, looking at me so earnestly it hurt. How could I say no to that?

'Copy me,' Nonna said, producing what looked like some kind of medieval knife out of her coat and running it quickly across the palm of her hand, causing a sudden stream of blood to form. I gasped and took another step back.

'It's fine, I promise,' Mum said, soothingly, taking the knife from Nonna and etching her own palm, before handing it on to Bella. Bella took one deep breath and followed suit, then passed the knife to me. I held it, looking at their expectant faces. My mind told me it was wrong, but an unexpected instinct, something from somewhere inside me, told me it was absolutely right. I made a quick, light cut.

Standing right in front of the monument, facing it, Nonna held out her arms, palms blood red from where she'd rubbed them together and placed them on the stone. I looked at Bella, at Mum. Mum nodded, as if this was an everyday occurrence. I couldn't help but think we were all sleep-deprived and should've stayed at home, but also (clearly) I had no choice.

Reluctantly, I pushed my body up against the stone, the coldness instantly creeping through my clothes. I thanked the gods it was stupid early enough that no one was here to witness this. Once we were all splayed out, bloodied hands on the monument, Mum and Nonna started speaking in low, booming voices:

'Uplifted ancestors of the Downer Coven, we come before you today to present our coven's daughters. May you protect them, heal them, support them and help them in all that they do.

So shall it be.'

I was cold and tired and feeling silly. I was essentially dry-humping a massive stone. But just as I was about to ask how long we needed to stay like that, a surge – bold and strong and electric – crashed over and through me, like a wave. I felt like I was being dragged down, but also floating above, like I was on fire, but also freezing cold. I was in a whirlwind, I was lying calm on a beach. I was everything and nothing. I heard voices – chanting, laughter – like we were at a party. Calls of 'Welcome' came from distant, muffled voices and images of faces – of people who I just knew were Molly, Aunt Alice, others – flashed through my mind. And under it ran the squawk of seagulls, the crash of waves, the rush of the wind. I felt powerful and focused and alive. It was like my whole body was singing.

And then all of a sudden it was gone and Nonna was handing out sherbet lemons and brushing her skirt down.

'Group hug and home to some *Buffy*?' she asked.

CHAPTER TWENTY-FIVE

'Jessie! Wait up.'

Summer was weaving her way through the zombified faces of a Monday morning trying to catch up to me.

'Are you OK?' she asked, lowering her voice. 'I've been texting you all weekend, you didn't reply. I was worried, I nearly came round to check on you.'

'Oh yeah, sorry. Mad family weekend,' I said, imagining what would have happened if she'd come when the house was full of a thousand locusts or when none of us had hair or when all the saucepans were floating round the kitchen.

'So you're all right? I heard about what happened on Friday.'

'On Friday?' It took me a second to register that she was talking. The showdown with Coach – it felt like a lifetime ago. 'Oh, that thing with Coach? That was nothing, I'm totally fine.'

We'd been walking and talking, but as we reached the school gates, Summer paused, looking at me earnestly. 'Are you sure? Because it sounded ...' She searched my face for signs of an imminent breakdown or outpouring of tears. 'It sounded bad. But if you say it was nothing, it was nothing. I just wanted to catch up with you to see if you needed some moral walking-in support.'

'I'm all good,' I said. And I absolutely meant it.

***

In fact, I wasn't just good. I was positively *radiating* kickass. This morning I hadn't needed to repeat into a mirror that I was strong; I actually felt it. I was no rhino – I could have defeated a rhino with a sneeze. The incident with Coach felt hazy, like something I'd seen in a film, or something I'd seen happen to someone else from a distance. It was not quite tangible, but it had a certain aura, it was drenched in meaning – it was the thing that had got me to here, to *this* point, to strength. When I thought of Coach now, I thought of fun and possibilities and retribution. Revenge.

It just so happened that Monday was a prime day for it too – Media Studies with Marcus this morning, Maths with Callum later, and PE with Libby and Coach last of all.

I was so lost in thought, I nearly missed my first opportunity.

'Ignore her,' Summer was saying. 'The singular lemming-like brain cell she has renders her incapable of independent thought.'

I glanced around to see who Summer was talking about. It was Sadie, who was standing in a small huddle with a couple of boys, looking at something on her phone. I could hear my own voice coming from the speaker and realised that it must have been the video from Friday, of me freaking out in Coach's face.

'Proper pyscho,' Sadie said, making eye contact with me as she spoke.

Thanks Sadie, I thought, *for that guilt-free pass. My first take-down*.

I was prepared: a weekend's worth of practice, a new understanding of my powers and a Super Plus tampon – plus pads. I didn't concentrate, I channelled. I pictured my anger as a ball, and let out a deep breath.

'Ow! What the—!' A girl near Sadie yelped as a locker door slammed into her head. She looked around, confused, while everyone laughed at her.

Damn. Right action, wrong target.

Sadie was still laughing at the video on her phone. I desperately wanted to try hexing her again, but didn't want to risk hurting any other innocent bystanders.

'Are you *sure* you're OK?' Summer said. I'd totally forgotten she was still with me. 'You just seem a bit . . . I don't know. Different somehow.'

'I'm absolutely fine, I promise,' I said, watching as Sadie began walking off down the corridor away from us.

The bell had gone and more and more people were making their way to registration, pushing past us. I had missed the opportunity.

'OK, if you're sure,' said Summer. 'See you at lunch?'

'Yep, see you at lunch.'

***

'Your first filming days are this week,' Ms Simmons said in Media. 'You will not be allowed to film unless you have everything on the checklist done and everything's been signed off by me. Is that understood?'

The class let out a collective murmur that was supposed to signify understanding.

'I'll take that as a "Yes, Ms Simmons". So, by the end of this session I need the checklist completed, including the running orders for your filming days, and a storyboard, please. Be thorough, work together, and remember, this is your chance to have your voices heard – make it count. Off you go.'

'Are you all right?' Tabitha whispered, as we settled in our groups.

'Me? Yeah, fine,' I said. 'Not particularly looking forward to this, but you know . . .'

'I heard about Friday. It sounded terrible.' She spoke even more quietly. 'You should make an official complaint to Mr Harlston.'

'Like that would do any good. Honestly, I'm fine,' I said, sensing the rest of our group was trying to listen in.

'Jessie, why don't you take the interview with Coach?' Marcus boomed, sitting up and puffing out his chest like a chairman of the board. 'Maybe you could scream the questions in his face in that really subtle, madwoman-on-a-period interviewing technique you have nailed.'

I smiled. A neutral, nothing-to-see-here smile, a biding-my-time smile, a please-witch-ancestors-make-me-able-to-control-my-powers-and-inflict-some-retribution smile.

'Cut it out, Marcus, we've got a lot to do,' Tabitha said, more meekly than I imagined she meant it. It was sweet of her to even try; I knew she hated anything that drew attention to her.

'Sorry, miss, you're right, miss,' said Marcus. 'Why don't you girls get on with filling in the permissions and we'll work on the content.'

Tabitha blushed and we shared an eye-roll.

'I'll get the sheets,' I said, going over to the front desk where all the photocopies were.

Freddie was there. He gave me an awkward smile.

'Hey,' he said, shifting from one foot to the other. 'You OK?'

185

'Why wouldn't I be?' I asked, flat-toned. *Would everyone stop asking me that?*

'No reason,' he said, speeding up his sheet selection.

He paused, his sheets in his hands, hovering. 'Good luck,' he said finally, nodding towards my group, before turning and scurrying back to his table.

'Jessie, could I have a quick word with you please?' Ms Simmons said. 'Outside, maybe?'

'Sure.' I followed her out. Was I in trouble for how I had spoken to Coach? We stepped into the corridor and she pulled the door to the classroom closed. I could hear noise break out as soon as the door shut.

'I meant to catch you in registration, but didn't get the chance. I just wanted to check everything's OK with you. I heard about the incident with Mr Bowd on Friday.'

I looked at her face, trying to work her out. I liked how she had two piercings on each earlobe, like a low-key teacher rebellion. She was wearing hoops with small silver moons dangling from them today, next to little star studs. I bet she had a tattoo somewhere too. She didn't look cross, or like she was about to give me detention.

For a split second I thought about telling her all about Callum and his cronies and the relentless bullying I'd had from all directions. But then I realised that wouldn't make it go away, or make me feel any better. I was going to do things my own way.

'Yeah, I'm fine,' I said firmly.

'I'm really sorry that happened to you,' Ms Simmons said. 'It's never easy adjusting to a new school at the best of times but

I feel like you're having an especially hard time here at the moment.'

'It's not been a walk in the park, but honestly I'm fine,' I said, calling on my rhino strength. Her face, all warm and sympathetic, was making tears prick at the back of my eyeballs. I needed to remind myself I was not a victim, not any more. I had powers.

Ms Simmons went on. 'I wasn't there on Friday, Jessie, and I don't know exactly what happened. But my sense is that it was not handled appropriately, and I would like to speak to Mr Harlston about it.'

I hesitated. I did like the idea of having someone in my corner, someone fighting for me. But it would only lead to more trouble in the end. Mr Harlston was a wet fish who wouldn't lift a finger against Coach or those boys – how could he? They brought the school more glory (and probably more funding) than anyone else. As opposed to me, Little Miss Trouble-maker. It was never going to come to anything. I did love Ms Simmons for trying though.

'Thanks for the offer, but I think I'll be fine,' I said. And I would be, just as soon as I got my witch on.

'All right,' she said reluctantly. 'Well I'm here if you change your mind, or if anything else happens – please do come and see me. I mean that, Jessie.'

We walked back into the classroom, the chaos subsiding instantly.

'Good feminist society meeting?' Marcus asked. 'What was on the agenda today – how to manage your PMS so you don't scream at teachers?'

'Shut up, Marcus,' Tabitha said.

'Maybe they were planning a bra-burning,' Harry suggested with a cackle.

'I'd be up for that,' Marcus said.

They all thought that was hysterically funny and started belly laughing like they'd never heard anything so witty. I couldn't bear to look at them – all smug and full of themselves. I felt sick. And then . . . I felt pain. Of the useful kind.

What should I try? I wanted them to suffer, to look foolish and be embarrassed . . . a rash, I'd give them a rash – I'd done that before, it must be a basic hex.

Come on, Jessie, you can do this.

I tuned out the sound of their laughter and closed my eyes.

Deep breath, channel, feel the pain, release. But their laughter kept getting in the way. *Fine*, I thought, irritated. *Laugh, if you think it's so funny.*

'Enough now,' Ms Simmons said. 'Get on with your work, please.'

But the boys didn't stop.

They carried on laughing. I opened my eyes, searching their faces for redness, spots, any signs of a rash. Nothing.

They still carried on laughing.

Ms Simmons walked over, looking angry. 'I said, *that's enough. This is not a comedy club.*'

Their eyes were looking at her saying, 'We know we need to stop' but their continuing laughter was effectively saying, 'Sod you'.

The rest of the class watched in a stunned silence.

How could they defy her so blatantly?

And then it clicked. This was *me*. My powers. OK it hadn't

been exactly what I'd been aiming for, but for a group of boys who used laughter to make everyone else feel bad . . . it was pretty fitting. Maybe the universe knew what it was doing after all.

Tears were coming with the laughter now.

'Enough is enough!' snapped Ms Simmons. 'Get out of my class – straight to Mr Harlston, now.'

They stood up instantly, furiously red, desperate to escape, not understanding what was going on and still hysterically, uncontrollably laughing. Ms Simmons stomped over to her computer to register the incident, looking dumbfounded by the whole thing.

I sat quietly, gently cradling my abdomen, trying not to laugh myself.

***

Oh what joy I felt all day! My heart was singing and I really did feel like a Disney character. But not one of the feeble princesses who waits for someone to rescue her. I was a powerful, capable (nearly) witch and nothing could touch me. My only disappointment – and it was a big one – was that Callum was off sick today. Part of me wondered if I'd accidentally done something to him, but I figured I hadn't even seen him, so surely that wasn't possible. And anyway, he could wait. I had three days left of my period and there was a big match coming up on Wednesday. He'd be back for that.

At lunch I magicked my coffee hot and my pizza tasty, made the end-of-break bell ring ten minutes later than usual and cleared up a big spot on Tabitha's forehead for her. I forced Jay Grove to stand up in the canteen and tell everyone he'd been lying about going all the way with Harriet Bircher and I made

Dave Pearce's moobs lactate (as he seemed so obsessed with discussing every Year Ten girls' boobs in such detail). I had a few mis-shoots – like making Holly Wells bark instead of speaking up for herself and exploding poor innocent Eli May's juice box instead of Oscar Dent's (they were sitting next to each other, it was an easy mistake to make) – but they were minor and inconsequential. What teachers would call 'stepping stones to success.'

I was flying high and no one could stop me.

Down with boys, down with lies, down with girls being made to feel rubbish – I was single-handedly going to sort out this school. No one could stop me.

Until PE.

'Ms Jones,' Coach said, evil glint in his eye. 'I hope you're feeling calmer today.'

I couldn't look at him. Even though my powers were more under control now, my feelings towards Coach were still so off the charts that I was worried I might accidentally blow him up. I ignored him and carried on pretending to warm up.

'Paired pass practice this afternoon, ladies.' Ugh. I hated the way he called us 'ladies' in that patronising, smarmy, jackass kind of way. 'Jessie and Libby, you can be our first pair. Come up here and demonstrate for us, please.'

Was he kidding? Me – demonstrate? And with Libby? Did he know she hated me? Or did he just wanted to humiliate me by pairing me with the best player in the class? Or both? Probably both. There was a wave of stifled laughter and murmuring as Libby and I took our places in front of the rest of the class. She glared at me, looking as unhappy as I was.

'One ball each,' Coach said, throwing us both a ball. (Mine narrowly missed my head.) 'You're going to continuously pass to each other, always keeping one ball high, one ball straight. The key is to focus on both balls and to keep your hands moving.' He took a step back, barely supressing a grin at the anticipation of me falling flat on my face. 'Off you go then.'

Every muscle in my body wanted to throw the ball right in Coach's smug face, but I knew I couldn't. Libby and I started passing. I was managing to catch and release and wasn't making a complete fool out of myself. Progress. Not having to concentrate so hard on passing meant I could focus on my scheming. What could I do to Coach? I'd been waiting to see him, waiting for the right moment – but to do what? What would be a suitable revenge? I could magically stick his whistle somewhere it definitely shouldn't be …

And then, interrupting my thoughts, a ball – coming hard and fast towards my head. Before I knew what was happening, the ball had boomeranged away from me and hit Libby square in the face. I heard gasps. Then Libby was in front of me, shoving me hard in the chest.

'You bitch!' Libby screamed.

I pushed her back, just to protect myself, but she went flying, way further than I would have achieved with any normal push. My body was humming and buzzing. My period pains were coming on strong, but not like the sharp sudden pains I'd been getting before; this was a more constant throbbing. I felt out of control. *Oh crap, was this me doing some kind of a Hulk? Was I about to transform into a mega-strong Super-witch?*

Libby sprang back to her feet and was on me before I could

think, grabbing my hair, kicking my shins. I wanted to defend myself, but I was worried my Super-witch powers might destroy her. Where the holy hell was Coach?

'Break it up, break it up,' he said, sauntering over, looking amused. 'Let's all calm down and stop the hair-pulling shall we, ladies?'

Libby stepped away, breathing heavily and looking stunned. I attempted to smooth my hair down and put myself back together. Everything hurt – my head was stinging, my shins were peppered with little darts of pain and my period pains had me nearly doubled over. I was numb with the cold too, which I hadn't noticed before now. One of the many joys of outdoor PE – standing around in the freezing cold wearing not much more than essentially a pair of big knickers. The sky was a dark grey, threatening and loaded. I had a sudden urge to go home and curl up under my duvet.

'You, young lady, have earned yourself a detention after school today,' Coach said to me, trying and failing to hide a smile.

'*She* attacked *me*!' I said, incredulous.

'After you threw a ball in my face!' Libby said.

'That was an accident,' I said.

'Yeah, right!'

'Fine, detention for both of you,' Coach said, like the whole thing wasn't worth his time. Then he added, 'Sorry, Libby, but I can't be seen to be unfair.'

Whaaaaaaaaat?

That was it. I felt drained, and nowhere near as powerful and indestructible as I had when this stupid lesson had started, but I was sure I still had enough left in me to do something.

Deep breath, channel, release.

A moment later, the rain started. No warning, no slow start, just heavy, hard rain pouring from the sky. It was not quite what I had in mind, I thought, as I watched Coach stroll back in, dry under an umbrella he'd pulled from his kit bag. As the rest of the class scurried inside, I stood, letting the rain drench me, looking forward to the day I had honed my powers enough to make Coach bleed spiders through his eyes.

CHAPTER TWENTY-SIX

'It says here to give you an activity that develops communication skills and teamwork,' Mr Deacon said in detention, his bug-eyes peering over his glasses to read from the computer screen. 'I would have had you collecting litter but, sadly, the weather being such as it is, that's no longer an option. So, toilet graffiti it is.'

'But, sir,' Libby said, protesting, 'we usually just sit and do work.'

'You've obviously never had detention with me before, then,' Mr Deacon said. 'Go and find Mr Blake in his office and he'll give you the materials required.'

Libby opened her mouth to say something, but he'd already moved on, doling out a task to the poor sod standing behind us. I wondered if I could magic my way out of it somehow, get him to change his mind, but I felt thoroughly depleted, like an empty crisp wrapper blowing in the wind. I just wanted to do whatever would get me home and under that duvet fastest – if it was going along with this Victorian school punishment, then so be it.

***

'This is all your fault, you know,' Libby said, once we'd collected the cleaning products from the grumpy caretaker, Mr Blake, and were walking down the corridor to the bathroom.

I said nothing. The truth was too wild to explain.

The stink as we opened the door was rank.

'This is so gross!' Libby said, putting a pair of the gloves on like they were radioactive. 'You take that stall, I'll do this one.'

I nodded, held my breath and faced my fate. To be fair, this stall seemed fairly low key – there were a few declarations of love (*JT 4 WG, L&T4EVA*), a few insults (*Ellen is a liar, Carrie is a bitch*), a few teacher burns (*www.GoFundMe/get-Mr-Anstead-some-deodorant* – that one made me chuckle) and a few drawings of willies, but it wasn't like the door was covered. It felt achievable. I sprayed the solution we'd been given generously. The chemical smell rose up my nose, catching at the back of my throat. I was sure it was totally illegal making us do this. I could sue. I made a mental note to keep an eye on any future health issues that might arise, especially with my lungs, and started scrubbing. I heard Libby's phone ping and the tapping as she replied. And another ping – she let out a frustrated sigh before replying this time. The pinging and the sighing and the replying barely stopped the whole time I scrubbed at my door. I could sense the increased frustration through her muttering and frantic tapping. I thought about saying something – either telling her to focus on the job in hand or asking her if everything was OK – but I decided silence was my best course of action.

I was taking stock of my progress and toying with the idea of leaving the Mr Anstead one for posterity, when Libby suddenly spoke.

'Were you telling the truth about Callum kissing you?' she asked, her voice small through the cubicle partition.

'Yes.'

I heard her downing her tools.

'I knew it.'

She knew it? Seriously?

'I thought you didn't believe me?' I asked, trying to level the anger in my voice.

'I didn't *want* to believe you. Who wants to admit that yes, their boyfriend is such a high-level arsehole that he'd leave his girlfriend behind to go chasing after a girl he barely knows to try to get it on with her – against her wishes, as it turns out.'

I was silent. I didn't know how to respond to that. I knew I should feel sympathy, on some level, and yet I mainly felt anger.

'I'm sorry,' she said. 'Though, to be fair, it was mainly Sadie that was actually mean to you.'

'You encouraged her. And you threw a ball in my face – twice if you count today.'

'Well, you got me back for that.'

'Hardly. Why are you asking me about this now, anyway?' I asked.

I heard her sigh and stand up, then open the door to her cubicle. I did the same, my knees stiff from squatting for so long. The air outside the cubicle felt relatively fresh compared to the stench of the inside.

'I'm having a spin-out,' she said. 'Callum's been up in London, staying with family friends. He'd gone all quiet on me and he was being weird, and then Sadie showed me a post this girl had put up on Snapchat of her and Callum in a bed. She's kissing his cheek. When I messaged him about it, he said she was a family friend and they've known each other forever and they just fell asleep in the same bed, talking. And then he said I'm a psycho girlfriend and too controlling and he doesn't know if he can be with someone who has outbursts like this for no reason. And now I just don't know what to think. Am I being unreasonable?'

She looked so confused and helpless, like a kicked puppy. Not at all like the confident, self-assured Libby I was used to. And all because of that stupid douchebag. I wanted to rant and rave and tell her he was a good-for-nothing idiot boy who didn't deserve her and that one day he would be a boring middle-aged man, reminiscing about his glory days back in high school playing football because he would have nothing else going for him and would have driven everyone away.

But I'd been here before. I'd had heart-to-hearts with girls and warned them off horrible boys and it seriously backfires if they get back together because then you're the bad guy for being so mean (honest).

'Sound like he's gaslighting you,' I said cautiously.

'What do you mean?'

'He's making you doubt yourself. You know he's done something wrong – but rather than admitting it and apologising, he's turning it round and making you feel like *you're* in the wrong – calling you crazy, threatening to break up with you . . .'

Libby considered it, scrolling through her phone with one hand, biting the nails on her other. Her lip was beginning to wobble. I wasn't prepared to deal with Libby crying.

'What's your gut telling you?' I asked.

'That's he's a bad boyfriend,' she said, her voice cracking.

I paused, letting her soak in her choice of words, pleased that she was the one to reach that conclusion for herself.

'You can do so much better than a bad boyfriend,' I said, gently.

'I really can, actually.' Libby had a different look in her eyes now. Glinting, defiant. No wobbly lip. This was good.

She typed a message, fast and assured. I heard the whoosh of it being sent then she showed me her phone, beaming.

> Whether anything happened or not, I've been thinking, and I don't want to be with you any more. I deserve better. We're over. Have fun in London.
>
> PS I know it was you who came on to Jessie, not the other way round.

Had I just helped Libby come to her senses over a bad boyfriend? Encouraged an epiphany about knowing your worth and not putting up with less? Had we just had . . . a bonding moment?

I was proud of her, though also a bit terrified she had mentioned me. Would it read to Callum like it was *my* idea she did this?

'God, I better go,' she said, checking her phone again. 'My folks are picking me up and my Dad is not impressed – my detention has apparently messed up some kind of sacred pre-match honorary dinner for my brother. He'll be even less impressed if I keep him waiting.'

'You have a brother?'

'Yep, he's in Year Eight – the Golden Child. He's not at this school though, oh no no – he goes to Falcon Manor, the private school over by Cowes. Because of course he deserves the best, just by virtue of the fact he has a penis.'

'Wow. That's . . . harsh.'

'Yep. Anyway, I don't want to make my dad angrier by having him wait for me. I've got to dash. Are you all right to drop these back?' she said, handing me a bundle of the cleaning stuff.

'Sure, but have we done enough time?'

'We're only ten minutes short of the full hour, and I've scrubbed off at least three dicks and four teacher insults so I reckon we're good. Thanks!' she said, halfway out the door. Then she stopped, looking back.

'And thanks for the advice,' she said. 'Genuinely.'

***

I was dutiful – it's a trait I can't help – and stayed the extra ten minutes, half-heartedly making a start on the third stall, before returning the cleaning products to Mr Blake and checking out with Mr Deacon.

I braced myself for the wet walk home. Rain hadn't been on the forecast today, so of course I had nothing helpful like an umbrella or a coat, just my old hoodie. The rain had picked up, so heavy now it was ricocheting off the tarmac ground, and pond-like puddles had amassed all over the car park.

I stood under the covered entrance, aching all over, bone-deep tired, waiting for a lull that looked like it would never come. A sleek, fancy car pulled up and I watched as Libby, who must have been waiting under a walkway, went to put her stuff in the boot.

The man in the driver's seat stomped out of the car and started going off at Libby, who now seemed like a shrunken, meek version of herself, struggling with the boot, in the rain, while he stood under his umbrella shouting at her. I couldn't hear most of what he said over the wind, just the odd words and phrases: *'stupid girl'*, *'what do you expect'*, *'ruined our day'*. A boy sat in the front, staring intently out of the windscreen, and a woman, I guessed Libby's mum, sat in the back, eyes to the floor. Libby didn't seem sad or mad, just resigned.

But *I* was sad. *I* was mad. It wasn't OK. Maybe it was because I felt it was partially my fault she was having to endure this crap or maybe it was because of the venom in her dad's voice, but I felt compelled to do something. I needed to bring out the witch, pronto, but I didn't know if I had anything left in me. I was still so drained.

Deep breath, channel, release.

I was focusing on the dad, trying to get him to shut up.

Nothing.

It wasn't going to work. All I could feel was a hardness, a black wall.

I tried again.

Deep breath, channel, release.

My stomach cramped and I doubled over in pain. Surely *that* meant I'd done something. But when I looked nothing was happening. Libby was closing the boot, her dad was still shouting at her. I'd failed.

And then, out of the blue, it happened. Libby's dad was still gesticulating, still moving his mouth, but it was as if someone had put him on mute. Nothing was coming out.

He looked confused, started frantically grabbing at his throat. He was getting redder and more hysterical. Everyone else looked on, confused and there was definitely a flash of relief in Libby's face. I hadn't fixed everything – Libby's dad was still horrible and her mum was still in the back seat, but at least, for now, he was quiet. Maybe that would have to be enough. I just hoped he wouldn't find a way to blame Libby for it.

After a few more minutes of silent shouting, he gave up even trying to speak, got back into the car and screeched out of the car park. And, as they drove off, I was pretty sure I saw Libby smile.

CHAPTER TWENTY – SEVEN

After that day in the apocalyptic rain, I was ill for two days.

Proper ill this time – horrendous period pains, full-on chills and fevered dreams of me turning Libby's dad into a frog and Coach's hair all falling out. It took me a minute when I first woke up on the third morning to reality-check that I hadn't actually done those things – I was pretty sure I hadn't. Had I dreamt the bonding moment with Libby too? That felt pretty real. If I thought about it hard enough I could still smell the toilets.

When I finally emerged from my room, blinking into the brightness with a light crust of two days of sweat on me, I wasn't even sure what day it was. That would teach me to remember an umbrella.

Hungry, I padded down the stairs, and was met with chaos. Random shouty men were walking about with varying levels of purpose, a wall in the hallway was in the middle of being knocked down, approximately a tonne of dust covered every possible surface and good old Handy Andy was in the middle of it all, directing everyone and looking important. I guess the building work had started then. Fabulous timing.

'Hi, Jessie,' Handy Andy beamed. 'How're you feeling? Your Mum said you've been under the weather.'

'Uh, better thanks,' I said.

'You take care,' he said. 'I've been trying to get them to keep the noise down a bit for you, but it's a losing battle, I'm afraid.'

'Thanks,' I muttered, keen to keep moving.

I was barefoot and wearing just a T-shirt (though thankfully one long enough to cover my knickers and vaguely pass for a nightie). I probably should have headed back upstairs, but my need for food overpowered everything else. I not-so-elegantly tiptoed my way as fast as possible through to the kitchen, the dusty floor feeling gross on the soles of my feet.

The kitchen was a mess too, full of discarded tea mugs and dirty plates with remains of bacon sandwiches teetering in stacks on the table, making me think, again, that Mum really should try magicking the housework. At least there was no work going on in here yet and therefore no workmen to dodge. I checked there was bread left and retrieved the bacon from the fridge, my mouth watering.

The incessant pounding and shouting paused briefly, and I heard Mum's voice coming from somewhere – low and urgent. Despite my hunger, it was the kind of tone that you know you need to eavesdrop in on. I dropped the bread on the counter and followed it.

She was in Nonna's annexe, and the door was ajar.

'We need to speak to her. She could do herself – and others – serious damage if she carries on like this,' Mum was saying. 'I mean, she's already depleted. Not to mention the effect it's had on you.'

'I'll be fine. She needs to work it out for herself,' Nonna replied. 'Like you did.'

'The circumstances were different.'

'Hardly. She needs to learn for herself. It won't mean anything if we push it on her.'

'And what about in the meantime? What if—'

At that moment the pounding kicked off again, catching me so off guard that I let out a little noise – part gasp, part surprised cry.

'Jessie? Is that you?' Mum said, hurrying out of the annexe.

I couldn't help but look guilty.

'I was just . . . food,' I mumbled, lifting up the bacon packet in my hand as evidence.

Nonna came over and started fussing over me, feeling my forehead, then putting her hands on my temples and closing her eyes.

'How are you feeling?' she asked. She looked pretty terrible herself, dark circles under her eyes, skin pale.

'Uh, yeah, much better, I think,' I said.

'Hmmm,' Nonna frowned. 'Not a hundred per cent yet. But we can work on that. Here, come in the annexe, it's the most dust-free place. Your mum will make you a sandwich and I'll run you a special bath.'

'A special bath?'

'You'll see, now scoot. There's a blanket on my sofa, go and snuggle under that.'

**

Nonna's baths are the World's Best. Fact. She has a knack or maybe she actually uses magic, who knows. Whatever it is, she gets it just right – the water hot enough for it to feel like a warm hug, but not so hot you start sweating and have to get out after two minutes. She puts the right smells in it in the right quantity, so you breathe in the gorgeousness and feel relaxed and enveloped, but not like you're sitting in a liquid potpourri.

This particular bath, after my two bedridden days spent writhing in my own sweat, was a definite twelve out of ten. It felt so good I almost had a little weep after I eased myself in.

'Nice bath?' Nonna said, hobbling into the bathroom. 'Rosemary and clary sage.'

I scrambled to cover up all the bits that needed covering up. 'Nonna! I'm having a bath here.'

'Don't be such a prude, child, I've seen it all before – many times! You'll need to loosen up before you go to any meets. We're all as nature intended there.'

'Well, for a start, I won't be going to anything that requires me to be naked. And secondly, could you maybe give me *some* privacy . . .'

'I'll look the other way,' she said, sitting herself down on the toilet seat. 'I just wanted to check in with you, love. How are you doing?'

'Much better,' I said. 'My period pains are still bad, but my temperature definitely feels like it's gone.' *Though not fully loving this bathroom set-up*, I wanted to add.

'And how are you doing with the *other stuff*, petal – since the weekend? Are you feeling like a beautiful witch butterfly yet or are you struggling to break out of that chrysalis? Any fat caterpillar left in you?'

How was I feeling about the *other stuff*? The truth was, I hadn't really thought about it the last few days – too busy sweating myself inside-out. That Monday at school when I'd tested my powers out, I'd felt . . . not necessarily 'beautiful witch butterfly', but pretty badass, even though I hadn't been completely successful. I'd definitely felt powerful, and in control – just about.

I thought back to the look on Marcus's face when he couldn't stop laughing. That had felt amazing. But then Coach's smug face flashed before me, him sauntering back into the changing rooms unscathed, because I hadn't managed to unleash any decent retribution. I definitely still needed to hone my powers – I was nowhere near done with Coach or Callum.

'I feel pretty good,' I decided. 'It's nice to know I'm not going to injure anyone.' *By accident*, my mind added. *On purpose* would be great.

'You know, it's a very delicate balance,' Nonna said.

'What is?'

'Nature, Earth, Witchcraft. We work as one and we can only thrive if we are respectful. If we bow to nature.'

Was Nonna having a senior moment? 'Uh, yeah. You said that at the weekend already.'

'I know, just repeating it. It's important.'

I held my nose and slipped my head under the water, letting the warmth fully envelop me. I thought I might just stay in this bath for ever, topping up with fresh hot water and fresh oils every few hours, getting Nonna to bring me food and drink. It seemed like a perfect plan.

When I came back up for air, Nonna was lighting a red candle and murmuring something under her breath. Was she chanting? I assumed – hoped – it was some kind of get-well-soon incantation.

My gaze caught a photo of her and Gramps on the wall. They were standing in front of their cottage on the beach, both laughing – full-on belly laughs by the looks of it – right into each other's faces like they were in a bubble, like they thought the other person was the funniest they'd ever met. They looked so happy, so together.

'Did Gramps know you were a witch?' I asked, once Nonna had sat back down.

'Of course he did,' Nonna said. 'He was very supportive. A big fan of our craft. Respectful, too. He had to be really, we helped him out enough.' She chuckled to herself.

'What do you mean?'

'Put it this way, it wasn't just natural talent that led to him being the best fisherman around.'

'Is that allowed?'

'It's give and take, Jessie. You can take, as long as you give back. That's the fine line of nature.'

'And how exactly do you give back?'

'Lots of ways – planting trees, cleaning the ocean, healing a plant or animal – it's all about nurturing and balance and respect.'

I studied the photo again, wishing I'd had more time with Gramps, that he was here now. Maybe he'd have some words of wisdom. I loved the fact that he'd known – though of course he had, I couldn't imagine those two ever having any secrets and lies between them.

'Did Dad know, about Mum – and me and Bella? I mean, *does* he know?'

'It's not my place to say. Have you washed your hair?'

It was always the same when the subject of Dad came up with Mum though – an impenetrable wall, questions blocked, subject changed. But Mum was different now – she was Mum 2.0, motto: family first. It might be worth asking her again.

'Yes, I've washed my hair,' I said, knowing there was no point pushing Nonna on it.

'Come on, you'll be getting as wrinkly as me in there now,' Nonna said, pulling herself up slowly from the toilet seat. I had a flash of realising she was starting to get old. 'Get yourself out and I'll make you a special tea.'

'Will it be one of your special teas that taste of mud and ditch water?'

'Yes, but it will do you the world of good – and if you're lucky I'll add some cinnamon for you, you big wimp.'

***

'It's alive,' Bella said, coming through to the kitchen and hanging her bag up neatly (as always), her arms piled high with parcels for her (as always).

'Nice to see you too, sis,' I said.

I was huddled on the armchair in the corner – the only dustless seat in the house – slowly starting to feel human again. Whatever magic mud Nonna had put in her tea, it had worked.

'It's looking good out there, Mum,' Bella said, as she worked her way through her stash, taking out various glamorously packaged freebies and inspecting them. I was used to it by now – the constant gifts, the shiny new products, the invites to exciting launch parties. I couldn't care less about a new 'dewy glow' highlighter or 'perfect peach pout' lip gloss, but there was still a teeny-tiny part of me that always felt a flutter of something like jealousy when they arrived. Jealousy at what, I wasn't quite sure – the freebies, the attention, the fact people think she's special enough to send things to?

'Don't lie,' Mum said. 'But it's fine, it's allowed to look like a building site for now, because it is a building site. That's what I keep telling myself anyway.'

'I've had lots of comments on this today,' Bella said, pointing to the headband she was wearing, which I hadn't even noticed. It had the same floral print as the dungarees Mum had made, so I guessed it was another one of her creations. 'Think you're on to a winner. We should set you up with an online shop, people love this kind of thing at the moment – turbans, headbands. Even scrunchies are making a comeback.'

Mum grinned, a coy but chuffed grin. 'Oh, I don't know about that, but it's nice that you got some positive comments.'

'Honestly, you should think about it.'

Mum was over by the stove, stirring some concoction. We hadn't had the dahl again, which was a blessing, but my hopes weren't high. Bella went over to her and gave a kiss on the cheek. 'Everything OK?' she asked her, quietly.

'All fine,' Mum said, in a forced cheerful tone that we could both totally see through.

Bella gave me a look. It was fleeting and subtle, but definitely *a look*. I wasn't sure what I was supposed to have done. Last I'd checked, we'd had a good sister-bonding weekend and our stock was on the rise – I was even managing to not cringe at all her sucking up. And I'd been ill! So unless, in my fevered state, I'd sleepwalked into her room and messed up all her precious make-up, I had no idea what her beef was.

'How was school?' I asked.

'Fine,' she said, flatly. Normally, given the smallest chance, she'd run through a blow-by-blow account of the latest contouring and highlighting techniques she'd tried out on her friends that day. Something was definitely up.

'Do you need a hand with anything, Mum?' Bella asked.

'Actually, if you could just stir this for me, I could do with popping up to get changed.'

'Sure,' Bella said, taking the spoon.

'OK, what have I done?' I asked, as soon as Mum was out of the room and safely out of earshot.

'Besides nearly causing a natural disaster, you mean?' she hissed.

'What are you on about? What natural disaster?'

'Classic Jessie! You haven't even noticed.'

I stood up from the chair, ignoring the light-headedness, and edged closer to the stove, trying desperately to get my fuzzy brain working. Natural disaster? Had I missed something?

'Just tell me, Bella. If I did anything, I didn't mean to, so maybe dial down the meanness?'

She turned around to face me, still holding the spoon. Her eyes were dark and serious, not an ounce of sisterly jesting in them. 'You didn't mean to? So you didn't *mean* to make a guy confess to lying in the canteen, made some boy's boobs produce milk? Ring any bells?'

My brain caught up and my face must have shown my horrified realisation.

'Exactly,' she went on. 'And there we go, typical self-centred

Jessie, not thinking about Mum, or Nonna, or me or – God forbid – greater consequences. Just yourself.'

'But . . . it was hardly anything,' I said, doing a mental tally of what it actually had been: the lying and the milking that she'd already mentioned, the random girl and the locker, Marcus and Tom and Harry and the laughing, making my food nicer, Tabitha's skin . . . oh, and Libby's dad . . .

'They specifically told us magic is *not for fun*. It's for doing good and healing and working with nature.'

'I didn't do it for fun,' I said. 'I did it out of self-defence.'

'It's serious, Jessie,' she said, waving the spoon at me now. 'You messed with nature! We had a two-day storm because of you. Nonna and Mum had to try and undo some of what you did and Nonna's too old for that crap, she was in bed all day yesterday, she's exhausted.'

'But . . . But I . . .'

I didn't know what to say. I felt terrible about Nonna. I hadn't realised. I mean, yeah, I'd noticed the rain, but I didn't think that had been anything to do with me. And I didn't know that Nonna had needed to fix it somehow.

It couldn't have been as bad as Bella was making out. Storms happened all the time without magical interference – it was probably some random weather pattern coming in from Bermuda, nothing at all to do with me. She was using this as an opportunity to play reprimanding grown-up again.

'And what have you been using your magic for, Ms Perfect Witch of the Year?' I said. 'Because I don't think magicking flawlessly applied foundation or the perfect French plait is allowed either, just FYI.'

She opened her mouth to answer, then shut it and just stared at me with stone-cold hatred – with an edge of pity. I didn't enjoy it. Luckily, just then Mum came back and I took the opportunity to fight my way through the dust and retreat to my room for cuddles with Dave. Dave didn't judge me.

CHAPTER TWENTY-EIGHT

Nonna made me stay off the rest of the week, saying I needed to rest and feeding me up with all kinds of gross teas and tinctures – which I gladly took over going back to school.

Summer came to call for me after school on Friday. I couldn't remember the last time someone had come to call for me – probably not since primary school. I was caught off guard, and given half the chance I would've firmly avoided anyone coming to the house, but it was nice to see her.

'Mate, you're alive!' she said, stepping cautiously into the remnants of the hallway.

'Just about.'

'I wanted to take you surfing but I figured if you've been ill again it's probably not the best time. Though my nan always says sea water is the best cure for everything. Apparently when my mum was young, every time she got ill, Nan would make her go for a swim, whatever time of year it was. She made her go with tonsillitis once.'

'Sounds like *my* Nan,' I said. 'Batshit hardcore.'

Summer laughed. 'It's an Island thing.'

'I'm probably not up for surfing – yet – but I am pretty desperate to leave the house. Fancy a walk? Sea air, instead of sea water?'

***

213

'Maaaaan, it feels good to be out of the house,' I said a few minutes later, striding ahead of Summer down the road.

'All right, slow down though. Don't make me run.'

'Sorry, I'm a bit over-excited.'

'What's been wrong? At this point you've probably been off school more than you've been in.'

'God, I know,' I said, realising she was right. 'I had a mega temperature – I think from getting drenched in the rain the other day. But I'm feeling better now.'

'Good, we've missed you.' She gave me a friendly elbow nudge. 'So the building works have started?'

'Yeah. It's full on – noise and dust and builders and builders' bums and man alive, those builders like to have their constitutionals in our toilet. It's gross.'

'Ugh!'

'Yep. And I think my Mum fancies the builder, who is actually called *Handy Andy*, and is a boring middle-aged man-baby. It's making me feel nauseous watching her be all flirty and grim. And Mum and Bella are having an exclusive mutual love-in, which is also making me feel vom. Hence the excitement at escaping. I've been going out of my mind.'

I took a breath. It felt good to have a rant. We'd walked up to the headland and were out on the open grass now, up high. I was feeling better already, calmer. I slowed down for Summer to catch up and we fell into stride. She had her hair down for once, the wind whipping her long blonde waves into her face.

'Anything wildly interesting happen at school? I know I missed my filming days, though I'm not sure how 'interesting' they would've been.'

'Yeah, I think Tabs was mega gutted about that – she's been enjoying having a comrade. Will you be OK? It won't affect your coursework?'

'I don't know, I hadn't thought that far ahead – I was just pleased I didn't have to spend the whole day listening to Marcus and the gang bore on about sport. I do feel bad for leaving Tabitha to fend for herself though.'

'Tabitha can hold her own,' Summer said, trying unsuccessfully to fend off her hair. 'Well, sort of. She does a good line in dirty looks.'

We walked on towards the monument at the top. I took deep, lung-filling breaths, relishing the tinge of saltiness.

'Have you seen Libby at all? Does she seem OK?' I asked.

I could sense a hesitation before Summer replied.

'Libby's fine. Libby will always be fine,' she said. 'You shouldn't be worrying about her.'

'She's not that bad, you know,' I said. 'Underneath, I think she's pretty decent. I think she made some bad choices and she doesn't have the best home life and it's made her seem harder than she actually is.'

'I've known her since we were five. Trust me, she's that bad.'

'You've known her that long? I didn't know that.'

'Island life,' said Summer morosely. 'We were all at primary school together – me, Libby, Tabs, Callum, Marcus. Libby and I were actually best friends for a while, not that you'd think it now.'

'No way!' I said, stopping and turning to face her.

'I know, right? But it was primary school – I guess our personalities and, you know, our moral compasses, hadn't kicked in yet.'

'So why aren't you friends now?'

'Lots of reasons.'

'Expand, please,' I said, walking again, but slowly.

'We were fine up to about Year Seven. But, I don't know, high school changed Libby. She started caring more about what other people thought of her, how she looked, her popularity rating. Libby never wanted to hang out with Tabs any more – Tabs had joined the Model UN and was into her writing and Libby deemed that too geeky, so she started being a real bitch to her.' Summer shrugged, but I could tell she wasn't telling me everything.

'And?'

'And what?'

'And what else happened? I don't believe it was just that.'

Summer sighed. 'There was something else, but it was just the nail in the coffin – we were drifting apart already.'

'Go on . . .'

'So, around the start of Year Eight, a thing kind of happened. Back then, I was trying to get my head round my sexuality. I'm pretty out about being bi now, but at that point I hadn't told anyone – mainly because I hadn't figured it out myself. Libby and I were hanging out in my room one day – because yes, we used to do that BFF stuff – and I confided in her that I thought I might be gay . . . Alice Portland had just joined and I was having all these . . . feelings. Libby was really understanding and helped me talk it through. Then she suggested that we kiss. She said it might help me make my mind up. I explained I wasn't sure it worked like that, like any girl would do, and politely – very politely – said thanks but no thanks.'

216

She sighed, twisting a strand of hair. 'The rest of the day seemed totally fine – we chatted and watched some TV and she helped me do dinner for the kids. Except when I got to school the next day she was being really weird.'

'Weird how?' I asked.

'She basically ignored me – unless other people were around, and then she acted all chummy. But she'd drop these mean digs into conversations – so if I was talking about boys, she'd say "like you'd know". Eventually she made enough leading comments that people starting asking the question – mostly behind my back.'

'So, she effectively outed you?' I asked.

'Not exactly, but, like I said, she got people talking. And it wasn't a nice feeling. Especially as I hadn't figured anything out for myself.'

'Why would she do that? Did you ever talk to her about it?'

'I tried to. I figured maybe she was embarrassed about offering to kiss me. I explained that I was really grateful for the offer, and I knew she'd done it to be a good friend. She just laughed at me and said she'd been joking. So yeah, I don't know – maybe she was worried I'd tell other people. She's not exactly one for breaking the mould. But anyway, that was kind of that. I certainly didn't want to be friends with her any more, and she's just become nastier and nastier since then – doing similar things to other people. She's a bully, simple as that.'

A hardness came onto Summer's face, but not before I'd seen the genuine hurt there.

'God, that's cruel,' I said. 'I totally understand why you don't like her now.'

'So you get why I can't get on board with the idea that underneath she seems pretty decent?'

'Yeah . . .' I said, pausing. 'It's just . . . I had an unexpected chat with her the other day in detention. She opened up a bit. For the first time I felt like I saw a different side to her – a decent side. Do you think there's a *chance* she might have changed?'

'Never. Some people are beyond redemption at this point, and I think she's one of them,' Summer said. She stopped suddenly, facing into the wind so her hair was swept off her face, like something from a Beyoncé video. Her eyes were bright and intent, her cheeks pink from the walk. 'I can't tell you who to be friends with, obviously, but just be careful. Please. And don't trust her.'

'OK,' I said, understanding her intensity a bit more now, but still wishing she could have seen what I'd seen in the bathroom that day. I knew Libby wasn't a saint, that much was obvious, but shouldn't we all be allowed space to grow and improve? But what did I know? Maybe I was just clutching at straws.

A dog ran over to us and starting darting between our legs excitedly.

'Kimye!' I crouched down to try and stroke her and got knocked off my feet. Summer turned round, saw Freddie running towards us and rolled her eyes.

'Arsehole alert,' she muttered.

'Hey,' I said, standing up and wiping off some of the mud.

'God, did she do it again? Sorry!'

'That's all right, it's not my favourite ball gown.'

'Hi.' He nodded to Summer. She nodded back, not making eye contact.

We all stood there awkwardly. Despite my residual dislike of Freddie via his association with Prime Arsehole (and my embarrassment over him being the one to alert me to my period being all over my trousers), he still had some kind of soft focus on him when I saw him – especially outside of school. I concentrated on Kimye, squatting down to stroke her, letting her lick my face excitedly.

'Are you guys coming to Harry's tonight?' Freddie asked finally, filling the silence.

'What's happening at Harry's?' I asked.

Summer shot me a glare.

'Ah, you've been off, I forgot. He's having a house party for his birthday. I think most of the year are going. You should totally come,' he said, the enthusiasm in his smile nearly enough to make me forget what a grim prospect a party with Callum and his cronies in attendance would be.

'I can't, I've got . . . family. A family thing. My sister . . .' I trailed off. I really needed to get better at spur-of-the-moment excuses. Lying – I needed to get better at lying.

'I'm busy too,' Summer said. 'We'd better get going.' She grabbed my hand and pulled me off like we had an urgent appointment.

'Bye,' I called out to a bemused-looking Freddie. 'Bit rude?' I said to Summer, once we were far enough away.

'*He's* rude. All the time.'

'He seemed all right then – and when I saw him up here the other day.'

'That's him being Jekyll. At school he's Hyde – and that's the one that hurts. You're not going to that party, are you?'

'Not a chance in hell,' I said.

'Good. Definitely don't. Promise me you won't,' she insisted, giving me a long, serious look.

'Copy. Roger. Yes, sir, Roger, sir,' I said, letting her march me down the hill.

CHAPTER TWENTY-NINE

I absolutely meant it when I told Summer I had no intention of going to Harry's party. Why would I? It would be full of people I didn't like (and who clearly didn't like me). I wanted nothing to do with it. I would have rather spent the night at home, watching one of Nonna's rubbish detective mysteries and putting up with Bella's side-eye than go to Harry's party. Which was in fact exactly what I was doing when I got a notification that Libby had added me on Snapchat. Very tentatively, I added her back. A second later a message came through.

Are you coming to Harry's tonight? Callum will be there and I could really do with some moral support.

It seemed like a message that called for a fairly straightforward answer:

But she wasn't having it.

> I need to go to prove to him I'm awesome. Please come. He's so mean. Mean, but handsome. I don't trust myself around him. Please.

There wasn't the tiniest atom of my body that wanted to go to that party. The thought of it made me feel like vomiting my insides out. But I felt like Libby breaking up with Callum was partly because of me. I couldn't desert her when she was trying so hard to be strong. I wanted to text Summer, to ask her to come along too, to ask her advice, but I knew she was down on Libby and wouldn't give her the benefit of the doubt, wouldn't see that it was a pretty big deal for Libby to be asking for help at all.

What was the worst that could happen?

I could handle a bit of name-calling and laughing at me if it would help Libby stand up to Callum and, judging by my newly insane period action, I probably had a bit of magic left if I needed it – in an emergency. Only in *proper* self-defence this time though. Of course.

> OK. What's his address? I'll meet you outside.

Five Things About House Parties:
1. They are a form of torture . . .
2. . . . unless you're popular or best friends with the person whose house it is.
3. The house will ALWAYS get trashed.
4. There will ALWAYS be sick clogging up a sink.

222

5. There is no easy way to enter a house party solo – safety, as always, is in numbers.

Harry's house looked nice. It was set back from the main road out of town, in a small cluster with two other houses. Not big, but not small. There was a discarded kid's scooter out the front and a basketball hoop that looked like it hadn't been used in a while attached to the garage.

I could hear the music and the general hubbub of a party from the bottom of the driveway. It felt wrong being here, but I told myself I wouldn't have to stay long. I'd do a quick in and out, be there by Libby's side when she first saw Callum, and just stay until she felt comfortable. I kept telling myself I was doing this for the greater good, for Girl Power, for girls all over the world in relationships with mean boys, for feminism itself. I was going to Harry Benn's party for feminism.

I texted Libby asking if she was here yet, but she didn't reply. I loitered outside, intently scrolling through my phone so that anyone else going in didn't think I was some saddo stalking a party. I tried texting again. Still no response.

Twenty minutes of pretending to be busy and purposeful later and I *still* hadn't heard back. I had decided to give it two more minutes and then leave, when Freddie arrived.

'Hey, Jessie,' he said. 'I thought you weren't coming?'

I would have preferred to see Libby and get this over with, but it was nice to see a familiar face I didn't outright hate. Standing there in his black jeans and checked shirt with a big smile on his face, he looked like the nice, friendly, Jekyll-Freddie from outside of school.

'I'm not. I mean, I wasn't, but I'm here for Libby. Except she hasn't turned up yet.'

'OK,' he said, looking confused. 'She might already be in there. You coming in?'

I glanced at my phone. Still no messages.

'Sure, but just to find her.'

'You could also, you know, have some fun?'

'I doubt that,' I said, more loudly than intended. Luckily, he laughed.

***

We squeezed our way through the bodies in the narrow hallway, walking towards the noise, my stomach fizzing with every step we took. *Feminism. I'm doing this for feminism*, I reminded myself.

As we walked into the kitchen, which was full of pink-faced people, the noises and comments started. A few 'oooh's and 'aaaah's and 'has she tried it on with you yet, Fred?' and one 'psycho bitch'. I made out some faces I recognised – Sadie, Marcus, Harry, a few others – all staring and taking me in, the evil grins on their faces worthy of Disney villains. I sensed Freddie stiffen with embarrassment. He'd obviously not factored in how much being seen with me would drop his stock.

'Shut up,' he mumbled to them, making a beeline away from me. 'She was outside.' Like I was some kind of turd he'd found on the floor.

I was mortified, but extremely thankful that the side lamps and fairy lights were dim enough to cover my deep blush. I felt sweat form on my upper lip. What was it Bella called it? SULA – Sweaty Upper Lip Alert. Yep, that was me. Serious

SULA going on. *Feminism. Focus on the feminism. You're here to fight the good fight.*

'Is Libby here?' I asked, trying to style out the fact Freddie had dropped me like a hot potato.

'Have a drink,' someone said, passing me a disposable cup with some kind of fruit punch in it.

'I'm fine, thanks.' Drinking was definitely not going to help with tonight.

'Don't get your tits in a twist, Boring Brenda,' Sadie said. 'It's non-alcoholic.'

'Is Libby here?' I asked again, scanning the room.

'Yeah, somewhere. With Callum, probably,' a random I hadn't met before said.

With Callum? That wasn't great. I half-heartedly muttered some thanks and pushed my way through to the garden. I could hear the laughter and gossip kick in before I'd even left the room. I was used to people talking about me behind my back by now but I'd underestimated how horrible it would be having it so in my face. Their expressions stayed with me when I blinked, like glaring headlights I couldn't shake off. Why was I putting myself in this situation? I wanted to be here for Libby, I wanted to help her stand up for herself, but I had my limits and I'd pretty much reached them. If I couldn't find her in the garden, I'd leave.

I had a sip of the drink I realised was still in my hand. Non-alcoholic my arse! It had a nice buzz to it though. Maybe it would actually help, chill me out a bit – no Boring Brenda here. I took another gulp as I surveyed the garden. It was long and narrow, with fairy lights strung all along the fence on one side and a trampoline covered by the shadows of big trees at the very bottom. There was a firepit to the right of me, with people huddled round it talking in low voices, occasional bursts of laughter. I thought how nice it must feel to be part of a group, to have that security, the ease of it.

I glanced at their faces, lit up in the glow of the fire, but none of them were Libby. Most of them I didn't even recognise. I took another sip of my drink. There were some other people, further down the garden, but I was nervous about going down there when I didn't know anyone. Not that standing here on my tod was doing me any favours. I took another sip, readying myself.

I headed down the garden, taking long, slow, reluctant steps. I saw someone on the trampoline but as I got closer I realised it wasn't one body, it was two – intertwined and definitely *not* to be disturbed. I did a quick turnabout and headed in the other direction, towards another group of people. I recognised the tall silhouette among them as Freddie's and felt a ball of anger form in my gut. He was talking animatedly to a couple of guys I didn't recognise. Probably debating the intricacies of the angle of some footballer's goal at the weekend or moaning about a referee's bad decision.

'People need to give the guy a break, he's got mental health problems. Plus, he's a genius,' Freddie said.

'Nah man, he's lost his talent by being sucked into that parasite family,' someone replied.

'You're as bad as the rest of them.' Freddie said. 'Geniuses are always misunderstood.'

'Hang on, are you calling the Kardashians geniuses now?'

Freddie laughed. 'Yeah, let's go with that. They're definitely geniuses when it comes to making money.'

Without realising it, I'd edged closer and I was practically right beside them now. They turned and looked at me. Great, now I looked creepy.

'Hi,' I said, feeling the need to do an accompanying wave.

'Oh, hey,' Freddie said, caught off guard. 'Uh, this is Matt and Sam, they're friends from the cricket club. This is Jessie, she goes to Queen Vics.'

They both said hello, in a totally normal, genuine, pleasant way – there were none of the usual raised eyebrows or shared glances that I was used to receiving. It felt good, like this was an alternate universe where I was totally normal and could just casually meet new people.

'We're going to go get refills,' Matt said. 'You guys want anything?'

'I'm good thanks,' Freddie said, holding up his beer.

'I'm fine,' I said.

'Have you seen Libby?' I said, once they'd gone. 'I've been looking for her everywhere. I can't find her.'

'I didn't know you guys were friends now,' he said, confused. 'But no, I haven't. Have you tried upstairs?'

'No, feels a bit weird, going upstairs when I don't know Harry. But whatever.' I started walking away, towards the house, considering whether I had the energy to try upstairs. Then that ball of anger, plus the punch, made me stop and go back. 'I thought that was out of order, you know, when we came in. You practically sprinted away from me, you were so keen to make it clear you didn't come with me.'

Freddie looked shocked. He glanced down at his feet.

'I know,' he said, quietly.

I stood still, waiting for more. There must be more, surely?

'It wasn't only selfish though,' he said. 'I didn't want them to think anything was going on for your sake too. You don't need to deal with any more rumours.' He paused, his face all pained and pensive. 'But yeah, I did it to protect me too, and I'm sorry for that,' he finally added. 'Though if we're being totally honest, I'd probably do it again.'

'What?' I shout-asked.

Freddie looked around him, checking for people, checking we weren't being watched. Was it *that* embarrassing to be seen with me?

'Can we?' He gestured to the swing seat by the fence. I wanted to be standing up and pacing and ranting, but I sat down, perching myself on the edge of the seat, ready for all possibilities.

'Look, I get it,' he said. 'Trust me, I do. It's hard to join a new school, I've been there. And do you know how I survived? How I still survive? I play along. I fit in. It just so happens I like football and that's a ready-made in – the universal language of football is always a winner.' He fussed with his hair, rubbing a patch at the back of his head, a habit I'd noticed before. The fairy lights acted as a good filter, lighting him up nicely, making him seem softer.

'And fitting in requires being a dick to me?'

'Well . . . yeah, kind of,' Freddie said, at least having the good manners to look embarrassed by it. 'In my defence I've never actually joined in when they've been having a go at you.'

'Wow, proper Prince Charming, thanks. And, for the record, standing there and doing nothing is the same as joining in. It's called joint enterprise.'

'Ah! You see!' He looked delighted, like I'd offered him up some kind of evidence. 'You're smart – super smart. I've noticed. But you pretend not to understand everything straight away. You hide it, don't you? Why? I'm guessing it's to fit in. You're doing the same thing as me – you hide, you fit in, you're a chameleon.' He looked pleased with himself, his dark eyes shining.

I was surprised. How had he even picked up on that?

'Hiding's not the same as joining in – or standing by – while someone's getting hurt,' I said.

'And you've never done that? You've always taken a stand, have you? Fought the bad guys, even if it meant putting yourself in the firing line?'

I knew as soon as Freddie said it that I was as guilty as he was. Only a few weeks ago Tabitha had been crying her eyes out in the cubicle next to mine. I specifically hadn't gone to her, hadn't even checked if she was all right, because I was too worried about the implications for me, about getting dragged down by association. Exactly the thing I'd just had a go at him for. I swung my legs under me, staring at my battered Doc Martens like I might find the answers to the universe there.

'They used to call me "Albert",' I said, pulling my coat in tighter and having a gulp of punch, the sweetness sticking to my lips. 'In Year Six, a few schools ago. My mum has always told us to blend in, to not draw attention to ourselves, but I guess back then I was too young to realise what she meant, or maybe I didn't care yet. I'd started a new school, another one. I did what I always did, answered all the questions, always super keen, always with my hand up, always getting them right. I'd *always* been like that . . . but this time it didn't go down well.

'They started calling me Einstein, and from there it ended up as Albert. But not in a nice way. It was mean. Hurtful. So I learned my lesson, and now I hide it. Self-protection.'

'Exactly,' Freddie said, understanding lighting his eyes. 'Self-protection.'

'But I wasn't hurting anybody.' I pushed the thoughts of Tabitha to the side. 'The only person I'm hurting by hiding that I'm smart is myself.' As I said it, I realised it was true – I *was* hurting myself by hiding who I was. Did that mean Mum was right? About the moving back, needing to be our true selves? I filed that epiphany as a think-about-it-tomorrow-while-not-drinking-potent-punch note to self.

I could tell Freddie was thinking. I had a point, and he knew it. I studied his face, his jaw tight, his brows lowered in a frown. It's funny how people get better-looking to you when you like them more as a person. Take Callum – he's a conventionally good-looking guy, he has the chiselled jaw and the perfect hair and the deep, dark eyes, but to me, he's ugly. Ugly on the outside, because he's ugly on the inside. I used to think the same about Freddie, but the ice was thawing, slightly.

'That's all I've been trying to do since I got here,' I said. 'Fit in. Not even fit in actually, just survive. I have literally done nothing wrong.' *I mean, not strictly true, Jessie.* 'I know you won't believe me, but it was Callum who kissed me that night and Callum who lied to everyone and Callum who basically is to blame for everything.'

230

Saying it out loud made it all crystal clear. It really was all Callum's fault.

'I believe you,' Freddie said quietly. He looked like he might be about to say something else, but he didn't.

'How can you even bear to be around him? He's such an arse,' I snapped.

'He can be, for sure, but he can also be decent. He's not had it easy, at home. His mum left when he was young, his dad's . . . not a nice guy. It's tough for him.'

'That's not an excuse for making other people's lives hell.'

'Mmm,' he said, non-committal.

'For the record, I think you're being a coward. There's keeping quiet and fitting in, and then there's allowing bad shit to happen. There should be some things you feel the need to stand up to. You have a little sister – imagine how you'd feel if people were treating her like some of the boys treat girls at our school.'

I paused, thinking back to my own actions. I hadn't helped Tabitha out, and that was bad. But I had stood up to the boys and their scoring to Coach. Or tried to anyway. Not that it had done any good.

'There's a limit, you know. We all have a limit. Maybe you just haven't reached yours yet. Anyway, rant over.'

Freddie looked up now, straight at me. I wondered if I'd gone too far, if the punch combined with the angry ball had given me stupid courage and a big mouth. I couldn't entirely work out his expression, but it didn't seem outraged.

'It was more like a lecture, really,' he said, a smile creeping on to the corner of his mouth. 'But point taken.'

Now it was my turn to stare at my feet. I studied my boots,

following the line of the laces as they curved and criss-crossed. They kept seeping into one another and evading me. The swing came to a stop, but my head was on a delay, still moving, swirling. I thought about going to look for Libby, or just going, full stop, but something was keeping me.

'Was that Kanye you were talking about earlier?' I asked.

'Yes. And?'

'And nothing. I love the Kardashians, and by extension, Kanye, but "I'm not averse to a spot of *The Kardashians*" was, I think, the phrase you used before. It's just that you seemed a little bit more . . . enthusiastic rather than merely "not averse". Almost like, you're a *superfan* or something?'

'Yeah, you got me,' he said, holding his hands up in surrender. 'I mean, it's not something I broadcast to everyone, but Matt and Sam are cool. I like having heated discussions with them.'

'I'm not averse to a heated discussion myself,' I said, smiling. 'Especially about the Kardashians.'

***

We talked. And talked and talked. We covered *The Kardashians*, reality TV in general, books, music (we continued the Kanye debate from earlier), pets (he's Team Dog; I, clearly, am Team Cat), the Island and a whole lot more.

What we *didn't* talk about was school or Callum or anything even close. And that was fine by me. Other people came and went around us, more drinks got put into my hand and I was vaguely aware of music and talking and the general party noise getting louder. There were whispers and sniggers every now and again, but I didn't pay them too much attention, I was in a bubble. I felt bad for keeping Freddie from the fun, but not bad enough to stop. I drained my punch and let the warm, fizzy feeling wash over me in an all-consuming wave of happiness and confidence.

'You're pretty interesting, you know,' Freddie said. 'And not what I expected.'

'Ditto,' I said.

'And I dunno, I feel like I can be myself around you and not . . .'

'Ditto again.'

'My dad's in prison,' he blurted out. 'That's why we moved down here.' He paused, the air between us still. 'God, it feels good to say that out loud. I've never actually said it to anyone before.'

When I turned to look at him, he was concentrating firmly on the ground. 'Prison? What for? I mean . . . no, you don't have to answer that. Are you . . . do you see him?'

'It's a long story, which I'd rather not get into. He's back in Lincolnshire. We left to start afresh, to get away from everyone knowing our business and talking about us – which is pretty ironic given what a hotbed for gossip the Island is. And no, I don't see him.'

I didn't know what to say. The fuzziness in my head didn't feel warm and fun any more. It felt foggy and dense. I felt like I should definitely be saying something supportive, or comforting, but I couldn't think what. The silence stretched out between us.

'Oh God, I totally shouldn't have told you. I shouldn't have said anything. Please don't tell anyone. I just . . . I . . . It felt like I've been walking round carrying a cannonball. A really heavy one.'

'I'm a witch!' I half-shouted.

He laughed, which slightly burst the lovely intimate, bonding bubble I'd thought we were in. At least I had cheered him up a bit.

I must've looked disappointed because he adjusted his expression from mocking to faux-interested. 'A witch, huh? OK, so what witchy things can you do?'

I hesitated. I didn't want to tell him I had given Callum a rash or made Marcus's nose grow. Neither showed me in a good light. 'Well, I can heal people . . .'

'Healing's good,' he said, clearly just humouring me. 'Are we talking high-level healing like cancer and terminal illnesses, or cuts and grazes?'

'I know you don't believe me, but it's true. I'll show you,' I said, determined. I wanted to share a secret with him like he had with me. I wanted to stay in the intimate bubble, this circle of trust we had created.

I didn't stop to look around me and assess the situation.

I didn't even think to look for other people.

I didn't think (once again) about the consequences of using magic. All I thought was that I needed him to believe me.

I hoped I had enough power left in me to prove it.

'Watch that piece of wood,' I said, pointing to a small branch beside us that had dropped from the tree. 'I'm going to make it catch fire.'

He forced a serious expression on his face and looked at the branch. 'Watching.'

Deep breath, channel, release.

Nothing happened.

Dammit.

I'd still been bleeding, lightly, this morning. I should have been able to do something small, at least!

I tried again. *Deep breath, channel, release.*

Nothing.

I couldn't believe it. I'd made my big declaration and now couldn't even prove I was telling the truth. This was a disaster. Another one. Now he'd think I was crazy and totally to be avoided. My only hope was that he wouldn't tell anyone.

I looked at him, embarrassment radiating from all points of me. He was smiling. Not a mean, you're-a-fool smile – a kind smile. A he-thought-I-was-still-interesting smile. It made me smile too.

'Thank you,' he said.

'For what?'

'For finding a way to make me feel better. For not making me feel awkward.'

I didn't quite understand what had just happened, but then he moved his little finger over until it was overlapping with mine and he smiled at me and his eyes were all dewy and intense and suddenly, understanding didn't matter. I leaned in, feeling warm and woozy, and kissed him. Or he kissed me. We kissed. A gentle kiss that was both quick and slow. My fingers tingled, my heart gave a thump and my head swirled a bit. Was it the punch or was it love? It was over before I'd properly registered it. We both leaned back and avoided eye contact. I didn't know what to say, or do.

'I swear, I am a witch,' I heard myself saying. 'It's just . . . only . . . only when I'm having my period.'

Before Freddie could respond, I heard a voice shouting my name.

'Jessie!' Libby was marching towards me full speed. She looked angry. 'What are you doing here?'

I glanced between Freddie and Libby.

'You asked me to come,' I said, confused.

'What? No, I didn't!'

'Yeah, you messaged, you said you needed help to face up to . . .'

More people were gathering round now, drawn in by the shouting. I heard some sniggers, some whispers – the soundtrack to my life.

'You need to go,' Libby said, grabbing me by the arm and practically dragging me towards the house, leaving Freddie on the bench.

Libby was pulling me through the bodies in the kitchen, the hallway, speaking quickly and quietly. 'I'll talk to you on Monday, but you really need to go now,' she said.

I probably should have demanded answers or stood up for myself in some way, seeing as no one else was up for the job, but the warm buzzing feeling from earlier had turned to a sinister, cold throbbing and the drama of the night was becoming too much to handle. I let her push me out of the front door, glancing back as she retreated behind it without a word.

Standing alone on the driveway, the tears came instantly, along with shock and fury and a deep-as-a-gorge shame. And underneath it all, fear. What fresh hell had I just managed to stumble into now?

CHAPTER THIRTY

I don't remember much about my dad being around. He left when I was young, so now I can't be sure if the memories I do have are actual things that happened, or are things patched together from photographs and snippets of stories, like mismatched jigsaw pieces jammed where they don't fit.

Most of these memories – or false memories – are from when we were living in Manchester the first time. Before the move to the Lake District, before the move to Derbyshire – before he left, obviously. It was a small bubble of time when I thought everyone was happy. Not that I was consciously thinking, at the time, about whether people were happy or not, but I don't remember arguments every evening, or Mum crying quietly in the bedroom and making out she had a cold when Bella and I asked her what was wrong. I remember smiles, and family outings, and Dad dancing round the kitchen while he cooked and Mum gazing adoringly at him while sipping her wine and playing games with us.

One of the clearer, less-pixelated memories was from when I was about five, possibly younger – I was running, racing against Bella I think, and I fell over, face first, on to gravel. The kind of gravel that takes a layer of skin off and stings like it never won't hurt again. I remember Dad scooping me up, telling me that *it's not the fall that's important, it's the getting back up when you've been knocked down.* At the time I just wanted a plaster and a hug, but I remember him saying it.

He was a dictionary of motivational quotes like that: *shoot for the moon and even if you miss, you'll land in the stars*; *dreams only work if you do*; *do the right thing even when nobody is looking.* Mum used to laugh and roll her eyes at him – before the frustration at his empty words crept in and the eye-rolling stayed but the smile disappeared. Bella would always question him to try and understand what he meant and I tended to just nod and move on.

It's funny how they've stayed with me though, those quotes. I didn't think they had. Yet, there I was, venturing into the breach that Monday morning, repeating to myself: *it's not the fall that's important, it's the getting back up when you've been knocked down.*

I felt like I was on a never-ending hamster wheel of horror, but I was getting back up. What other choice did I have?

I couldn't stay home – things at home were bad. Only Nonna was acting normal towards me. Bella was stomping around, shooting me daggers and Mum just looked at me with exhaustion and worry in her dark-circled eyes. I was hoping, stupidly, that school might be better. At least there I could seek solace in Summer and Tabitha, and maybe something else controversial and gossip-worthy had happened at the party *after* I was aggressively kicked out.

Though at school there was also Freddie. In the post-party haze, in the cold light of Monday, how was I feeling about Freddie? I had no idea. My head was like a blender at high speed – one minute I was having swoony daydream flashbacks to our kiss, then the next instant I was getting an anger sweat at him for not sticking up for me when Libby dragged me out of the party. Though what had I been expecting him to say?

I had deep flashes of embarrassment remembering our conversation – saying I was a witch, trying to *prove* I was a witch, even. He definitely wouldn't want anything to do with me now. I cringed at myself and thanked God I hadn't had any powers left to actually prove anything. However mortified I was, revealing my family's secret would have been worse by approximately three hundred per cent.

And then there was Libby. I felt a wave of discomfort whenever I thought of her. I didn't understand her reaction at the party. Why had she been so angry? What had I missed? Whatever it was, I'd obviously been completely wrong in thinking she'd turned a corner. It seemed she was what Summer had said all along: a straightforward mega-bitch who would never change. I was embarrassed that I'd been so taken in.

As I got closer to school, the green bodies multiplied. I kept my head down, occasionally glancing up to try and find Summer. I'd carefully chosen my music – a killer female boss pop playlist: Little Mix, Beyoncé, Spice Girls, and right now, Taylor Swift. The current song pounding in my headphones, *The Man*, seemed particularly fitting – all about having to work harder than men to get the same things, dealing with double standards and not being believed – so on point. I turned it up, focused on the lyrics and prepared myself for the worst.

I tried to concentrated on Tay Tay, letting the music drown out everything else. Taylor knows. She's been through some shit. She's been publicly bullied, had a man (and his wife) try and keep her down. And she's still strong. I could sense the stares though. I made like a horse with blinkers on and headed straight to the toilets, seeking solace in the familiar dirty grey walls of the cubicle, my second home.

I checked the time on my phone and saw I had three messages from Summer. I opened them eagerly.

Jessie! WTH?!?

Why did you go to that party?! I told you not to go.

Are you so far up Libby's arse you'd ignore someone who was actually looking out for you (aka ME)??

I felt a stone form in my stomach at the thought of Summer being pissed off with me. She was my last hope, my safety blanket, my one true friend – ish.

I texted her back.

I'm not up Libby's arse, I thought I was trying to help her stand up to Callum. Being supportive.

The responses came immediately.

She's back together with him. It was a set-up.

WHICH IS WHY I TOLD YOU NOT TO GO!

'*It was a set-up*'. The words stood out as though bold and gold and dancing on the screen. I think deep down I'd known it was the only explanation, but a tiny, stupid, naïve part of me had been desperate to believe that it was something else.

Another text from Summer.

> FYI – there's a video of you doing the rounds. Thought you should know.

I sat on the toilet seat and put my head between my legs, adopting the brace position like you're supposed to do in a plane crash. I sure felt like I was plummeting.

A video? Of what?

It could only be of Saturday night. But surely it couldn't be that bad? I went to a party I wasn't invited to and got thrown out. Yes, it was embarrassing, no, it wouldn't help my already abysmal, non-existent street cred, but I could ride it out. It could be worse.

Before I had a chance to search the video out, I heard the bell through my headphones. I stared at my phone, willing Summer to text me again. I could really have done with one of her positive, 'this too shall pass' type messages.

Nothing.

I took a deep breath and emerged from my cubicle, reluctantly making my way to registration. At least it was with Ms Simmons, I thought. I'd be safe there at least.

***

Except, of course, it wasn't Ms Simmons because that would be too much like luck, or good karma. It was a supply teacher, one who looked about twelve years old and like she was crapping her pants at the sight of a room full of teenagers.

Fabulous. No one in the classroom was even pretending to listen as she shouted at them to take their seats. People were huddled round phones laughing, nudging each other, clasping hands to mouths. I sat down quietly, rolling my eyes at the chimp-like behaviour and wishing everyone else would shut up and let the poor, now red-faced woman take the register. Apparently, no man's an island, but holy crap I felt like one right then. A deserted, desolate, barren island. The weight of getting through the next few hours without Ms Simmons or Summer lay heavy on me, like I'd been buried up to my neck in sand and was just managing to keep my head from being covered.

The bell went without the register having actually been done. Half of the class filed out, and others, including Freddie, filed in for Media. We had the briefest moment of eye contact, before both of us looked to the floor, my feelings swirling and fizzing around my body like an Alka-Seltzer dropped in a glass of water.

The supply teacher managed to herd us to the edit suite where we took our seats in our groups, huddled round screens. Tabitha gave me a sympathetic smile, a *I'm feeling your pain but I'm not sure how to help you* smile. I attempted one back, though the thought of sitting through this next hour made me want to curl up in a ball and cry.

I was completely unattached to this project, and didn't have an ounce of interest in what they'd shot while I was away. I kept my head down, but I could see Marcus was gearing for a fight. His eyes were shiny and excited.

'I was thinking, Jessie. How about you just *magic* this edit for us?' he said, chuckling. 'How does it go again, is it like this?'

He took a breath and screwed up his face in an exaggerated portrayal of concentration, then held his hand to his stomach and breathed out slowly, mimicking me.

My own stomach lurched.

I felt the flame of a fierce blush.

How did he know about that? Had Freddie told people?

'Clearly, I was joking,' I said, concentrating on the screen like my life depended on it.

'Were you though?' he said. 'You seemed pretty convincing – other than the fact you didn't do any magic.' All the boys in the group laughed. 'Unless, of course, you bewitched Freddie into kissing you – I mean, why *else* would he? Let's ask him.'

I ground my teeth, feeling sick, the whole room morphing into some kind of swirling, spattered abstract painting.

'Hey, Freddie,' Marcus yelled across the classroom. 'Did you mean to kiss Jessie or did she magic you into it?'

Freddie ignored him. The teacher gave Marcus a glare from where she was working with another group. 'Sorry, miss, just some important business to work out, for the film.'

'Shall we maybe do some work?' Tabitha asked.

'Sure thing,' Marcus said. 'Don't let me stop you.'

Ugh, he was so infuriating, sitting there with his smug, smarmy, knowing grin. I wanted to tell him to stick it, but I had to ride this out. Focus on the screen, ignore Marcus. It was the only way through.

Tabitha got the log sheet ready and I forwarded the tape to the start of the interview with Coach, sweat forming just at the sight of his horrible face.

While Marcus and Tom and Harry chatted among themselves,

Tabitha and I watched the whole boring interview, which was predictably a love-in between Coach and Marcus about football and not at all relevant to how sport is helping young people. I had basically zoned out, still obsessively running through the events of Saturday night in my head, wondering how bad it really had been – when I was pulled out of my daze by the sound of my name on the video.

'You're lucky, Coach, Jessie Jones was supposed to have been here today too – you would've got a much harder grilling,' Marcus was saying on-screen.

I leaned closer to watch. The boys were all packing up, the interview clearly finished, backs to the camera – but the camera that was still running.

Coach laughed. 'Thank God for that. She's a feisty one, that's for sure.'

'Probably just her time of the month,' Tom added.

'Seems to always be her time of the month,' Marcus said, chuckling.

'What's Miss Jones on now, then?' Coach asked, all chummy and down with the kids. 'Does verbally assaulting a teacher get her a higher or lower score in your books?'

'When you're the teacher, lower for sure. What do we reckon, boys, shall we put her on a minus five? Better check with Callum.'

I could see their shoulders shaking with laughter. They gave Coach high fives. 'You lads'll get me in trouble one of these days,' he said.

The screen went black. Tabitha had closed the video. 'Ignore them, Jessie. They're total arseholes,' she said, quietly.

Behind us, Tom and Harry were laughing at something on Marcus's phone, paying no attention whatsoever to the work. 'Go on, do it,' Tom said.

I stared at the screen as Tabitha loaded the next set of rushes. My throat was tight, not sure whether it wanted to sob or scream. I felt like I was watching myself on a TV screen, my life a blur between reality and fiction. Had that really just happened? Was *all this* really happening? I looked at Tabitha for confirmation, to check I hadn't lost my mind thinking that it was *not* OK. Her face was a telling mixture of quiet anger, hopelessness and sympathy.

'Uh, guys,' Marcus boomed. He was now standing at the front of the class. 'Ms Simmons wanted everyone to see this as a good example of documentary-making.'

A video came on the big screen. The supply teacher, over at the other end of the classroom working with another group, looked confused and mildly panicked. Marcus looked like he was going to burst with excitement.

And I knew. Instantly, I knew.

Before I even looked and saw it – Harry's garden, the shot panning from the fire to the fairy lights, closing in on the bench – I knew.

It was a video of me. Me with Freddie, at the party.

'I'm a witch,' I declared on-screen.

It cut to me saying, *'I'll show you'*, me taking a breath, then . . . the kiss. Then the whole sequence again, and again, jump-cut like a boomerang this time. Then a piece to camera with Callum, looking all serious and faux-scared.

'I had no idea. She got me when I was alone, cornered me. Before

I knew it, she'd kissed me, and I didn't know how it had happened. I realise now, she'd bewitched me. Witch-kissed me. It could happen to anyone. It could happen to you! Be vigilant, boys. No sudden movements, no eye contact and carry these at all times.'

He held up a bulb of garlic and a makeshift cross.

The teacher was up at the front now, fumbling with leads in an attempt to turn the video off. Marcus, Tom, Harry, and a lot of the class were hooting with laughter and looking at me, watching for my reaction. I caught Freddie's eye but couldn't read what was there. Pity? Embarrassment? Tabitha tried to take my hand, but I pulled away.

I felt like I was on a delay, like my eyes had taken the video in but it hadn't computed to my brain yet. I could feel the pinch of tears, but I could also feel the tidal wave of rage. My ears were buzzing, my skin prickling with an energy, an electricity. If anyone was to touch me right now I might explode – or they might. I felt adrift, like a tiny sailboat in the middle of a stormy sea with no land in sight, nothing to hold on to, no harbour, no hope.

I stood up, the chatter and laughing sounding like static around me, grabbed my bag and walked out of the room as calmly as I could, while inside, my rage burned like hellfire.

CHAPTER THIRTY-ONE

I stood in the corridor, taking huge gulps of air. Air that was too thin, air that wasn't touching the sides. I focused on the weave of the beige carpet, trying to distract myself, following its threads, dull and flat from years of stampeding teenagers. How many years had the carpet been there? Ten? Twenty? Thirty? More? How many mean boys and upset girls had trodden down this path?

It wasn't working; if anything the waves of anger were getting stronger. I looked up, searching for something else. Lockers – I honed in on one with something etched into its door, looked closer, straining to make out the letters. SLUT. Seriously? My skin started humming again, my whole body whirring. I felt . . . charged.

I had to do something. None of this was OK.

Suddenly my legs were carrying me down the corridor like they knew what they were doing, even though my mind hadn't caught up with the plan yet. This wasn't just about me being bullied. This was about the whole sodding female population of the school – even the female teachers – and it had been going on for a long time. I wished Ms Simmons was in today, I wished there was someone who got it, who could see it, who knew I wasn't being a crazy, paranoid, 'hysterical' girl.

I thought of Summer. She always says it's not enough to moan about it, you have to *do* something about it. *Be the change you want to see*. She was right. We had to do something or nothing would ever change.

I was angry. I was boiling over, a kettle screaming steam, ready-to-burst sort of angry. And I was sick of pushing it down, turning it into something else more acceptable – shame, shyness – like girls are always made to do. I wouldn't let them dismiss my anger. I would scream and shout. I would make everyone pay.

Yes, I was angry, and hell yes, I had every right to be.

I needed to own it, to express it, to use it. My legs carried on, picking up the pace as I leaned into my anger, using it to propel me forward, to fuel my intention.

I reached Mr Harlston's office and paused, deep-breathing outside the door one last time. *You've got this*, I told myself. Once he knew the extent of what's been happening, he would have to act.

I barged past the admin staff, who were chatting and distracted, through to the inner office, where he was sitting at his desk.

'I need to talk to you urgently,' I said. 'Sir.'

He looked surprised, glancing past me to the receptionist, who was now standing in the doorway looking apologetic.

'Please,' I added. 'It's important.'

'Have I got time, Miss Pierce?'

She nodded.

'You'd better sit down then, Miss...?' He looked at me, questioningly.

'Jones. Jessie Jones. I'm in 10S. I joined a few weeks ago.'

'Ah, yes,' he said, a shadow of something – doubt, dread? – crossing his thin, weasel-like face. He gestured again for me to sit down. I didn't want to – I had too much pent-up energy – but I needed to keep him on side, so I perched on the edge of the seat.

'I'm glad you're here, Miss Jones,' he said. 'I was thinking we should maybe have a chat. I've been hearing reports of inappropriate behaviour towards teachers.'

Was he kidding?

No. Focus. Get your point out, Jessie. Don't let him derail you.

I took a deep breath. *Stick to the facts, don't be emotional.*

'Since I have been at this school,' I began calmly, 'I have had to deal with a number of incidents that I consider to be bullying of a sexist nature and today, just now, another incident occurred.'

He narrowed his eyes at me and if he could have got away with rolling them I'm pretty sure he would have done. 'We take bullying very seriously at Queen Victoria Academy,' he said coldly. 'We have a zero-tolerance policy on bullying, as I'm sure you know. Any allegations are a very serious matter that will be looked into with due diligence – including any actions on your part. Are you sure you want to go down that road?'

Actions on my part? What possible actions on my part? Existing? Trying to go to school and stay out of trouble?

'Yes,' I said firmly. 'I want to go down that road.'

'Ms Simmons has already spoken to me about some issues that were taking place between you and some Year Ten boys. I have looked into it and assured her, as I'll assure you, that it is misplaced humour on their part. They have been dealt with accordingly.'

'Dealt with how?' I asked, feeling the rage bubble working its way up from the pit of my stomach.

'How we choose to discipline other students is not your concern, Miss Jones. The issue has been addressed and resolved. So let's not dwell on the past, shall we?' His eyes flickered to his computer screen.

He was essentially checking out of the conversation – not even giving me a chance to explain what had happened today. Anything I said now wasn't going to register – I was a trouble-maker, a silly, emotional girl who was just giving him extra hassle to deal with and wasn't worthy of his time. He'd reel off the standard lines, promise to look into things, while effectively just shutting me up.

An image came to me of him and Coach in the staff-room, talking about me in low voices. *'She's a handful.' 'Overreacts.' 'Treat with caution'.* It was so clear, like I was watching it on TV. Was I seeing something that had actually happened? Was this a *witch* thing?

The hairs on the back of my neck stood on end and a cold wave ran through me, replacing the heat and the steam. Mr Harlston was looking at me like I was a stain someone had left on his chair. I couldn't bear it. I couldn't bear *him*. What was the point? What was the point of even trying when arseholes like him were in charge?

And further up, even more arseholes. They were in charge of everything: schools, businesses, newspapers, law courts, governments. A whole world run by misogynist arseholes in cahoots with *other* misogynist arseholes, forming a perfect breeding ground for yet *more* misogynist arseholes. In a world where a man who bragged about grabbing women's genitals got to be President, really, what hope was there? How was anything ever going to change?

Mr Harlston looked back to his computer and I felt a sense of utter despair seeping through me.

And then, like a switch had been flicked, I didn't.

It changed. Suddenly, it changed. My despair morphed into something else, something powerful. Angry and powerful and desperate. My buzz turned into a hum, turned into a current – full and forceful. It needed to be let out. I stood up, leaning over the desk. Mr Harlston looked up at me, startled.

'Today, I wanted to discuss the fact that this school is full of sexist, misogynist, boys – and men. They are bullies, they are liars, they are emotionally abusive, they wield their invisible power over all of us. It's not fair and IT NEEDS TO CHANGE!'

I didn't realise I was shouting – or screaming, more like. My skin was on fire and I could feel the anger taking me over, but I had no control now. It was an untamed beast breaking free.

How was this even happening? I wasn't on my period. But this was definitely the witch in me speaking. Roaring, more like.

I could hear voices, whispers, encouragement – the same voices I'd heard at the monument, my ancestors spurring me on, giving me power. I knew I was losing control, but it felt good – right and pure, a release of the sweetest kind. I let the anger flow right out of me.

I took a breath and the room came back into focus. Mr

Harlston was huddled in his chair, holding his hands in front of his face to protect himself. His desk was empty, everything that had been on it now on the floor – a smashed lamp, papers, a keyboard and phone. Like a bomb had gone off.

And I was the bomb.

CHAPTER THIRTY – TWO

I fled. Wholesale, full-on, fast as I could. What else could I do?

I knew I was in trouble beyond anything I could imagine. Big, giant, scary, black-hole, whirlpool trouble. The snapshot of Mr Harlston's face as I left stayed with me – wide-eyed shock and disgust.

I wasn't sure what exactly he had seen – an angry girl sweeping his desk clear, or objects flying at him of their own accord. I had to hope it was the former.

The truth was, it had surprised me as much as him.

I wasn't on my period. That wasn't supposed to be able to happen. Plus, I had been learning how to control my magic, to be intentional. None of that, whatever *that* was, had been intentional.

I ran through the staff car park and out of the gates on to the road, my heart thumping so hard I half-expected it to burst out of my shirt. I dodged the pensioners, the dog walkers, the day trippers, ignoring the tuts and the comments. I felt like I could have run a marathon, like I was being driven forward, a gust of wind pushing me onwards and onwards and onwards. I wasn't sure where. All I knew is that I had to get away. Far. Away. I had an overwhelming, deep-in-my-bones need to get off this island. I needed stable ground.

As if by magic, there was a bus heading for the boat at the bus stop.

I sprinted and got to it just in time, boarding and making my way to the top of the bus, my legs weak and wobbly, struggling with the stairs. Sitting down, I managed to take a breath. But only a small one; a big one would have led to tears. Not just normal tears either, an unstoppable, never-ending outpouring of them. I could feel them pooling inside me, gathering, rising, ready – and I really couldn't handle that right now.

Now that I was sitting still, the energy and strength and whatever else had been powering me disappeared like a light had been turned off. Instant darkness. I was utterly drained, a bag of skin with some bones holding it upright.

My phone vibrated. With shaking hands, I retrieved it from my bag. Eleven missed calls from Mum. There were voicemails too – the red dot notification glared at me like a silent death knell. Once I listened to those, there was no going back. The trouble I was in would be official and would require a response, and I wasn't ready for that.

I leaned my head against the window and closed my eyes, trying to rest. But under my eyelids the flashbacks started – Callum kissing me, Coach dismissing me, Marcus laughing at me, Callum on that video, Mr Harlston looking down on me. All these faces, like a terrifying Halloween montage, twirling and merging into a giant ball of nasty. Mean and nasty.

I opened my eyes again and stared out of the window to the sea in the distance, grey and churning. The bus wheezed its way up the hill, past houses with names like 'Sea Breeze' and

'Seascape' and 'The Lookout', front gardens that featured sea shell art or driftwood furniture that all looked ridiculous on a day like today, with the rain lashing down like it was straight out of the Old Testament. They felt like empty promises, or flattened hope.

By the time the bus pulled into the stop by the boat, the rain had become even more Biblical and the rising waves of the sea seemed in competition with it. I pulled my hood up and walked up the pier, into the wind. I had to look down in order to keep my eyes open. I bought my boat ticket – one way – and found a seat tucked around the corner to wait for the next boat. The waiting room wasn't the sweet relief I'd hoped it would be. It was cold and wet, pools of water forming under seats, everyone umbrellaless, caught off guard.

Caught off guard.

There wasn't supposed to be rain today. It was supposed to be nice today. It *had* been nice today. It had been sunny when I left for school, I remembered because I wished I'd thought to bring my sunglasses. It had been sunny first period, we'd had the blinds drawn in the edit suite. It was only when I ran out of school that I noticed the weather had turned. Then it had been raining and grey and angry. Like me. Had I done this, again?

This was bad.

My troubles lined up at me like a grim-faced greeting procession at a wedding: Mum, Bella, Nonna, Summer, Libby, Marcus, Coach, Mr Harlston, Callum. I would be expelled, for sure. Mum would be livid. Bella would hate me. Summer already thought I was a lost cause. I had no one on my side. I was standing – sinking, in quicksand – alone.

It was all this stupid island's fault. If I wasn't on the Island, I wouldn't have powers at all. Not as a juvenile witch anyway. Not according to Mum and Nonna. And if I left now, I might never develop into a full-fledged witch. I might never have to deal with having powers, as long as I didn't come back to the Island. I would be normal again.

I thought back to Dad, to his advice to get back up when you get knocked down. Which was all well and good, but I hadn't just been knocked down, I'd been knocked *out*. I was lying, battered and bruised on the floor of the ring, with a broken nose and concussion.

The thought of Dad flashed in front of me like a lighthouse in a storm, hopeful, promising, guiding. A complete change, somewhere different. No rain or winds or sea in Dubai, no Callum or Marcus or Coach or Libby, no witchcraft, no powers – just dry, desolate desert and a cleansing, raw, sauna-like heat. I could start again as a normal teenage girl, make friends I couldn't accidentally inflict injury on, have teachers who weren't misogynist pigs, live a normal life full of normal teenage things. That was what I needed: a new start, a blank page.

I had money in my savings account. Flights weren't that much. I'd message Dad to say it was an emergency and I needed to see him. I knew he had a whole other family and a new life, but I could slip into that, I could blend in – I'm used to that. I was his daughter, after all. Maybe I should wait until I was in Dubai to contact him, then he'd really have no choice. Or maybe I should contact him now and he might offer to buy my ticket?

An announcement came over the tannoy: 'Due to severe

weather conditions, we're sorry to report that the 11.15 departure to Portsmouth Harbour has been delayed. We apologise for any inconvenience this may cause to your onward journey.'

My new-found excitement plummeted and a fresh wave of panic that I would never get off this island kicked in. I needed to leave – I would grease myself up with goose fat and swim if I had to. I got my phone out to text Dad and saw that dozens of notifications had filled up my screen. Social media ones that I assumed were to do with the video, voicemails from Mum and Bella and Summer, and a string of text messages.

I looked at the messages from Mum first, mentally preparing myself as if I was about to watch a horror movie, tempted to put my hands in front of my face and read through my fingers.

I've just had a call from school. Call me ASAP.

Jessie, where are you? Call me.

You need to call me NOW.

If you don't call me within twenty minutes, I will be calling the police.

You are not in trouble, just call me.

NONNA IS VERY ILL. WE NEED YOU. CALL ME!

The cold sweat on my skin turned to ice.

Nonna. Nonna was ill.

My whole body dropped by five degrees.

'Jessie!' A loud shout from across the waiting room. Mum.

She came running to me – paint covered overalls, hair scrunched up in a turban, worry on her face, a blur of Mum-ness.

'Thank God!' she said, smothering me in a wet, hot hug, her shoulders shuddering as she sobbed quietly.

'Did you get my messages? Nonna's very ill.' She broke away from the hug, hands still on my arms. 'We need your help.'

'But – but what can I do?'

'I'll explain on the way.' She held out her hand to me. 'I know we need to talk – properly talk – but for now, let's concentrate on Nonna.'

'OK,' I whispered, letting myself be led by her, feeling a surprising amount of comfort in holding her hand, seeing her face.

CHAPTER THIRTY - THREE

We didn't speak in the car. There were a thousand questions spiralling round my head, but I didn't know where to start. Mum looked worried, her eyebrows drawn together, her mouth set in a firm, thin line.

The builders had cleared out for the day, leaving the house looking like it had been evacuated in a high emergency – half-drunk cups of tea on surfaces, tools in the middle of the floor – a building site Pompeii. I wanted to go straight to Nonna, but Mum insisted I change into dry clothes, saying I'd be no good to anyone if I got ill too. I flung on whatever I could find and rushed down to Nonna's annexe.

The lights were low in her bedroom, small shadows from candles flickering against the wall, and it took my eyes a minute to adjust, to find Nonna in the darkness.

I swallowed a sob when I saw her. She looked . . . dead. Pale, still and lifeless, lying small and helpless in her bed. The opposite of my big, loud, full-to-bursting Nonna.

Bella came bustling in with some more candles.

'Hi,' I said.

She glared at me and carried on.

Mum came in, looking focused, tense and worried. Her face was a dark shadow of pain and nerves, a reflection of how we all felt. She took a deep breath and shook out a long piece of rope.

'OK then, I'll begin,' she said, her voice shaking slightly. 'Let it be known that the Circle is about to be cast. All who enter the Circle do so in perfect love and perfect trust.' She lay the rope on the floor in a circle around the bed, which had been moved away from the wall. She walked over to the bedstead where a candle had been placed and lit it, chanting:

> *'Guardians of the East, I call upon you*
> *to watch over the rites of the Downer Coven.*
> *Powers of Knowledge and Wisdom, guided by Air,*
> *we ask that you keep watch over us*
> *tonight within this Circle.'*

She lit a candle on the shelf above the radiator, next to the photo of Nonna and Gramps on their wedding day, and spoke again:

> *'Guardians of the South, I call upon you*
> *to watch over the rites of the Downer Coven.*
> *Powers of Energy and Will, guided by Fire,*
> *we ask that you keep watch over us*
> *tonight within this Circle.'*

Then she moved to the end of the bed:

> *'Guardians of the West, I call upon you*
> *to watch over the rites of the Downer Coven.*

> *Powers of Passion and Emotion, guided by Water,*
> *we ask that you keep watch over us*
> *tonight within this Circle.'*

And lastly, she moved to the other side of the room, where Nonna's bedside table had been moved to accommodate a fourth candle:

> *'Guardians of the North, I call upon you*
> *to watch over the rites of the Downer Coven.*
> *Powers of Endurance and Strength, guided by Earth,*
> *we ask that you keep watch over us*
> *tonight within this Circle.'*

I focused on the candle on the bedstead. I couldn't look at Nonna, not yet.

Mum took a step forward until she was standing before Bella. 'How do you enter the Circle?' she asked, adding in a whisper, 'With perfect love and trust.'

Bella took the cue and stepped into the Circle, repeating, 'With perfect love and trust.'

Mum motioned for me to step forward. 'How do you enter the Circle?' she asked.

I glanced at her, questioning and she nodded. 'With perfect love and trust,' I said, uncertainly.

We stood so that we were at three points around Nonna, making a loose kind of a circle within the rope. Mum placed a burner carefully by Nonna's head, lighting a candle under its bowl that held a small mound of herbs. We joined hands,

261

stretching to reach each other. Mum's hand felt dry and paper thin, cold, while Bella's were the opposite – warm, damp and soft.

Mum began to chant again:

'We call upon you, Ginerva, in a time of need.
I ask your assistance and blessing, for one who is ailing.
Edith is ill, and she needs your healing light.
I ask you to watch over her and give her strength,
Keep her safe from further illness, and protect her body and soul.
I ask you, great Ginerva, to heal her in this time of sickness.'

This was like whenever I attempted to meditate – I tried to switch my brain off, to surrender, believe, but I always got distracted by reality and trivia. Now, I was wondering to myself how long this would go on for, and what it was actually supposed to do. And then darker thoughts crept in too: how could I live without Nonna? Would she meet Gramps in an afterlife?

Mum was still speaking, words that felt other and alien to me. Her hand got warmer, Bella's sweatier. *Focus, Jessie, focus.*

And then I felt it. A jolt. A flash. An energy.

It came out of nowhere, and my immediate instinct was to pull away and break the circle. But the energy wasn't just in me; it was everywhere – it was in the room, in the weight of the air. The candles flickered, then burned brighter. Even the floor felt like it was humming. Mum was still chanting, her eyes closed now, but I managed to catch Bella's eye and I knew she'd felt it too.

The rest of it isn't clear in my mind. I guess I must have managed to surrender, to give in, but when I think about it, it's not so much a memory as a feeling.

The next thing I *do* remember was seeing Nonna stir. It was dark outside, my ears were ringing and my back was throbbing.

Mum rushed to Nonna's side, gently checking her over, offering her water, telling her not to sit up.

'Stop your fussing, woman, I'm perfectly fine,' Nonna said, her voice a dry whisper, like a breadstick ready to snap. 'Jessie. Where's Jessie?'

'I'm here, Nonna,' I said, moving forward and taking her cold hand.

'How are you, my love?'

'*Me*? I'm OK. Don't worry about me. How are *you*?'

'She shouldn't be talking,' Mum said. 'Stop talking, Mum. You need to rest.'

'I can rest when I'm dead,' Nonna said, making the whole room fall silent. She chuckled, weakly. 'Too soon?'

CHAPTER THIRTY-FOUR

When I was younger, I once got into trouble for scribbling on a boy's painting.

It was at primary school. He'd done something mean to my friend, I can't even remember what, but I decided the best way to get revenge would be to ruin his precious artwork that was due to be in the school exhibition.

I didn't own up to it. Everyone knew it was me, but no one could prove it. The whole class had to miss playtimes until someone confessed, and then my friend said she'd seen me do it.

The school called Mum. She sat me down at home, on a dining chair placed in the middle of the living room like some kind of war interrogation, and asked me to tell her the truth. I denied I'd done it. And denied it and denied it. I cried, said I was being set up. She believed me and said she'd fight for me.

And she did. In her full kickass lawyer way – emails to the class teacher, a meeting with the Headteacher, a strongly worded letter. It was off the chart. And all the while I sat there, a hard rock of guilt in my stomach, knowing there was no way I could ever possibly tell her the truth.

***

'We need to talk,' Mum said, later. The sky was darker now, the night quieter.

My body was still throbbing from the trauma of the day. The air was dense, the house heavy. I knew this would be horrible and painful, but also that I needed to be completely honest this time. I just hoped that I hadn't pushed her so far that she wouldn't fight for me.

'I don't really know where to start,' she said, rubbing her face. We were sitting at the kitchen table. She'd made us both a 'restorative tea' that I hadn't dared try yet, though the smell of it, all herby and floral, was wafting up into the back of my throat anyway.

'Is this my fault?' I blurted out. The question had been sitting heavy on me. 'Is it my fault Nonna's ill?'

She looked at me intently, maybe trying to work out how honest to be.

'Not entirely,' she said finally. 'She hasn't been right for a while, although she's done a good job of hiding it. But today didn't help. It took a lot out of her, trying to . . . balance things out.'

'I'm sorry,' I said, hanging my head. 'I'm so sorry. I was trying to deal with everything maturely and officially. I wasn't trying to do anything witchy this time. It just happened, out of the blue. And I haven't even got my period!'

She stared at me, her eyes widening. 'Really?'

'Really,' I said. 'And . . . that's not supposed to happen, is it?' I focused on a knot in the wood on the table, waiting for her response.

'Jessie,' she said, something else in her voice now. 'That's remarkable – *you* are remarkable. There are very few – and I mean *very* few witches who come into their powers so young. You are one of a handful. That really is very . . . rare.'

'Really?' I asked, daring to look up and meet her eyes.

'Yes, sweetheart. Rare in the best possible way.' She took my hands, squeezing them gently. 'Tell me exactly what happened. Everything.'

So, I told her.

I told her everything, from the beginning. I tried not to be too biased or one-sided or emotional – I tried to stick to the facts. And the more I spoke about it, the more I went through every little move, mistake and misjudgement I'd made, the more the facts spoke for themselves. I hadn't done anything I shouldn't have done (OK, apart from a few bits of mean magic). Most of my problems had come from trusting people who didn't deserve it – and, really, that was more about their failings than mine. The whole story came out of me in a long, breathless monologue and when it was done, I felt a release, as though a knot in my shoulders had eased, a lightness.

Mum was quiet for a moment. Then she said, slowly, 'Have I told you about how I found out about my powers?' I shook my head. 'Well, I mean, I'd always known. Nonna and Gramps had told me I was a witch from day dot, but I guess I didn't really believe it.

'I was at your high school, Queen Vic. I was a late bloomer, didn't get my period until I was fifteen. I was going out with a boy called Bobby Royce. "Going out" is too strong a term for it actually – we'd been to the cinema once and had got chips together a couple of times. I liked him though. At the end of one of our "dates", we had a little kiss, which was perfectly fine, until, out of the blue, he tried to put his hand up my top. I gently pushed it away. We carried on kissing and he tried it again, this time a little more forcefully.

'Well, I was livid – you can imagine. And a little bit panicked. Before I knew what had happened, he'd pulled away and was shouting in pain. His hand, the one he'd been so determined to get up my top, was covered in angry red welts. I still remember the look in his eyes now – scared, shocked, but also disgusted. He looked at me like *I* was the dirty, disgusting one.

'Word got around, quickly, and the next day the story was that I was both frigid *and* diseased, had given him some kind of lesions. Everyone joined in, of course, and I became known as a weirdo, a freak – not even anything original. That was the best they could come up with.'

'Wow,' I mouthed, the word not quite forming properly. The thought of Mum at my age, going through the same kind of heartbreaking crap, felt surreal. Mum the kickass lawyer, Mum the machine, Mum who always had it together. 'That sounds awful.'

'Oh, it was.'

'Didn't you have friends that stuck up for you? Or stuck by you at least?' I asked, thinking of Summer and Tabitha.

'I had friends, but none that were prepared to stick up for me. My best friend was actually Kate. Summer's mum.'

'And she didn't . . .'

'Oh no – the opposite. Kate was one of the loudest voices putting me down.'

'What? Why?'

'She was scared for herself and joining in was the safest thing to do. If everyone's busy pointing the finger and decimating someone else, they're not going to look elsewhere for a target. Survival of the fittest, pack mentality – that's high school.'

'So what did you do?'

'I did what you've been trying to do – I kept my head down, I made myself as small as possible in every way, trying not to leave any footprints, any marks that might draw attention to me. And, at the very first opportunity, I left the Island. It's easier to be invisible on the mainland, especially if you keep on moving, don't make any ties, don't put down roots, keep pushing people away.'

I nodded. 'You did what you've always told us to do. Blend in, fit in, don't lift your head above the parapet.'

'Exactly,' she said, her eyes all sadness and regret. 'And Jessie, I cannot tell you how sorry I am about that. I see now how my words, my actions, my insecurities have impacted on you. Made you so fiercely determined to not draw attention to yourself that you've been denying your true self.'

'Is that what happened with Dad?' I asked. 'Did you push him away?'

She sighed, a deep, long exhale. 'I don't for a minute regret what I had with your dad – obviously.' She squeezed my hand. 'But I was never open with him about the extent of who I was, which meant we could never really work.'

'So he doesn't know about our . . .?' I wiggled my fingers in a witchy way.

'He knew something, but I downplayed it, said I had experimented with Wicca and herbal remedies. I didn't let him in fully. I'm working on letting people in now though.'

'Andy?' I asked, tentatively.

'It's a bit too soon for that yet,' she said, a definite glint in her eye. 'But I'd like us to work on telling your dad together. He

268

loves you and Bella both, dearly, and it's important he knows the real you.'

She had the beginnings of tears in her eyes, that little wateriness that comes just before the waterfall, when there's still a chance of fending it off. Her hair hung in loose, dark waves, unruly like Nonna's.

'It sounds like it was a good plan – the leaving and the keeping moving and the no ties,' I said. 'Why did you come back?'

'I honestly never thought I would. I was so happy being rid of this place, and denying my powers. But being a witch isn't something you can leave behind. It's within you, as much a part of who you are as anything. It's like we're a stick of rock – you break us open, and we have *witch* running through us. But I probably would have just kept trying and trying – if it wasn't for finding that lump.'

Ah, the lump, the tiny little mass of tissue that had changed everything.

'When I found that lump and I feared the worst, I don't know ... something shifted. I felt like a fraud, like I'd been living a lie – which I suppose I had. I had been trying to heal a broken leg with plasters. I just knew, even before I got the results back, that the change I needed was to come here, to come *home*, to find a way to start again. I needed to embrace who I really am, wholeheartedly – no more living in denial, no more running away from myself. And I wanted that for you girls too.'

She looked so sincere it hurt me to look into her eyes. I heard Bella shuffling around in Nonna's annexe, wondered if she was listening in, or if she'd already had this talk.

'Well, it's not really going to plan,' I said. 'Everyone hates me, I'm pretty sure I've been excluded from school and I nearly killed Nonna.'

Mum took her hand away from mine, put her head in her hands and rubbed her forehead again.

'I know, sweetheart. I understand how difficult this is, I do. But if I could go back in time, and give fifteen-year-old me advice, I would say, as I'm saying to you now: don't run away from yourself. Find a way to embrace your differences, to see them as the strengths that they are, as the things that make you special and unique. Look at what you did tonight. We couldn't have done that without you and your strength. We healed Nonna. We used our differences for good. And yes, I know,' she said, 'this is all easier said than done and right now you feel like you hate everything about your life and want to leave it all behind. But I promise, from the bottom of my heart, you'll regret it if you do.'

'Embracing my differences isn't going to fix things now!' I said. It sounded nice, sure, but it wasn't a plan. It didn't *mean* anything. 'All bridges are burned. I'm at the point of no return.'

'There is never a point of no return,' Mum said, a glint in her eye. 'You'll find you have more support than you think. Starting with us. We're all here for you. And, as you've seen tonight, we're stronger together.'

'I'm not sure you're *all* here for me,' I said, quietly, nodding towards the annexe.

'Of course we are,' Bella called out as she came and leaned against the door frame. She'd totally been eavesdropping. 'You're an annoying spoilt brat most days and I could've done without the drama, but we're family.'

She smiled, then Mum smiled, and I found I couldn't help myself. The warmth trickled through me, contagious.

'Course we bloody are,' Nonna's cracked voice shouted from her room.

We all rushed in to her. She was pulling herself up to sitting, rearranging her pillows with difficulty.

'Mum, stop it, we can do that,' Mum said, trying to take over.

'I can do it myself.' Nonna flapped Mum away. 'Come here, Jessie.' She held out her hand and I took it, worried at how light and papery it felt. 'Now listen, I've been waiting for months for you to have your epiphany and it hasn't happened, so I'm telling you now. I'm not going to have another one on my hands who takes practically a lifetime to come to their senses and realise how utterly fabulous it is to be a witch. Especially one as rare and powerful as you're turning out to be, my girl!

'So you're not going to go running away like your mum did. We're going to work this out together, and if that means combining our powers and sticking it to the Man, daily magic lessons and family therapy, that's what we'll do. I'm not going to be around forever, not in this form anyway, so we need to make the most of each other. We love you, you're special, get on with it.'

I looked at her, still smaller than usual, but definitely with some essence of Nonna back. The pinch of devastation at the thought of her not being around still hung in the air, an aftertaste, sharp and sour. *She* was special, that was for sure, and so was Mum, and Bella, so maybe she was right. Maybe I was too.

'Enough of that,' she said, with a grin. 'Someone needs to sort their life out. So let's get brainstorming.'

CHAPTER THIRTY-FIVE

I took a deep breath and knocked on the door, doing a last-minute hair rearrangement like I was about to go on a blind date.

The wait between the knock and the door opening felt loooooooong. Four-seasons-have-passed, children-have-grown-up-and-had-their-*own*-children type long.

'Hi,' I said, an uncertain smile plastered on my face, when the door finally opened.

'Jessie.' Kate looked genuinely pleased to see me. 'Come in, come in. Summer's in the kitchen. Summer!' She led me inside. 'How's Nonna doing? I heard she wasn't well.'

I didn't even question how she knew. Island grapevine.

'She's doing better, thanks. Mum's not letting her get out of bed yet, but I don't think she'll manage to stop her for long.'

'Oh, I'm so pleased.'

I looked into those bright blue eyes that had always seemed so kind and open and warm and tried to imagine a teenage Kate who was mean. I couldn't. I wondered when she had changed for the better, *why* she had changed. I remember Mum used to tell me how high school is just a flash in the pan, and that the popular kids who seem like gods, like they'll always have a blessed life – a lot of the time it's those kids who amount to nothing special.

It's the science geeks who go on to develop life-saving medicines, the tech-heads who run huge Silicon Valley companies, the quiet introverts who become authors and artists. She said high school is a boiling pot of hormones and social anxiety and the best people in life always take longer to find themselves. I guess Kate took that bit longer. Mum too.

Autumn came running to the door, hiding behind Kate's legs when she saw me.

'Hello, Autumn,' I said, crouching down to her height. 'I got you something.'

I pulled a shell from my pocket. I'd spent an hour on the beach earlier searching for the perfect one. I'd had a few good options, but I was sure this one was pretty special. It was a perfect scallop shell – a rarity as they're usually chipped and broken. This one was whole and perfect and shiny on the inside. I held it out to her. She peeped out from behind Kate's legs, and when she saw it she couldn't resist, her podgy little hand grabbing it straight away.

'Wow. What do you say, Autumn?' Summer prompted, appearing from the kitchen.

'Thank you,' Autumn said, already running off with her treasure.

'I'll leave you to it.' Kate gave Summer a little rub on the back. 'Please send my love to your family, Jessie.'

There was a brief pause after she had gone. Summer and I looked at each other, trying to gauge where we were at. She didn't look angry. She looked like herself.

'Hey,' I said, my nervousness and jangly insides returning. 'Can we talk?'

'Sure,' Summer said, grabbing a coat and closing the door behind her.

We walked down to the concrete sea-wall next to the café, sitting down and dangling our legs over the side. I wished we were on the sand so I could run my fingers through it, or that I had a hot chocolate to hold – anything to fiddle with and focus on.

'I'm sorry,' she said, catching me entirely off guard.

Hang on. Wasn't it me who was supposed to be apologising?

'For what?' I asked.

'For the crappy text messages. I thought you went to that party to chase after Libby and try and get in with the in-crowd. And that you'd lied to me about not wanting to go in the first place.'

'That's *so* not why I went.'

'I know. I get that now. You were genuinely trying to help Libby.' She took a deep breath. 'I'd heard on the Queen Vic grapevine that Callum was trying to set you up and I did try to warn you, without saying as much. But I should've just told you – I'm such an idiot. I didn't want to upset you for no reason. I figured you didn't need to know if you weren't going – which, by the way, you told me you weren't.'

'I know, I'm sorry – I totally wasn't, but then Libby messaged. Was Libby in on it?'

'She says not. Apparently, he was raging that Libby broke up with him and blamed you. Persuaded her to give it another shot, then used her phone to message you to tell you to come.

And of course you didn't know they were back together as you were off school.'

'Wow. What a dick.'

'Dick on steroids. She's broken up with him for real now, so she says. Although I'm pretty sure everything that comes out of her mouth is a lie.'

I thought back to our chat in the bathroom, how sincere Libby had seemed. And how confused and hurt and fed up.

'I think she's a bit . . . lost,' I said. 'And unhappy. She's so used to seeing other girls as competition, she doesn't even think twice about it now. But deep down, underneath the meanness and the bitchy front, I really do think there's something decent to salvage.'

'OK, now you're sounding like a Disney movie. A feminist Disney movie, if there is such a thing.'

I shrugged, knowing that I probably wasn't going to convince Summer. Their history went deep. 'Just a theory,' I said. 'Sadie's totally a lost cause though, obvs.'

'Hell yeah. No Girl Code, morals *or* ethics there.'

'Just a blank, sheep-like space.'

'Your Mother Theresa mask is slipping there.'

'You're right,' I said. 'Maybe we shouldn't write Sadie off either. That makes us as bad. Maybe she deserves the benefit of the doubt.'

'Hmm, that might be a step too far.'

We sat, legs dangling, basking in the glow of the sun which had broken out from under a cloud.

'What are you going to do about school?' Summer said at last. 'The rumour doing the rounds is that you threw a chair at

Mr Harlston and he had to go to hospital. I'm guessing that's entirely exaggerated though?'

'It's all a bit of a blur to be honest, but there was definitely no chair-throwing involved. In terms of what I'm going to do about school, I actually have a plan – which I need your help with . . .'

CHAPTER THIRTY – SIX

Libby was going to be harder.

I knew Summer was inherently good and kind and would probably understand once I'd explained, but Libby? She was anyone's guess. She'd been hot and cold on me since I'd started here. It was a gamble thinking I could get her on side.

The fact that she'd got back together with Callum didn't bode well. Maybe she still believed I *had* tried it on with him and that I was after her boyfriend (the thought made me want to retch). But there was something about that moment in the toilets that gave me hope, and I was clinging on to that for dear life.

I'd have to face up to the finger-pointing and whispering soon, but there was no way I wanted to be seen near school grounds just yet. I knew she had netball practice, so I waited by the gates, half-hiding in a bush like some kind of cross between a stalker and a spy. The problem would be getting her on her own – Libby was not one for lone-wolfing. And sure enough, when she came down the road, it was with Sadie and Phoebe tagging along. But I had no choice; it was now or pretty much never.

'Hi, Libby,' I said, trying to step out from the bush without seeming too ridiculous. All three of them shrieked. *Oops.* 'Sorry, I didn't mean to . . . Can I talk to you for a minute?'

Sadie looked at me like I was a piece of turd lying on

the pavement, a particularly runny and gross one at that. Phoebe looked amused and ready for a show. And Libby looked . . . uncertain.

'Sure,' she said. 'You guys go ahead.'

'Um, no way am I leaving you with her,' Sadie sneered. 'You don't know what she's capable of. She might use her powers to . . . Oh yeah, that's right, what powers?' She laughed, clearly expecting Libby and Phoebe to join in. They didn't.

'Seriously, Sadie,' Libby said. 'I'm fine, go ahead without me.'

Sadie did not look pleased, but she walked reluctantly off, looking back over her shoulder at us while hissing something to Phoebe.

'Can we walk and talk?' Libby said. 'My dad wants me back in time to go and witness the wonder that is my brother playing hockey.'

'Of course,' I said, feeling the knot in my stomach loosen a bit. This was a good start – she didn't seem on attack mode at least. We started walking down the hill, side by side, and it reminded me of what Mum had said about having difficult conversations while not looking at each other.

'I've been messaging you,' Libby said, surprising me out of my how-do-I-start-this-conversation thoughts. 'On social. You haven't replied.'

'Oh. I . . . I haven't looked at my social media. I came off it after . . . '

'The video. Yeah, I figured. Look, I wanted you to know that I had nothing to do with getting you to go to the party. Callum sent you those messages from my phone, but I wasn't in on it.'

More knot-loosening. Libby wasn't in on it! Yay! A tiny

Summer-like voice in the back of my head suggested she could be lying, but I pushed it away. Why would she lie? She had nothing to gain. Unless there was an even grander scheme to get me I wasn't yet aware of.

'I mean, you totally shouldn't have come to that party,' Libby said. 'Bit of a masochistic move, going into that viper's pit willingly.'

'I thought I was being a good friend. Supporting you. Girl Power and that.'

'Well, clearly you're too nice – and trusting,' she said. There it was – the hint of a smile, a faint chink in the armour.

'What was Callum's plan, anyway?'

'Knowing Callum, probably a vague scheme of getting you drunk and embarrassing you somehow. It's not exactly hard to embarrass a girl publicly these days.'

'Mission accomplished,' I said, feeling like a gullible, naïve fool. And then that thought again, another creeper that had been haunting me since the party. 'Was . . . was Freddie in on it?'

'God no,' she replied, instantly. 'He was furious when he found out – even had a massive showdown with Callum in the canteen the Monday after the party. It was just Callum and his wannabe boy band. I haven't spoken to Callum since.'

'Really?'

'Hell, yeah,' she said, with such assurance and confidence that I wanted to give her a massive hug.

We hit the high street and took a back lane up towards Libby's road. It was busier than usual. We were getting closer to summer and nicer weather. It still wasn't bustling like the city, though. There never seemed to be urgency on the Island, at any time of day – no fast walking, or stressing in a queue, no fixed, grimly determined expressions.

Libby stopped and turned to me. 'Look, I shouldn't have believed Callum when he said you'd kissed him. I think I was just . . . desperate, clinging on to him. I'd wanted to be his girlfriend for so long – like, SO long, since primary school really. He used to be nicer, and funny – but in a decent way, not at everyone else's expense. I hadn't noticed how much he'd changed, or maybe I had but I was ignoring it because I still wanted to be his girlfriend. And I definitely shouldn't have got back together with him. If I hadn't, he wouldn't have got my phone, and you wouldn't have gone to the party.'

Was that an apology that had just come from Libby's mouth? Did she just . . .? Yes. It had definitely been an apology, even though she was clearly trying to pretend it wasn't.

We were nearly at her house. She checked her watch. I felt lighter, giddy even. I gave myself an internal high five – I had been right! Libby *was* decent, underneath all the hard layers of patriarchy-programmed bitch. I didn't want to get ahead of myself, but it felt like we'd totally turned a corner.

'I don't suppose you could get back together with him briefly one last time, could you?' I asked. 'For the greater good.'

CHAPTER THIRTY-SEVEN

'Do you think this will work?' I asked Tabitha.

We were sat in the (very originally named) Beach Café, nervously nursing lattes and jumping slightly every time someone came through the door.

'I really don't know,' she said, hardly taking her eyes off the door.

School had finished half an hour ago, and Tabitha had been here for at least half of that time, having come straight down, so they were due any minute. In my head, I ran through the lines I'd rehearsed to her earlier, channelling Oprah; I figured Oprah would know exactly how to handle this.

'There's no harm in trying,' she said. 'And honestly, I so hope we can pull it off. I know you've never seen them as friends, but they were really good together. I've missed us all hanging out.'

'And how do you feel about Libby? I gather she wasn't always nice to you, either?'

'She wasn't, but I don't know, it was kind of expected that we'd drift apart a bit – we had such different interests. It was more hurtful for Summer because it was so sudden, and they actually did have a lot in common. I just hope you're right about Libby having changed.'

'Me too,' I said, as the door burst open.

'Hey,' Summer said, coming through the door, pulling out a chair and dumping her many bags on the floor.

'Hi!' I said, way too enthusiastically. 'Have a seat.'

She already had.

'I thought you had UN today, Tabs?' She waved a waitress over and ordered a hot chocolate and a piece of chocolate cake.

'I do, I'm missing it.'

'Sorry, what?' Summer said, doing a double-take. 'Wow, you weren't lying when you said it was important, Jessie. Is this to do with the Plan?'

I stared at my mug.

'Kind of,' I said. 'Look, you trust me, yes? Because I want you to know that I've thought about this a lot and I feel absolutely sure this is the right—'

The door went again, and this time Libby walked through. Summer glanced at her, then back to me. Then back to Libby.

'*Really?*' they both said at the same time, giving each other death stares.

'Just hear Jessie out,' Tabitha said.

'No way,' Summer said, standing up.

'Please, don't go,' I said, standing up too. 'Just listen. One minute. Please, both of you, listen for one minute.'

The two sets of other people in the café, both elderly couples who had been sitting in silence, were now staring at us, intrigued at the teenage drama.

'I'll stay,' Libby said, managing, in that amazing way she had, of making it seem like she was winning at a competition no one else had realised was happening. I could see Summer's hackles go up.

'Please,' I said to Summer, using my best puppy-dog eyes.

'Fine,' she said, plonking herself back down. 'You have *one* minute.'

'OK,' I said. 'The thing is – I really like you both. I think you are both awesome, in your own ways. We've brought you here today because we need you *both* for the Plan to work. But aside from that, Tabitha has told me what great friends you used to be – even *you've* told me what great friends you used to be, Summer.' She grunted at that. 'And I *know* that you two should be friends again. You should all be friends again – I can feel it in my gut.'

'You need to take something for that,' Summer muttered. Libby shot her a look.

'I get that you guys have a history and I'm just sweeping in as a newbie and know nothing about it and I totally think you two need to have a chat on your own to work through some things, but at the end of the day, that's the past. People change. All of us change, one way or another.'

'You got that right,' Summer again. I'd never seen her this snappy, which made me think her feelings really had been hurt. Which *also* meant she really had been good friends with Libby, and that was worth fighting for.

'When I was in Year Eight,' I said, 'I used to listen to Justin Bieber, watch Blue Peter, wear crop tops and think the greatest thing that could happen in the world would be One Direction getting back together.'

'Really?' they all said at the same time, laughing. That was good.

'Yes! My point is, that it's practically a lifetime ago – teenage years are dog years like that. I know it's hard, especially when people feel hurt, but you have to find a way to work through the things that happened in the past – when we were all different versions of ourselves – rather than holding on to them. What you *really* need to hold on to is that you were friends – *good* friends. You grew up together, you made memories.'

'Not all of them good,' Summer said.

'OK, but you had a friendship and, knowing both of you, I think it was a friendship worth trying to save. Or resuscitate. Apart from anything else, we're going to be spending a fair bit of time together on what I've got planned, and it's not good for anyone to have bad energy hanging over them. I need all of you, and I need all of us to work as a team.' I looked at them expectantly, trying to read the room, feeling like I'd just delivered some Nonna-worthy wisdom.

Summer made a vaguely affirmative noise.

'But more than that,' I continued, 'and this is the big one, bear with me – we're girls and we need to stick together. Boys, school, society – they'll take every opportunity to turn us against each other, to make competition when there is none, to make us feel like one girl's success is at the cost of another girl's failure, like there's limited space we need to fight over and it can't be like that. We need to stick together, to support each other, to be allies – not enemies.'

I took a breath, feeling like I'd just word-vomited up a Model UN speech, hoping it had hit the mark. Tabitha smiled at me but I couldn't gauge Libby or Summer's reactions from their faces. They were just sitting, perfectly still, staring at me.

'Um, that's it. That's what I wanted to say.'

'OK,' Summer said, matter-of-factly. 'That all makes sense to me.'

'Sure,' Libby agreed. 'You make some good points. I'll give it a shot.'

'So . . . you'll try?' Tabitha asked, sounding shocked.

'We'll try,' they both confirmed.

'Really?' I said. 'I was expecting more . . . resistance.'

They shrugged.

'Amazing!' I said, feeling ecstatic, like I'd won some kind of prize, which I guess I kind of had. 'Group hug?'

'Don't get ahead of yourself,' Libby grunted. 'Let's get back to the Plan.'

CHAPTER THIRTY — EIGHT

'Knock knock.' Bella walked straight in, as usual without waiting for a response, carrying her enormous make-up bag.

I'd just put my uniform back on for the first time in a week. I shouldn't have been wearing it – I was excluded from school and Mum was in talks with them and the council. But it was the only way of getting into the building unnoticed.

'I know it's not usually your thing,' Bella said, lifting her bag, 'but I thought I'd see if you wanted any war paint? I do a good natural look – proper natural, not obscene-contouring and layers-of-foundation natural.'

She looked so open and genuine and like the old Bella that I didn't have the heart to say no. 'Sure, thanks. Just a bit though.'

The smile she gave me was worth it. She set about opening her many-levelled bag and laying everything out meticulously – I'd never seen so many different pots and brushes and make-up implements. She positioned me on the edge of my bed, getting a small ring light out. Dave wound round my legs reassuringly.

'Just relax,' Bella said, wiping some kind of cream under my eyes. 'Maybe try not to squeeze your eyes shut?'

'Sorry,' I said, trying really hard not to.

'How're you feeling about today?'

'Like I might throw up,' I said, acknowledging the seasickness in my stomach. 'And shit myself at the same time.'

'Ew, Jessie!'

'You asked.'

'Well, *I* think you're very brave,' she said, moving on to a new ointment. 'You're standing up for yourself, and others, and I think it's great.'

'Who are you and what have you done with my sister?'

'Ha ha. Sit still.'

'Anyway, you're the brave one. You talk to thousands of people all the time with your videos. Today will be nothing compared to that.'

'But that's an anonymous audience. I don't have to see their faces. Why do you think I went into it in the first place?'

'What do you mean?'

'My YouTube channel. It's my way of hiding in plain sight.'

'But – but that doesn't make sense!'

Bella paused, put down a pot, picked up a brush, stood back and looked at me. 'For someone so clever, you can be a bit stupid sometimes. I started getting into make-up in Year Eight when my skin was awful. I was getting teased, badly. I had days when I didn't want to go into school at all. Anyway, I started experimenting with foundation and concealer – anything to hide my spots. It just kind of grew from there. And now it's my war paint – an outer layer between the real me and the one the world sees.'

'How did I not notice that?'

'Because you're so wrapped up in yourself you don't ever consider anyone else?' she suggested, not unkindly. I gave her a friendly elbow. 'Hey, careful, you don't want me to smudge,' she chided.

'So I guess we've both been hiding, but in different ways?'

'There it is – she gets it!'

'Well, your way has turned out pretty well for you. Popularity, freebies, money . . .'

'Yeah, but, you know, it comes with its own problems. I do love it, but it's not always plain sailing. Some of the comments people leave, honestly – it's scary. People like that should lose their internet privileges and be made to do some kind of trolling rehabilitation programme.'

'Speak it, sista!'

'You're such a tool.'

'Love you too.'

'But look, what I wanted to say, in all seriousness, is that I admire you for putting yourself out there. And I know you'll smash it today.'

She stood back, downing tools, taking me in with a critical eye.

'Done,' she said, handing me a mirror. 'Battle-ready.'

I prepared myself for a virtual-reality, inch-thick-make-up me that I would somehow have to wipe off without causing offence, but when I looked in the mirror, I saw me looking back. A healthy-looking, radiant me – alert and wide-eyed and ready.

'Thank you,' I said, giving Bella a hug. 'Love you.'

'Who are you and what have you done with my sister?' she asked, squeezing me tightly back.

***

'There she is!' Mum said as Bella and I came into the kitchen.

The builders had already started with the hammering and shouting and Handy Andy was sat at the table with Mum having a cup of tea.

'Morning,' I said. 'Hi, Andy.' He looked grateful to be acknowledged, which made me feel guilty for being so ice-cold to him before.

'Hi, Jessie,' he said, smiling and standing up. 'I'll leave you all to it.'

'I'll come and find you with those tap samples later,' Mum said, a silly grin on her face. 'Right, what inspiring power breakfast can I get you ladies?'

Images of burnt toast and frazzled bacon filled my head. 'I might just grab a bowl of cereal,' I said.

'Oh no you don't,' Nonna said, coming in from her annexe. 'I've made you a power remedy. A powerful remedy for a most powerful witch.'

'God, here we go,' Bella said, teasing. 'Way to hog the family limelight, Jessie.'

'Ugh. I mean – yum?' I said, as Nonna handed a mug to me, her eyes gleaming, bangles still jingling defiantly. She was looking better every day, more like Nonna. The steam from the mug wafted up my nose and I had to resist the urge to gag.

'Trust me, drink it up,' she said, winking. 'And after I may have some monkey bread for you.'

I did as I was told, holding my nose to swallow it down.

'How are you feeling about today?' Mum said, putting her arm around me and kissing the top of my head. 'Are you sure you don't want me there?'

'Are you sure you don't want *us* there?' Nonna amended.

Mum gave her a glare that said there was no way she was letting her leave the house.

'I'm feeling nervous,' I said, in the spirit of honesty. 'And yes, I'm sure I don't want any of you there. I've got the people I need, hopefully. But thanks for the offer.'

'Even if it doesn't go the way you're hoping, know that we're very proud of you,' Mum said.

'Know that you're doing it for the right reasons and it *needs* to be done,' Bella added. 'And remember, you're the baddest-ass witch around.'

'Honestly, don't be such worrywarts,' Nonna said. 'She'll be fine. Better than fine. Go get 'em, Jessie. Go kick some patriarchal arse.'

Five Things About My Family:
1. They're sometimes (often) annoying, but 99 times out of 100 it's because they love me.
2. They've known me the longest and they know me the best, sometimes (often) better than I know myself.
3. They ALWAYS have my best interests at heart.
4. They will ALWAYS be there for me.
5. No matter how I sometimes (often) feel about them, I'm tied to them for life, so I may as well take comfort in Points 3 and 4 and enjoy them.

CHAPTER THIRTY-NINE

Summer and Tabitha were waiting for me by the seafront.

'Got everything?' Summer asked, as we fell into step.

'Think so.'

'Computer?' Tabitha said.

'Yep.'

'USB for back up?'

'Yep.'

'A ball-load of courage and determination?' Summer said.

'Not sure about that one,' I said, feeling my brave leak out of me a bit.

'You'll be fine, we've got your back,' she said. 'Worst case, what can they do to you? You're already excluded, and we're in 2021, it's not like the male population are going to band together and burn you at the stake. They might video it and put that out somewhere, but you're used to that.' She chuckled.

'True, true and true,' I said, inwardly wincing at how close to the mark she was with the burning at the stake comment.

The sea was glorious that morning. Sparkly and fresh and gently slurping at the shore. No harsh, angry crashing and not a tinge of grey in sight – just calm and silently powerful. The whole town felt different – awake, alive, new. For once, I didn't hate it.

'You sure she's coming?' Summer asked, as we rounded the corner by the school gates.

'She texted this morning to say she was. And why wouldn't she? She's done the hard work already, you'd think she'd want to see the grand reveal.'

'Uh, mate, I think the hard work is going to be standing up in front of the entire school and exposing an uncomfortable truth.'

'She'll be there,' I said, confidently, ignoring the reminder of what I was going to do.

We'd arranged to meet Libby in my 'office', aka, the toilet on the quad. It seemed a natural fit seeing as it was where I had spent a large proportion of my time at school, where I had first met Summer and Tabitha, and where I'd had the detention bonding session with Libby.

I'd wanted a code word we could use at some point in the operation (though I had no idea what we'd need one for). Summer had told me I was being overly dramatic, but if I really wanted we could call the whole thing Operation Sleazebag Shake-down, which was good enough for me.

We'd arranged the meeting for slightly before school started to avoid the mass entry. But, forced to do some people-dodging so as not to be spotted, Summer, Tabitha and I got to the toilet rendezvous five minutes past our meeting time at 8.50. There was no one in there. My heart did a dive.

'Libby?' I said, into the ether. Summer stood there with an expression that bordered (surprisingly) more on disappointed than *I told you so*. I looked at my phone; no text messages. We could still do it without her, but it would have been helpful to have her on side.

A horrible thought came to me – what if Libby had completely turncoated and was about to sell us out? What if it had all been a big double cross? The seasickness came back. I couldn't even look at Summer.

'Sorry, sorry.' Libby stormed in the door, flustered. 'I got held up, everyone's buzzing, it's crazy out there!'

I nearly cried with relief, and when I snuck a look at Summer, I saw that she was sporting an enormous grin. Libby stared at us impatiently.

'Well? Have you seen the post?' she asked.

'What post?' Tabitha asked.

'Agh, I forgot, you guys are social media deniers.' She rolled her eyes. 'Here, look.' She ushered us into the end cubicle (my personal favourite) and got her phone out to show us.

It was Freddie's Snapchat. Libby tapped on his story with all the excitement of someone opening a present on Christmas Day.

A few things I'm setting straight.
1. *Jessie and I were joking around that night about her being a witch. OBVIOUSLY.*
2. *That video was totally edited. And . . .*
3. *I saw Callum kiss Jessie all those weeks ago – totally unprovoked and uninvited.*

#stopthewitchhunt

I blinked to refocus my eyes and my brain, to try and process what I'd just seen, the words floating behind my eyelids. Freddie had *seen* Callum kiss me? Why hadn't he said anything before?

Anger rose up, but alongside it was joy. He had spoken up now, at least. Better late than never I guess. Maybe he'd reached his limit after all.

'Trust me,' Libby said, delighted, 'his Snapchat is usually all football scores and lads' nights out – this is a big deal.'

'I don't know how that makes me feel,' I said.

'Validated?' Tabitha said.

'A bit. But won't he lose his friends now, because of me?' As much as I appreciated Freddie standing up for me, I didn't want anyone to have to experience the hounding I'd been subjected to.

'He would have known the risks when he posted it,' Libby said. 'Honestly, I've seen it coming for a while. Freddie's never been the same as that lot, he just plays along most of the time.' She grinned. 'We played Seven Minutes in Heaven once in Year Nine and all the other boys tried it on when they made it into the cupboard, but Marie said that Freddie just wanted to chat. He would've stood up for himself eventually, this just gave him a little nudge. That's a *good* thing, don't look so downcast.'

Tabitha gave me a little rub on the back and a reassuring smile. Maybe Libby was right and Freddie would have done this anyway. Long live the revolution.

'OK, let's recap the plan,' I said, aware that time was slipping away. 'Libby, you keep Marcus and Callum and any other football minions out of the way. Summer, you get ready to record the whole thing. And Tabs, you find Ms Simmons and tell her this is the final version of the film, that the one she has is an old version.' I felt bad lying to Ms Simmons, but I knew she'd understand. At least, I hoped she would.

'What if she says it's too late to change it?' asked Tabitha. That could be a disaster.

'If you have to, tell her the truth,' I said. 'She'll get it, I think.'

'You *think* or you know?' Summer pressed. 'Because really this whole thing rests on her.'

'I know,' I said, with more confidence than I felt. 'But we have our Plan B, if needed.'

'Plan A is much better though,' Libby said. 'Putting it online is . . . risky.'

'So let's make the A-plan work then,' I said. 'End of term assembly is after registration, so we should be on at about 9.10. Text me once you've spoken to her and I'll come for the big show.'

'OK,' Tabitha said, her expression serious and set.

The bell rang, loud and proud. It felt like a call to action. My stomach did a three-somersault, twisting-tuck dive.

'Here, quick,' I said, grabbing the laptop case out of my bag and handing it to her. 'It's already open so you should just need to press play, but any problems, it's saved in iMovies as #hastostop.'

'Still think you should've gone with #FreeJessie,' Summer said.

'Quick group hug?' I said as second bell went, opening my arms the short distance the cubicle allowed. They edged in, reluctantly. 'We've got this,' I said, trying for enthusiasm, 'and if nothing else, if it all goes horrendously, end-of-the-world wrong, we've got each other.'

Summer rolled her eyes at me. 'I'm not sure you've quite mastered the inspirational pep talk.'

'Good luck,' I called after them as they left the cubicle, off on their mission, out into the big wide world. I'm pretty sure I saw a conspiratorial little shoulder nudge between Summer and Libby, and that in itself made my heart sing a bit, like a proud mum.

***

If I could have paced, I would have, but there wasn't enough room in the cubicle. As it was, my nervous energy had no outlet, so it just zinged around me like a fast-flying ball on that old-skool tennis game.

I tried meditation again, thinking now was as good a time as any, but, as before, all trying to clear out my mind did was open up a bigger space for more thoughts to come bulldozing in. I thought of what Summer had said – *Worst case, what can they do to you?* – and how really, in the grand scheme of things, it couldn't be anything that bad. I was fully prepared for a future of social media Armageddon and a lifetime of home-schooling. I'd still have Summer and Tabitha and Libby – we could meet in private, to protect them from being tainted by my stigma; I could live vicariously through them. Eventually I would learn to accept my life as a hermit and be grateful for the company of Mum and Nonna and Dave (Bella would be off somewhere exciting, being all successful and socially acceptable).

It felt like I had waited an eternity, but when I looked at my phone it was only 9.08. Tabitha should've spoken to Ms Simmons by now. Just as I thought that, a text came through:

S not here! People saying she resigned. And no USB in the laptop case!! Can't escape to get back to u, Metcalfe herding us into the hall now. Computer under a pile of papers on side of room 201. Get the USB to me before our group goes on!!

Oh bugger. Bugger, bugger, bugger.

I checked my bag and there was the USB stick. I had forgotten to put it with the laptop! Of all the rookie mistakes to make, this one seemed too stupid. I was so angry at myself.

Bad. Bad, bad.

But it was fine. All fine. I just needed to get it to Tabitha before she went into the hall. Which was . . . now.

I opened the cubicle door, clutching the USB, my hands shaking like I'd caned a crate of Red Bull. I didn't trust my legs to keep me upright. The corridors were eerily quiet and the sound of my uncertain footsteps rebounded off the walls. I glanced down towards the hall, where a few stragglers were wearily shuffling in. The door closed behind them. I looked around for Tabitha, hoping she'd managed to slip away somehow, but she wasn't anywhere to be seen. I heard Mr Harlston's reedy voice, muffled through the door, telling everyone to settle down. Damn! I was too late.

I had no idea how to get the USB to Tabitha or on to the projector.

Then it came to me like a cartoon light bulb idea – I needed to blend in, which I'm a total champion at. I was wearing my uniform for exactly that reason – not being noticed. What if I just . . . walked out on stage with the rest of my group? Mr Harlston always leaves the hall after the introductions and he would be the only one who would know for certain that I wasn't supposed to be there.

I didn't even need much time, just long enough to get me to the stage and get the USB to Tabitha. Aside from freezing time or bewitching the whole school (which I had no idea how to do anyway), this was the only option I had.

Whatever happened next, I was going to have the whole school staring at me, one way or another, and I needed to get used to that idea, even though right now all I wanted to do was flee back to the bathroom, lock myself back up in my cubicle and assume the foetal position. My phone beeped again, this time a message from Bella:

Good luck. Sending you power vibes.

I suddenly wished I *had* asked them to come, to support me. I don't think I'd ever wanted to see Bella's face more than I did right then. But it was too late. I was flying solo.

Come on, Jessie, you've got this. Greater good, Girl Power, Vive la Révolution.

I could hear the hum of the assembly – everyone quieter now, Mr Harlston whining into the microphone.

I stood outside the doors, waiting. There were small glass windows in each door that I dared not peer through yet, but I knew they'd dim the lights for the media presentations soon and that would be my chance to sneak in.

I caught snippets of Mr Harlston's rambling introduction:

'The Media students have all worked so hard to capture the . . . the uh . . . important issues facing young people today . . .'

It should have been Ms Simmons up there – and I knew for a fact she would have been doing a much better job of it. I heard the first group get up from their seats and traipse dutifully to the stage. Someone – Bianca maybe? – gave a heartfelt speech about why they had chosen the environment as their subject.

Finally, I saw the lights dim and heard their piece start playing, a muffled blur of words coming from beyond the door. Even if I'd been in the hall, I don't think I would have heard a word over the loud pounding of my heart. A door from the back of the hall crashed open into the corridor I was standing in. It must be Mr Harlston leaving. I moved a few steps to my left as silently as I could, crouching behind the water fountain, closing my eyes like a toddler playing hide-and-seek – *if I can't see you, you can't see me*.

Luckily, the Head's office was in the other direction and I heard his shoes click-clack their way towards it, away from me. A wave of bored clapping came from the hall, the first group's video obviously finished. I chanced peering in the small glass window, trying to make out shapes in the dimmed light, searching for my girls. A group of students from the front row stood up and began walking towards the stage. One tall, beefy shape – all swagger and strut – stood out instantly. Marcus. This was it. My chance.

I tried to swallow, my tongue lying fat and heavy in my mouth like a beached whale. The closest door to the stage was the one I was already standing at, but once in the hall, I would have to walk past the row of teachers peppered against the wall. I had no choice though.

Taking a deep breath, I waited until Marcus, Tom, Harry and Tabitha were nearly at the stage and then slipped in through the door, falling into step behind Tabitha with as much certainty and purpose as I could muster. She climbed the steps to the stage, turned her head slightly, barely perceptibly, and gave me a tiny smile. From the audience, I felt the glances, the double-takes, the teachers murmuring to each other, questioning, and the Mexican wave of realisation among the students. But I kept my eyes fixed ahead of me.

Marcus was already up on the stage, playing to his crowd, assuming (I was sure) that the increase in attention and the excitement in the air was down to his presence. It kept him occupied, and that was fine with me. I scuttled up the stairs behind Tabitha, trying to shield myself slightly behind the edge of curtain to the side. She put her hand out behind her, taking the USB like a relay baton, and let me retreat into the shadows. The rest of the group took their places on the seats set up for them on the stage.

'The latest version is on here,' she said assuredly to the supply teacher, holding out the USB stick.

The teacher looked confused. 'But they're supposed to all be on here . . .' she said, pointing at the computer screen.

I saw Summer a few rows back, on high alert, phone at the ready. She caught my eye and gave me a nod.

'What's *she* doing here?' Marcus said, noticing me for the first time.

We had to move fast. I inched closer to the computer.

'It's rude,' Tabitha blurted out to the supply teacher. 'That one you've got. It . . . there are some swear words on there and Ms Simmons says you can't show it.'

The teacher hesitated. I took her pause as an opportunity and gently moved her out of the way, taking the USB from Tabitha and sticking it in the laptop

'Thank you,' I whispered to Tabitha.

I am not, in any way, good with computers, and my hands were shaking so much I could barely drag the mouse. As I did, I looked up, and saw Coach standing out of his seat. He was frowning and squinting, as though unsure whether it was me. He took a step towards the stage.

I felt sick. Like, I-might-actually-throw-up-all-over-this-computer sick.

'Coach,' I heard a low voice say. Freddie. He was standing right in front of Coach, blocking his way. 'Mr Harslton said he wanted to see you, urgently.'

Coach paused for a second but then took the bait and stomped off purposefully in the direction of the office.

Nice one, Freddie. A fake summons wasn't going to stop Coach for ever, but I didn't need long. I prayed to the witches, to all that was good and magic and right. *Please let this work.* I took a deep breath and carefully dragged the file again, dropping it squarely in the centre of the video player.

It loaded and a 'play' button appeared.

I pressed it. No going back now.

My face came up on the screen. And the recording of me began speaking, my voice ringing out clear and calm.

'For this project we were asked to make a film about an issue that is important to young people today, something that we feel strongly about, an area in which we don't feel our voices are being heard.

Our film is about the appalling way girls are treated. Still. Every day. Especially at Queen Victoria Academy. I wish we hadn't needed to make this particular film, that it was something we didn't still need to highlight or talk about, but sadly that's not the case.

People say that there's no need for feminism any more or that we've achieved equal rights or that feminists are just bitter man-haters, but the truth, as you'll see, is that we still live in a society where girls are valued less than boys, where they're judged largely by their appearance, treated like property, and worse.

When we started this project, we didn't know how many stories there were, or how many people would be willing to come forward and share theirs, but once we started asking and word spread, we had so many we couldn't fit them all in.

Let's start with mine.'

The kerfuffle was instant from the minute the video started playing – excited murmurs, chairs scraping, phones out recording, a surge of interest. I focused on the audience. The teachers mostly looked confused, unsure whether this was the actual project. They started to consult with each other, and one sceptical-looking male teacher left, probably in search of Mr Harlston. The girls were shushing people around them, grinning at each other. A girl near the back even called out, '*Yas Queen!*'

The boys looked less sure – some looked uncomfortable, some angry, and some seemed to be finding it hilarious, including, of course, Callum Henderson. I didn't need to search him out; he was the centre of attention as always, sitting loud and proud in the middle of the room, a smug grin on his face, patting the backs of boys around him, fist pumping, laughing out loud.

If Coach got wind something fishy was going down and came back with Mr Harlston before the end of the video, they'd shut it off for sure. I knew we had limited time.

The photos Summer had insisted we take of my vandalised locker were up on the screen.

'But it didn't stop there. There was more specific and targeted harassment to come — including using another girl's phone to invite me to a party, spiking my drink with alcohol at that party, filming me without my consent and cutting together footage that was then spread over social media.'

Summer had come up to the side of stage and was standing beside me, squeezing my hand. Tabitha was the other side of me. I felt stronger with them there, like I had stepped into a suit of armour. I caught Libby's eye from the side of the hall, she gave me a thumbs up and a big grin. I gestured for her to come up and join us.

'Well done!' Summer whispered. 'You did it.'

'But look at them,' I said. 'The boys — they don't care, some of them are laughing!'

'Oh, they'll care in a minute,' Summer said darkly.

'We've all known about the scoring system for ages,' Tabitha was saying from the screen. I was so proud of her. It was totally out of her comfort zone to do this, but she had stepped up. *'The whole school has known about the scoring system, and no one does anything about it.'* She held up the piece of paper Callum had drawn the pizza face on. *'This is just one instance of it, but there have been many.'*

I looked around the hall. The teachers were looking much more uneasy now, but also rapt and concerned. No one was making a move to stop us.

Georgia Wells was speaking now.

'I complained to Mr Harlston. He said it's just "boys being silly" and he'd talk to them, but that I should just ignore it.'

Bryony Tate now.

'I told Coach about the boys leaving notes in our lockers with scores on. He said he would deal with it. But he didn't.'

Me again. Footage of me walking through the playground, paper planes landing at my feet. Footage that Libby had persuaded Sadie to forward to her.

'Coach witnessed an incident where I was harassed by boys throwing paper aeroplanes at me with scores on and did nothing to stop it.'

And then it was Libby's turn. The real Libby stepped onto the stage and squeezed my hand as the screen-Libby started talking.

'Here is the WhatsApp group, started by Callum Henderson, called "Stat Chat" and, as you can see, they discuss at length what scores girls should have according to their looks, breast size, and how likely they are to let you hook up with them. Here are just a few examples:

Callum: Deffo a seven with a rack like that
Marcus: Eight I reckon
Eli: Nah, too frigid – never wears low-cut tops
Harry: Putting her down to a three, didn't let me put my hand up her top
Callum: Dude, epic fail! But good news, L let me get to second base – up to a six!'

I felt Libby cringe next to me. I was so grateful to her for being brave enough to get the proof from Callum's phone and (more specifically) for letting us use the bits that mentioned her. I knew it wasn't easy. The WhatsApp group chat was long and demeaning and disgusting and part of me hated giving those words any more air, but it had to be done, and I think we all knew that.

On-screen Libby continued.

'Teachers were repeatedly told about this scoring system and failed to stop it or even punish the boys involved. Shockingly, we have footage of a teacher participating it in himself.'

At that very moment, the door at the back of the hall swung open with force and Mr Harlston came storming through, closely followed by Coach, closely followed by the (male) teacher I'd seen scurry out of the hall earlier. Their faces looked a satisfying mix of angry, horrified and ashen. The footage on-screen now was the out-takes from the original interview with Coach. I'd made myself watch that tape through to the end. And it had got even worse.

'What's Miss Jones on now then? Does verbally assaulting a teacher get her a higher or lower score in your books?'

'When you're the teacher, lower for sure. What do we reckon, boys, shall we put her on a minus five? Better check with Callum.'

'You lads'll get me in trouble one of these days, but yeah, go minus five. Update me, then. Libby? Still a six? Sounds about right . . .'

And on it went. The boys reading out the stats and Coach laughing, sometimes agreeing or adding comments. Never reprimanding, never telling them to stop. Participating.

Coach and Mr Harlston were on the stage now, red-faced and panicking, desperately pulling at the leads of the laptop and shouting at the terrified supply teacher to make it stop. It didn't matter what they did now anyway, I'd sent the video to the *County Press*, the school governors and the council. We had proof, he had not a leg to stand on.

All the same, I wanted the video to finish. I wanted everyone – especially the boys – to watch it to the end. Coach eventually just ripped the leads out, the laptop crashing on the floor, his face twisted and pulsating. He was breathing hard.

The video stopped.

I had been determined not to use magic, but now I had no choice. And this time, it really was for the greater good.

I focused, breathed. I thought of everything Nonna had taught us about using our energy, feeling our power. I used my anger, rather than letting it use me. I didn't want the chaos from Mr Harlston's office. I needed precision and control.

Focus, deep breath, channel, release.

The video started back up again.

***

When I first came up with the idea for the video, I'd been worried there wouldn't be enough material, that it would end up being mainly me moaning. But once we started asking for contributors, we were inundated.

There were testimonies from pretty much every girl we'd approached and then once word got out, people started coming to us, desperate to tell their story. There was the everyday, wear-you-down stuff: boys speaking over girls; ignoring them in a group setting; teachers dismissing their contributions in favour of a boy's opinion; tasks being divided based on gender, with girls being assigned admin-based roles and boys getting the important tasks.

Mansplaining, manspreading, manterrupting – boys and men taking up more than their fair share of space in every way possible. Then, of course, there were the other stories: girls being kissed – or worse – against their wishes; pictures of them being shared on social media, without permission; girls being slut-shamed for doing what boys are celebrated for; girls being spoken about like pieces of meat, or property; girls being judged solely on what they looked like, their physical 'assets'. None of this was unexpected, we lived it with it every day. But what was surprising was the extent of it, the far and wide reach. It had touched every girl in school. And when I'd explained what we were planning, they were all on board, all keen to find a way to make a change, together.

The hall was on fire. Everyone had phones out recording, talking, shouting, buzzing. Some members of staff – all male – were on their feet, attempting to calm the room. The female teachers, I noticed, were sitting perfectly still.

'In conclusion, we have identified there is deep-rooted, institutional misogyny and sexist behaviour in this school, within both the student and teaching bodies. It is directly impacting the lives of hundreds of female students and affecting their educational experience. It must change and it must change now.'

The screen went to black and there was applause – slow and steady and a bit uncertain at first, then gaining in strength, and finally, hard and frantic. There was a standing ovation by most of the girls (and to be fair, some of the boys). Mr Harlston was trying, ineptly, to restore order, looking like he was about to explode. Many of the boys were sat there, stunned, wondering if they were implicated, if they were going to have to pay for this.

I sought out Callum, longing to see the look of shame and horror he must be wearing by now. But when my eyes finally found him, he looked exactly the same as always. Nothing had changed – he was still smiling an assured, nothing-can-touch-me smile, that made my skin prickle and my stomach drop.

I wanted, overwhelmingly, to make him pay. If the film hadn't worked, my magic would. I could bring him out in a rash – a permanent one this time. Or I could cut him down to size – literally, take some height off him, so he at least didn't walk quite so tall. I could turn him into a sodding frog. I could . . .

He caught me looking at him and offered me a mocking smile and a salute and in that moment it took all of my energy, every ounce of every part of me, not to magic the shit out of him.

But I didn't. I looked away, knowing that he wasn't worth my magic. I took a breath and I trusted in the universe. One day, somewhere along the line, Callum Henderson would get what he deserved and, for now, what we'd done was enough.

Libby, Summer, Tabitha and I gave each other one more hand squeeze, then readied ourselves to deal with the inevitable fallout. I hoped we'd managed to make a difference, in some small way. But if nothing else, we had each other, and right now that felt like all I needed.

TWO MONTHS LATER

Five Things About Me:

1. I'm a witch, and that's OK. Better than OK, actually – it's pretty damn cool.
2. I'm very intelligent – and I'm especially good at Maths and Science.
3. I'm learning to surf.
4. I make documentaries. I want to study film at uni – somewhere nearby like Southampton or Portsmouth (I want to be close to my family).
5. I still hate black pepper and parsley. Some things never change.

Sometimes I like to think of my life now like a movie montage, played out with a soundtrack. I crank the music up loud; it's a kickass female boss pop playlist, of course. This is what it looks like:

Me, actually wanting to get out of bed of a morning, hating the seagulls slightly less – they're still annoying, and loud and relentless, but their noise doesn't sound like nails on a blackboard to me any more. Me, breezing into the kitchen, which, while still somewhat chaotic, is shaping up into quite a nice space. Me, greeting Mum and Nonna and Bella in the style of a Disney character with birds tweeting round my head.

Nonna, who hardly ever feels the need to waft the bad energy away from me these days, giving me big, squashy bosom hugs and telling me to 'stay true'. (It's a new catchphrase she's working on; I'm not convinced.) She's back to functioning at about eighty-five per cent Nonna capacity and it is such a relief.

Bella and I actually cracking a smile at each other most days, which is new and nice. The day of the Reckoning (that's what we call the film-showing now), she put up a make-up free video about skin problems and how to deal with them, which proved to be her most popular ever and has got her a bazillion more subscribers. I like to credit myself with some of that success.

And Mum, who now has slightly less-dark circles under her eyes, and is normally humming and wiggling her hips to some old-person radio station when I make it downstairs, but always pauses to give me a squeeze. She is truly embracing the kaftan and turban, free-flowing kind of vibe, which makes me wonder how she ever managed in those stiff business suits for all those years. She's reconnected with Kate and the two of them are really making up for lost time – lots of coffees and dinners, art classes, dance classes, yoga classes and deep and meaningfuls. They've even been surfing together, which Summer gave me stick about as Mum braved it before I did.

Mum and Andy are moving towards being an official thing. I still find it hard not to call him Handy for short, and I'm avoiding meeting his bad-taste-in-T-shirts children, but it's hard not to warm to him when I see him and Mum together –

310

being all goofy and loved-up and dancing in the kitchen – and realise how happy he makes her.

The magic is coming along nicely, now that I'm beginning to get to grips with what a magical rarity I am. Nonna's taken me and Bella to a few Island-wide coven meet ups – they're actually a blast and I'm kind of enjoying being treated like a local celebrity in those circles. Bella's very gracious about the fact I have my powers all the time, when she's limited to just having hers on her period – I think she likes that I have my own 'thing' now. Nonna's a great teacher. She's very strong on the whole 'with great power comes great responsibility' message, but I get it now. She's also super patient with us (mainly me), despite numerous 'accidents' – exploding trees, reproducing frogs, purple hair, that kind of thing.

After breakfast, on my way out I feed Chicken – I can't be sure she's Chicky returned but when a solo chicken kept appearing in our garden I had a strong sense it probably was. Then I'm out the door, picking up Summer on the way to school.

The walk into school, through the corridors, is much improved. I don't have the fear of what I might find on my locker, or what people might be saying about me any more. I have more friends, get more smiles.

Of course, there are still some groups of people hunched over phones looking at things online, whispering about someone who did something. The difference now is that it's not acceptable. Or not *as* acceptable, anyway. Mum says it's a bit like smoking – when she was younger everyone smoked because it was the cool thing to do. But now, hardly anyone our age smokes – it's frowned upon and smokers are shunned to cold outside spaces.

311

I get the feeling that's what's slowly happening now with sexism at school – the posting of photos and videos and the general being mean to girls. There are still rumours, and judgements – that's human nature – but more of us are calling people out on it now and refusing to participate in it.

Our Media Studies effort made the front page of the *County Press* (which wasn't a surprise – a sheep crossing a road makes the *County Press*). It also led to a massive overhaul at the school. Mr Harlston resigned with some BS, save-his-arse public statement about how he had not been aware of the level of harassment that was happening in the school, was outraged it had been taking place under his management and, as such, felt he should step down as Head.

Coach was fired.

Ms Simmons (who, it turned out, *had* resigned and complained to the local authority for exactly the reasons our film highlighted) agreed to come back and set up an equality policy and task force. I was allowed back too – after many emails and meetings and agreeing to do an anger management course.

I walk into Maths on my first day back from exclusion with my head held high, taking my seat directly behind Callum Henderson and his overly gelled hair. Oh yeah, he's still here. *Of course* he is. He and Marcus and a few others were suspended and not allowed to return until the internal investigation had been wrapped up – an internal investigation that was led by three men and one woman and cleared by the local MP, Callum's dad. So yes. *Of course* he's back, because that's the way the world works.

Is he humbled? Has he changed? Is he nicer?

Not really. A bit, and not really.

He managed to ride the waves of notoriety and make it work for him. He's not as open about being a dick, and he has less friends who just want to bathe in his light, regardless of what he does, but he still walks around with that innate arrogance. He may stay that way for ever, never change, end up a CEO of some important company, or even Prime Minister.

Or maybe, just maybe, people along the way (people like me) will chip away at him, bit by bit, and one day he'll finally see the error of his ways. It's doubtful, but you have to have hope. Because otherwise what's the point?

Baby steps, that's what I tell myself. Things *have* gotten better: the acting Head has established a genuine zero-tolerance policy for sexist behaviour; fewer people are making sexist comments about girls; no one is posting pictures they shouldn't be on social media; boys like Callum are less loud and proud; and boys like Freddie have found their voice and personalities and aren't following the herd quite so much. More importantly, there's less competition among the girls. We're standing together, and that kind of feels like the biggest victory of all.

I put my hand up in Maths, not caring if people know I'm clever and capable. Freddie catches my eye and smiles – I'll see him later.

I sit with Summer and Tabitha at lunch. Libby joins us pretty often, and sometimes even Sadie and Phoebe come too. We talk about lessons, and coursework, and weekends, about how Phoebe's auditioning for the musical, and when we should get together to help her run lines. We congratulate Sadie for getting a distinction in her Textiles coursework, and Tabitha for her blossoming writing career. Summer and I make plans to go surfing again at the weekend, something I'm embracing now the weather is warmer (and when I say embracing, I mean 'finding more bearable'). We talk and support and moan and cry and joke and laugh.

And, when no one's watching, I magic my pizza into something edible. There have to be perks, after all.

AUTHOR'S NOTE

Though it's wrapped in some jokes, at the heart of this book is an important issue. We are living in a very worrying time for women. Our reproductive rights are being threatened, domestic violence against women is rising, the number of reported rapes is rising, while the number of those successfully charged is down and that is just scratching the surface. In a world where the Prime Minister refuses to openly acknowledge how many children he's fathered and a man who openly boasted about grabbing women's genitals was elected president, it's easy to see how this disregard and dismissal of women and women's experiences is reinforced.

I'm amazed that some people ask if we still need feminism and my answer to those people is always the same – a big, resounding, YES, YES, WE DO. And if this book helps even one girl stand up and call out unacceptable sexist behaviour then I will be one very happy feminist.

Sadly, we aren't all blessed with Jessie's magical powers (much as I would LOVE to make a boy's nose grow every time he lied), but there are still lots of things we can do. At the back of the book are some brilliant people doing brilliant things and some brilliant resources – please do check them out – and luckily, this is also just scratching the surface.

ACKNOWLEDGEMENTS

It feels so unbelievably surreal to be sat writing actual acknowledgements after the many years of writing would-be ones in my head. Unbelievably surreal and amazing!

First and foremost I have to thank my brilliant, talented, insightful and all-round fabulous writing group, The Flugels – Catherine Coe, Claire Wetton and Zoe Boyd-Clack. Thank you for reading that first one so many times you forgot your own names and for reading everything I have sent your way since, thank you for telling me, kindly, when it was probably time to move on and for always encouraging me to keep going. Thank you for not losing your patience with my endless texts and wobbles, for reassuring me the bijillion times I needed it and for making me laugh. Your generosity and love and support are astounding and I know for a fact this book would never have happened without you. Here's to many more 'writing retreats' full of laughs and strange drinks and slightly creepy strangers who are good for anecdotes.

Thank you to my first writing group, The Black Sheep Writers – Barbara Mackie, Crispin Keith, Jo King and Jan Carr. You gave me the confidence to read my work out loud and the idea that it might be something worth pursuing. And oh, how I loved those starter pieces! Special thanks to Cath Ouston for suggesting I go along to the writing group in the first place and to Jan for pointing me in the direction of SCBWI.

And what a direction it was! SCBWI (Society of Children's Book Writers and Illustrators) – where to start?! What an absolute dream of an organisation. The children's book community is a very special place and SCBWI is a bright star within that community. I have developed my skills and my knowledge and met friends for life (still working on learning to like fancy dress though – I'll get there!).

Thank you to my Winchester buddies – Danielle Dale, Laura Williams and Claire Symington. You are all so talented and I can't wait to read your books in the future.

Thank you to Alice (Ball-Breaker) Ross and Becca (Industry Expert) Langton – more talented, insightful writers who have been so generous with their time and feedback and general encouragement. We have some serious celebrating to catch up on, girls – by order of the Deadline Madam! Thank you to Nicola Penfold for our catch-up walks and your invaluable debut author insight. Your writing is beautiful and I can't wait for your next book. Massive shout out and thanks to The Goodship 2021 Debuts – you have all been so supportive and generous with your advice and general cheerleading. I feel so lucky to be part of such a talented group and I cannot wait to have all of your beautiful book babies lined up on my shelf. We did it guys!!

Huge, heartfelt, slightly weepy thanks to my incredible agent, Helen Boyle. I still remember that first email you sent me – the enthusiasm and passion you expressed then and that you have sustained since, even when the chips were down, so to speak.

Thank you for your thoughtful feedback that has helped me shape this book, for dealing with my often ridiculous questions and concerns and for sticking with me. You are a gorgeous human being and agent, and I am lucky to have you in my corner.

Thank you, thank you and thank you again to my superstar editor Lena Macauley for connecting with Jessie and her story, for getting (most of) my jokes and for believing that the world needed to hear about a teenage period witch taking on The Patriarchy. Such is the world at the moment that we still haven't met in person, but when human contact is allowed again, maaaaaaan, I'm going to give you the biggest hug.

Thank you to everyone at Hachette and beyond who has helped get *Hexed* alive and kicking – Lucy Clayton, Beth McWilliams, Alice Duggan, Ruth Girmatsion, Genevieve Herr and Cat Phipps.

I feel like I'm delivering my Oscar acceptance speech and I'm about to get cut off so here are some last ones: thank you to my English teacher, Mrs Matthews, who graciously endured many, very boring, early stories of mine (including an eight pager about ants, if I remember correctly) and always asked for more. I still have your original Sylvia Plath books that I feel guilty for not returning so please get in touch so I can!

Huge love and enormous thank you hugs to my mum and dad and my sister, Carly – for the Storyteller tapes that totally ignited my love of story and for always encouraging me to keep writing. (Will you promise you'll actually read this one, Carly?)

Much, much love and hugs to my Isle of Wight friends and family, especially my teenage consultants – Dee, Livi and

Nathan – without whom lots of nineties slang and references would've stayed in the book. The Island is a very special and unique place and, like Jessie, I have grown to love it. I hope that comes across in the book, which is in part, my own love letter to the Island.

Thank you, thank you, never-ending thank yous to my best friend, Danielle, for commiserating and celebrating with me along the way, for always saying lovely things about whatever I send you (because sometimes, lovely things, whether true or not, are what you really need to hear as a writer) and for 4 a.m. kitchen discos when required – which is basically, always.

Thank you to the many women I admire who are writing and creating and putting out content and have been an integral part of this book without even knowing it. Laura Bates, Holly Bourne, Dolly Alderton, Pandora Sykes, Dawn O'Porter, Emma Jane Unsworth, Bryony Gordon, Caitlin Moran and all *The Real Housewives of Beverley Hills*, *New York* and *Orange County* – but especially Lisa Rinna who is my spirit animal. I dream that one day we will drink cocktails and dance on tables together.

And I saved the best for last – thank you to my gorgeous boys, Huxley and Cooper. I've never been shy about the fact that I found being a mum to small children extremely hard, but it was that experience that gave me the opportunity and the need to develop my writing and for that – and the fact I have you two wonderful humans in my life – I am eternally grateful. And Will – where do I start? We've been through so much together. You have always been there for me, and I know you always will be. I adore you. Thank you for everything and everything and then some.

LOOK OUT FOR THE NEXT BOOK FEATURING JESSIE JONES, COMING JULY 2022!

After a summer of surfing, sunbathing, helping Summer out down at The Cove and fine-tuning her witch skills, Jessie starts Year 11 with high hopes. She feels like her life-ducks are finally in a row – Nonna is back to being full force Nonna, the haunted house of horrors is feeling less deserted naff 70s hotel and more like home and she and Bella can actually bear to be in a room together again. Best of all, at school, Jessie has her sisterhood of Summer, Libby and Tabitha supporting her, so this year should be a breeze, right?

Wrong.

When a new witch arrives on the island, Jessie quickly realises that a new year just means new troubles.

After a brief (but fun) stint working in television and as a primary school teacher, Julia Tuffs decided to take her writing dreams more seriously. She lives in South West London with her family and ragdoll cats (Billy and Nora) and spends her time writing, reading, dreaming of holidays and watching too much reality TV. She aims to write the kinds of books that shaped and inspired her as a teenager.

HEXED is her debut novel.

Find her on Twitter @JuliaTuffs

ADVOCACY, RESOURCES AND FURTHER READING

WEBSITES

everydaysexism.com
The Everyday Sexism Project was set up by Laura Bates as a place where women could record instances of the everyday sexism they experience no matter how big or small, knowing that it helps to feel heard and that we're in this together.

ukfeminista.org.uk
UK Feminista supports students and teachers to promote gender equality across education. Their website has lots of great resources for schools and individuals, and they also provide training and campaign for gender equality.

thefword.org.uk
An online magazine that covers all aspects of contemporary feminism including books, film and TV, politics, music and more. Run by volunteers and open to submissions.

fawcettsociety.org.uk
One of the OGs of feminist organisations, the Fawcett Society is a membership charity that campaigns for equal rights for women in all areas of life.